C. St. John Sprigg
THE CORPSE WITH THE SUNBURNED FACE

C. St. John Sprigg's life was tragically cut short on February 12th, 1937 in the valley of Jarama, just east of Madrid. Like many of his literary contemporaries, such as Hemmingway and Orwell, he joined the anti-fascist forces in the Spanish Civil War. Although he was a highly-trained pilot he joined the fight as a machine-gunner and instructor. He died a hero while manning the last held machinegun nest on "Suicide Hill" at the Battle of Jarama, providing cover for his retreating comrades. Sprigg's hilltop post was overrun by fierce Moorish fighters just as he was spiking his gun and preparing for his own withdrawal.

Christopher St John Sprigg was the real name of the writer 'Christopher Caudwell', who published poetry and philosophy under the Caudwell *nom de plume*. Parallel to this Sprigg kept the fun stuff, his detective novels and aviation writing, under his birth name. Sprigg wrote a handful of delightfully entertaining golden age mystery novels before he was thirty, displaying considerable talent and promise in that short span.

The Corpse With The Sunburned Face straddles two diverse worlds, a placid English village stained by murder and a hostile African landscape steeped in ritual and death, and although it sets up as a typical British cozy, the story becomes something quite savage and thrilling in its second half. *Pass the Body*, Sprigg's first mystery novel, is also available from Bruin Crimeworks.

THE CORPSE WITH THE
SUNBURNED FACE

C. St John Sprigg

BRUIN CRIMEWORKS
The Emerald Empire
Eugene, Oregon

THE CORPSE WITH THE SUNBURNED FACE
©1935 by C. St. John Sprigg

Edited by Jonathan Eeds
Cover design by Michelle Policicchio

Original cover art provided by the Viet Hung Gallery,
Ho Chi Minh City, Vietnam

This book was crafted in the USA but is printed globally

Printed in the USA
ISBN 978-0-9987065-4-2
Published September 12, 2018
Bruin Books, LLC
Eugene, Oregon, USA

For inquiries: bruinbooks@comcast.net

A
Special thanks to
David Margolies,
Keeper of the
Christopher Caudwell
Flame

Original NOTE from the 1935 edition:

Although the customs, history, and beliefs of Ashanti have been largely drawn on in depicting the kingdom of Balooma in the latter part of this book, the characters in this as in all other parts of the book are entirely fictitious, and their actions have no relation to the real history of that picturesque Confederacy.

Editor's update to the original NOTE:

The Ashanti of today live in central Ghana in western Africa approximately 300km. away from the coast. The Ashanti are a major ethnic group of the Akans in Ghana, a fairly new nation, barely more than 50 years old. Ghana, previously the Gold Coast, was a British colony until 1957. The kingdom of Balooma, which Sprigg locates further to the east in Nigeria, is completely fictional, and would have been a rival kingdom to the Ashanti Empire.

I

LITTLE WHIPPERING

CHAPTER ONE
Miser Into Wilderness

"I OUGHT to have been A Polar explorer," murmured the Rev. Samuel Wykeham, vicar of Little Whippering, in the County of Berkshire, as he slowly climbed the road that led to the Downs.

"Or an African missionary," he added as he breasted the slope, puffing a little. The vicar was A man of about fifty, with firm bronzed features, a scholar's stoop, and A short-sighted forward projection of his head.

"Nothing ever happens in Little Whippering," he finished irritably, murdering a dandelion with the thick end of his knobbly stick. He had an uneasy sensation that he had heard the complaint, or one like it before, but the occasion evaded his always unreliable memory.

At that moment the vicar was startled to hear screams of terror. A small boy shot down the hill, his head held low. Seeing the vicar's black legs in front of him, the child made a detour, without pausing to raise his head. But the Rev. Samuel's long arm shot out and arrested him. Then the vicar turned up the child's face. It was one of the Bundling boys, freckled little imps, but now the freckles had a peculiar mottled effect on the boy's pale face.

"Compose yourself, William! What is all this fuss about?"

"The Invisible Man's come," panted the boy. "I seen him." He was trembling in the vicar's grasp.

"Now, now, William," said the vicar kindly. "Your story shows a complete lack of logic from its inception. If the man in question was invisible, how could you have seen him?" The vicar patted his curly head soothingly.

"All the same I seen him," insisted William. "Just like I saw him on the pickshers in Wantage, with great gloves on, and a cloth thing over his face."

"And where did you see this remarkable phenomenon?" asked the vicar, realizing now that the child had certainly been frightened by something concrete.

"It's the new chap at *'Wilderness'*," answered the boy. "I saw him getting out of Harry Thompson's car. All smuvvered up!"

The vicar laughed. "Really, William, I'm surprised at you! A boy of your age frightened because a gentleman wears a muffler. Perhaps he's got a bad cold; in any case it is quite chilly today, and I would blame no man for taking precautions if he had a catarrhal tendency!"

William wriggled sulkily at this rebuke. Feeling that he must somehow justify his terror, he added: "Oo. He had a great nose on him like an elephant, a foot long!"

The Rev. Samuel looked reprovingly at William, and the boy reddened under the look. "I fear you depart from veracity, William! You know what happens to little boys who are mendacious. Not—" went on the vicar dreamily, following the current of his thoughts, "that I believe in threatening children with hell-fire for comparatively innocent fibs. After all—" The vicar was recalled to reality again by the wriggles of his captive.

"I were hiding in the bushes," William blurted out, "and the chap saw me, and twisted my arm, and he said he'd split my belly up if he cotched me round there again!"

"Ha, ha! William Bundling!" said the vicar, "*Now* we feel solid ground beneath our feet. The truth was that you were detected in the act of espionage, and were very properly rebuked. Evidently the new tenant is a person with a sense of humor. But he did not allow for the literalness of the Bundling temperament. Well, well, the warning was perhaps all the more salutary for being taken in earnest. You can accept my word for it, William, that you are in no immediate peril of life or limb. But all the same, take the lesson to heart! Never be inquisitive, my dear boy. Never. Never!" The vicar released the boy, who was now grinning. The vicar always spoke to children in precisely the same tone and manner as he did to grownups. As a result they all liked him, but had only the vaguest idea of what he said to them. In this case William understood in a general sense that there was nothing to be alarmed about, and, soothed by the vicar's gentle murmur, he trotted quietly home. Meanwhile the vicar resumed his walk up the hill.

So the new tenant of the Wilderness had arrived! The Wilderness was an eyesore of a cottage, with a violent pink asbestos roof, standing a mile from the village itself, on the edge of the Downs. Little Whippering itself was a charming old-world village without a jarring note, carefully kept so by the Marions, who had owned—and lived in—Little Whippering, ever since written record ran.

The Wilderness, however, had been built on land outside the Marion property by a crotchety old retired sailor, and its hideousness had always been a sad grief to the old squire, and equally of course to his son, the new squire. Since the sailor's death six years previously the cottage had been empty, but now, apparently, the executors, a firm of London solicitors, had found a tenant. A man with a liking for solitude.

"Though if he thinks a few threats will cure the inquisitiveness of Little Whippering villagers, he's sadly in error," thought the vicar, shaking his head and remembering the many sermons he had preached against this vice, "for when it is carried beyond certain bounds it becomes a vice."

"All the same," the vicar admitted to himself a moment later, "I think I will turn to the left here and go past the Wilderness. After all, he is a new parishioner. I owe him a call sooner or later."

Presently the Rev. Samuel arrived outside the front gate of the Wilderness. The cottage was built in a clearing in a copse, and so could hardly be seen from the gate. From the Downs its abominable salmon pink roof showed up all too plainly. The vicar hesitated with his hand on the gate, stopped; and then peered. There was no sign of occupation. The windows were still shuttered.

"Odd," thought the vicar, "very odd!"

"After all," he told himself, "now I am here, I ought to call. It will give the man, whoever he may be, a favorable impression of the zeal of our rural clergy."

With which comforting thought the vicar opened the squeaky gate, strode up the weedgrown path, and tapped smartly with his stick on the oaken door. Then, to his surprise, he saw that a kind of square hole had been cut in the door. The edges of the wood were still new. A grating and a little flap had been nailed in the hole. The vicar remembered that a builder had come in from Abingdon to do the place up. Evidently one of his duties had been to fix up this contraption.

"Quite like a monastery grille," thought the vicar examining it. "Dear me, I hope this person is not religious."

This hope, at first surprising as coming from a clergyman, was explained by a recent experience, when the Orchard had been tenanted by a self-styled "Master Nostradomus." It had been rechristened "The Abode of Love," and turned into a nudist colony, to the dreadful scandal of Little Whippering, and the perplexity of Police Constable Collop. The vicar had got up one morning recently to be told that "Master Nostradamus" had fled, leaving behind him several unpaid bills. And now this—

The vicar's reflections were cut short by a furious barking, and what appeared to be a large dog began to scrabble with its paws on the other side of the door. The vicar was fond of dogs. All the same he hoped that the tenant would not open the door wide and give this animal a chance to do what it evidently wanted to do, namely tear the vicar to fragments.

Then he heard approaching steps, and the grille in the door rattled. The vicar saw two eyes glimmering behind it, and realized that he was being scrutinized.

"What the blankety hell do you want?" said a rough uneducated voice.

"I want nothing," said the vicar with Christian meekness, "except—in a metaphorical sense—the pleasure of your company. I am the incumbent of this parish, and I came to call on you, as you have just arrived here. However, if the moment is inconvenient—no doubt you are unpacking your household gods—"

The vicar heard the new tenant muttering behind the grille, and realized that, whatever he might be, there was not the least fear that he was religious.

Suddenly there was a click, the grille was swung back and the vicar saw before him the barrel of a gun—or rifle, in his consternation he did not notice which. Its muzzle actually touched the vicar's chest. He stepped back hastily.

"I'll give you twenty seconds to get off my property," roared the voice, "and then I'll blast your blankety head off, devil-dodger or no devil-dodger! And that goes for any other blankety nosey-parker in this blankety village! so put that in your pipe and smoke it!"

The vicar's hand closed on his knobbled stick. He felt a sudden unchristian desire to be able to bang the owner of the voice over the head with it. Indeed the wish was taking the form of a prayer when he repressed it forcibly, heedless of what dire damage it might do in the realms of his unconscious. He bowed his head meekly.

"Very well, my good man." He walked slowly away down the gravel path, with the uncomfortable feeling the bravest man has if he knows that a firearm of some kind is levelled by a lunatic at his back. When he gained the gate, the vicar found to his surprise that he was quivering, and the palms of his hands were damp with sweat. He wiped them thoughtfully.

"Dear me!" he said to himself. "There must be something peculiarly alarming about that man! First William and then myself!"

~§~

By the time the vicar reached the foot of the hill again— for he had now given up his project of having a blow on the Downs, Little Whippering was already well informed about the new arrival. William Bundling was one source of information. Another, and more authoritative, was Harry Thomson, a youth with a lobster-red face and large hands. Harry Thomson ran the local garage and hire car, which he drove rather as if it were a plough, encouraging it with an occasional "Giddap!"

He had three days before received a curt note, signed "S. O'Leary," ordering him to meet the 4:15 from Abingdon, and asking for the number of his car. Mr. O'Leary had darted out of the 4:15, his face completely muffled up, and had shot straight into the waiting car.

"And it's my belief," said Harry Thomson weightily, "that he doesn't want his face to be seen."

"Why?" asked old Mr. Padding, who was sitting on an upturned oil-drum.

"Ar," answered Harry. "Ar," according to Little Whippering convention, is a sufficient answer to any question. It is impolite to press further.

"He's a murderer, that's what he is," said Mr. Padding, now revealing that his original question had only been a trap, which Harry had however evaded.

They were interrupted by young Herbert, Harry's assistant. Herbert was educated on two-penny bloods, and felt a simple murder to be rather flat.

"He's a leper, that's what he is!" said Herbert.

"A leopard, hark at the boy!" exclaimed Mr. Padding, spitting contemptuously. "Do you think he's escaped from the circus?"

"Not a leperd, a leper!" exclaimed Herbert. "One of those people with 'orrible diseases, like I read about, what they have to shut up."

"You can do a bit of shutting up yourself, young Herbert," said Harry severely, "we don't want no nastiness. You cut along and finish washing Mr. Horace's Austin."

Mr. Padding rumbled obscurely for a few minutes after young Herbert's departure.

"Him with his lepers. . ."

Then he hoisted himself to his feet, and with a mumbled farewell, departed to make sure that the village was not deluded by an absurd invention of young Herbert's morbid mind.

"Lepers indeed," he muttered as he walked past the Marion Arms to Mr. Gudgeon the baker's. Gudgeon himself was behind the counter, and Mr. Padding went in.

Gudgeon was one of the personages of Little Whippering, a large genial man with a walrus moustache and red arms, who held positive views about the equality of man, a Radical surviving in the backwaters of Little Whippering. Gudgeon prided himself on his independence, which meant being genially rude to everyone in the village, however rich or important, except the Marions. He was always ready to threaten people with the Law, that obscure menace about which he was believed by the judicious to have a knowledge rivalling that of old Fotherthwaite of Abingdon, with the added advantage that Gudgeon was always prepared to advise without charge.

Mr. Padding briefly told Gudgeon the story of the new arrival, and aired his theory.

"What I say is, Gudgeon, you ought to go up there and have a look at that murderer. You could pretend to have come about An order."

"You think that, do you?" said Mr. Gudgeon.

"It might be that there was a reward out of him," suggested Padding.

"Ar, it *might* be," admitted Mr. Gudgeon slowly.

There was a silence, during which Mr. Padding filled his pipe.

"On the other hand it might not," went on Mr. Gudgeon. "And as it happens I've already got my order from him, so I should look a precious fool going up there asking for one."

"What, has he been in here?"

"He has not, Silas Padding."

The two men were silent. Padding did not show any interest. When Gudgeon was ready to tell the story he would. Meanwhile there was plenty of time. He lowered himself gently on to a sack of flour, and his knee-joints cracked. "Rain," he muttered dolefully.

"Yes, I got a letter from him," said Mr. Gudgeon at last. "Just, *'Deliver a small loaf to me daily, S. O'Leary,'* that's all it said!"

Mr. Gudgeon fumbled beneath his apron and at last produced a floury piece of paper. He unrolled it.

"Deliver a small loaf to me daily," he read out slowly.

Mr. Padding took the note, smoothed it, and spread it on his knee. Then he put on his spectacles.

"Deliver a small loaf to me daily," he read out with an air of surprise. "Well, there's a proper caution for you!"

Mr. Gudgeon reflectively dribbled a handful of brown sugar through his large red fingers.

"Well, Silas Padding, I sent young Dick up there with a small loaf, and I'm blest if this chap didn't stick his hand out of a hole in the front door when Dick knocked, and took that loaf from him. You could have knocked Dick down with a feather, he was that startled!"

"Ar," said Mr. Padding. "Didn't want his face to be seen, see?"

"That's as maybe. But he's not a murderer!"

"So you say," said Mr. Padding, a little wounded by this defection. However, Gudgeon always was one to take up an independent line.

"He's a miser, that's what old Small-Loaf is," pronounced Mr. Gudgeon. "You mark my words; he'll bury his money in the floor of the Wilderness and just live there like a pig. I mind the time when they had a miser at my cousin's, beyond the town. Miser they calls 'em, but I say misery. And certainly he come to a miserable end, for they found him with his throat cut from ear to ear, bleeding like a pig."

"Well, now, and who might have done that? Or did'n do it hisself?"

"Oh, some tramp did it," answered Mr. Gudgeon, "and took all the money. Leastways they never found it."

Mr. Padding sucked his teeth in silent contemplation of this pleasant prospect. Then, after getting painfully to his feet, he tottered out of the shop, without another word, and set off to Miss Tipton's, the village Post Office and "grocery." Mr. Padding had a shrewd knowledge of village psychology and he recognized at once that the Miser theory would triumph over the Murderer theory. The throat cut from ear to ear would do that. There was still time to change . . .

"Have you heard about the new miser they've got up at Wilderness?" he asked, without preamble, as soon as he was inside Miss Tipton's.

"What, him a miser? Well, I never. But then what did I say? I had a letter from him this morning," she fumbled. Mr. Padding waited, but Miss Tipton's fumbling was without result. "There! I must have wrapped some lollipops in it."

Mr. Padding's bleared eyes showed no surprise. What else could you expect of a woman? Hens all of them!

"Anyways," went on Miss Tipton, "he's ordered butter and whatnot, and I sent Elsie up with it, poor child, and he stretched out a great arm from a hole for all the world like an ogre. The poor child's still a-shivering and shaking. He's no Christian, I said it at once."

"Christian! I'll lay he isn't!" exclaimed Mr. Padding. He sat down for roughly ten minutes, staring vacantly into space, and then moved on. The Marion Arms was now opening, and his story ought to be worth a bitter.

Meanwhile the vicar had, as he felt in duty bound, spoken a friendly word of warning to Police Constable Collop. "Not that I think he means what he says, Collop, but it might be as well to keep an eye on him. You might even go up and see him. After all the sight of the blue uniform of the law is not without its sobering effect."

P.C. Collop nodded and placed a broad toe on his bicycle pedal. "I'll go up and see him this moment, sir. A gun you say? Ho! We'll give him guns."

Collop swung a huge blue-swathed haunch over his ancient bike, and pedaled off with quiet dignity. The vicar looked after him. The broad and massive beam of the policeman seen from behind, supported by a narrow pedestal of steel and rubber, with the huge feet slowly reciprocating each side, gave him a feeling of reassurance. Collop lowered his head as if about to butt, rang his bell authoritatively, and swayed round the corner. The vicar turned and went on, past the low stone wall of the Marion's Park, with a feeling of relief. Collop would settle him!

Had Mr. Padding been beside the policeman when he

knocked loudly on the door of the Wilderness he would have seen confirmation of his wisdom in abandoning his original theory. So far from showing the terror of a hunted murderer, Mr. O'Leary gave no sign of alarm at seeing, on opening his grille, the tall helmet and imposing grey whiskers of Collop. On the contrary, above the wild barking of his dog: "God, is this village crazy?" he shouted. "First a devil-dodger and now a slop! What do you want, you blasted bluebottle? An Englishman's home is his castle, ain't it?"

P. C. Collop took off his helmet and wiped the inside carefully—it had been a stiff pedal up the hill—while he reflected on this. The insult he would pass, but he was not prepared to agree lightly to any legal maxim, without first looking in his book.

"That's as may be," said P.C. Collop.

"What's as may be, you blankety b—" said the mystery man, evidently unfamiliar with local idiom. "That will do, sir!" said P.C. Collop, feeling that the time had come to assert himself. "Not so much of the blankety, *if* you please. There's no call to be personal. Two can play at that game, without getting much further, and I has my duty to do, which I must remind you of, sir."

He was visited with a flash of inspiration. "Have you got a license for this animal?"

O'Leary made no direct answer, but he was heard stumping away into the interior. Meanwhile P.C. Collop cautiously applied his face to the hole in the door. There was a snap as a pair of canine jaws closed within an inch of the policeman's nose and he drew back hastily.

The footsteps returned and an arm, thrust through the door, extended two slips of paper. "There you are, nosey. And my gun license, see? Any come-back?"

Collop examined them with care. "They *appears* to be in order," he admitted, "but I'm not sure that I didn't ought to inspect the articles in question."

"Well, take a look at this," said the other, suddenly projecting a barrel from the grille. It was a shotgun, of large bore; "for shooting flocks of elephants I reckon," explained Collop afterwards, with stolid humor.

"As for the dog, I'll open the door and let him out if you like, but don't blame me if he 'as the guts out of you."

"Well, I won't insist," said Collop handsomely.

"Oh, thank you so much, officer dear," said the voice with sarcastic gratitude, and then abruptly, "And now clear off quick, you bastard."

"Bastard or no bastard, that's as may be," Collop was not the man to be hurried. He lifted his bicycle slowly away from the porch, watched by the unseen eyes behind the grille.

"I take it then," said Collop blandly before going, "that I can tell the village you don't want callers."

"Callers!" screamed the other, in a sudden burst of apparently uncontrollable rage. "You can tell your blankety village that if any parson, copper, district nurse, meddling old lady, snuffling brat, or any mortal soul but an errand boy or postman comes up this drive, they'll get the seat torn out of his or her pants by my dog, and a charge of buckshot in their gizzards to help them on their way as well."

Feeling that he had done his duty, and secured an interesting entry for his notebook, Collop left the Wilderness.

"There's a pleasant spoken chap!" he muttered as he shot down the hill. "Something fishy about him if you ask me. Just let him start letting off his buckshot, whatever that may be. You can't do that kind of thing in Little Whippering!"

However the new resident's message of goodwill was duly spread abroad, and was taken as proof of Mr. Padding's hypothesis. "Afraid someone will get his money, the old miser!" Heads were wagged in the Marion Arms and the Fox and Fancy. The miser legend began to grow.

~§~

Secluded in its fold of the Berkshire Downs, Little Whippering thereafter equally endured the changes of two twelve-months. The Miser had arrived, and though legend grew round him, so that any villager could have described to you his hook nose, his lean clutching fingers dribbling their hoard of notes and gold, he became accepted as a matter of course in his isolation, out there on the Downs, outside the kindly circle of the village, beyond the utmost pub.

The winds of winter howled cruelly round the pink asbestos roof of the Wilderness. Down below the villagers were snug and warm, but looking out of their windows, they could see the lights glimmering in the Wilderness windows, and could picture the strange demented creature huddled over his fire, stoking it stingily with the wood he had gathered from his copse at dead of night.

Well, there he was; but meanwhile there were more important things than the existence of a miser in Little Whippering. Old Mrs. Cabney swallowed her false teeth and asphyxiated herself. Farmer Bunn was swindled at Abingdon Market by a Londoner. The Misses Tibbie had a telegram telling them they had come into money. The young Bundlings got chicken pox. Young Squire Marion sold all his father's hunters. Tom Hand got a cold from falling into a ditch while tipsy. As long as Little Whippering was full—and was it not always full?—of such a ferment of events, fresh every day, events with a poignancy and excitement unknown to towns, it was natural that the Miser should be neglected, except by a few daring and shuddering boys peeping through the fence. Perhaps he might have mouldered away to death, years and years later and become only a dim legend—an ancient grey-bearded corpse found by a trades-man one winter's day, his emaciated arms clasped round his chest of treasure.

But—

CHAPTER TWO
Tuffy Samson Dead

IT was a cold spring morning. A black-bearded man, with a battered felt hat pulled down low over his forehead, and his coat collar turned up, trudged into Little Whippering. As he wandered from street to street, staring thoughtfully into shops, he was taken by the inhabitants for one of those cranky bodies who come to the village from time to time, generally with a guidebook in their hands. They peer vaguely at the church, and the disgraceful old tumbledown cottages in Cat and Dog Lane, and then depart again, ignoring the real glories of the village—for instance the fine new parish hall, the rebuilt "public" down by the common, and Harry Thomson's new petrol pump.

After wandering helplessly for an hour, the black-bearded man stopped diffidently near the vicar, who was talking to Mr. Jennings, the artist, at the corner of Telegraph Hill. The vicar was persuading Mr. Jennings to give his aid in the scenic decoration of the "Mikado" at the Church Hall. To the stranger, Mr. Jennings doubtless looked like a local farmer; at least that was the impression the artist always tried to give. He had a round red face with sidewhiskers, wore gaiters, and cultivated a slightly bowlegged walk. He was recognized in Little Whippering as a reliable source of free drinks, if properly handled, that is to say encouraged to give his strange views on rural topics. Mr. Jennings was at his happiest however on Market Day in Abingdon, when he could be seen walking round with a wise air and knowledgeably prodding cattle with his stick.

As for Mr. Jennings' art, it was touchingly faithful to life. No one except a few cynical horse-copers had ever been able to "fault" Mr. Jennings' horses. This was hardly surprising as he always worked from photographs. Indeed he considered the invention of the instantaneous camera had done more for painters of hunting scenes than any other product of the human mind.

Mr. Jennings never talked about his art. Indeed he seemed a little ashamed of it, practicing it furtively in a bedroom in his house. At dinner parties of hunt breakfasts (he rode to hounds of course) when paintings were mentioned, he would start, as if something in his remote past had been mentioned. "Oh, *that*," he would say vaguely. "Well. . ."

However Mr. Jennings was successful. An interminable succession of his notabilities, mounted on sleek bloodstock, had ambled, trotted, cantered, and galloped their amiable way through Exhibitions of the Royal Academy.

Mr. Jennings' reluctance to help with the "Mikado" scenery was a part of his affectation of robustiousness. If the vicar had asked him to slaughter a pig at the Harvest Festival or help plough his glebe he would have consented with alacrity, but painting—in public.

"Why not ask the squire to do it?" he said at last, with a heavy wink. Young Marion was known to be an amateur of painting. Incidentally he was a bitter enemy of Jennings who, for some reason best known to himself, was fond of referring to him as "The Sweet-smelling Flower."

The vicar, in his innocence, considered the proposition carefully.

"No," he said at last. "I don't think the squire's painting would quite do for Little Whippering. We are a little old-fashioned here, you know."

The Rev. Samuel remembered too clearly some of the

paintings shown him by young Marion. They had quite shocked him. He knew the nude was necessary to art but still was it necessary to *emphasize* . . .

It was at this moment that the black-bearded man interrupted them with an "Excuse me, sirs." The vicar nodded amiably.

"I'm looking for a friend of mine," explained the stranger in a slow uneducated voice. "An old shipmate.

"I believe he's come to this here place. I haven't seen him around, but he's a queer cuss, the sort that keeps himself to himself."

"What's his name?" asked the vicar reasonably enough.

The black-bearded man shifted uneasily from one leg to the other.

"Well, there's no knowing, you see. He got into a bit o' trouble a while back. Nothing to be ashamed of, you understand, just the kind of accident that might happen to any man. Except you, of course, sir, having your job to consider." The vicar bowed. "But it made him a mite standoffish. I could describe him of course, but he's an ordinary sort of fellow. He isn't short, and he isn't long. He's darkish but not exactly black—"

"Good Lord!" interrupted Jennings, "I wonder if it's our old miser up at the Wilderness?"

"Miser, eh? Why should it be him?"

"Well, we call him the Miser," explained Jennings, "but that's only a village nickname. His name's O'Leary and he certainly keeps himself to himself. He arrived here with his face hidden behind a scarf and nobody's seen him by daylight. If he's your friend, all I can say is, we don't like his manners. The vicar here went to call on him and the brute actually threatened him with a gun."

"His pejorative range," remarked the vicar thoughtfully, "argues a life spent entirely in low company, or else a remarkable facility in picking up undesirable locutions and metaphors."

"He swears like a trooper," translated Jennings.

"Ah, that would be my pal, then," said the black-bearded man, nodding.

"But you don't want to be frightened by his little ways," he said to the vicar. "It's all bark and no bite with him. He's got the 'eart of a child really, but he covers it up by swearing and blinding. You just want to kick him in the pants when he starts his games, and he'll calm down as quiet as a little lamb."

"Upon my word, I felt strongly tempted to try something of the sort," confessed the vicar, "but my kicking days are over. In any case rugger was my game, not soccer."

"Well, many's the time I've broken a bottle over Spike's head," said the stranger reminiscently, "and afterwards butter wouldn't melt in his mouth. Now where would this Wilderness be?"

"If you like," said Jennings, "I'll put you on your way. I'm going up to the Downs, and I can as well go past the Wilderness as any other way."

"That's uncommonly kind of you, sir," said the stranger without much enthusiasm. "But I don't want to trouble you."

"No trouble at all," Jennings assured him heartily. "Good-bye, Vicar! I'll let you know about that scenery when I've thought it over, but Marion's your man, not a doubt about it!"

The two tramped side by side up the hill leading out of the village, while Jennings gave a brief sketch of the Miser's arrival and subsequent history. He attempted to draw out the black-bearded stranger. But he was not to be drawn. In spite of his genial loquacity, Ire evaded all leading questions with a skill which showed a shrewd brain beneath his stolid exterior. Jennings soon realized that it was useless to press him farther. They turned off the main road to the Downs down the track that led past the cottage and when they reached the gate, the stranger hesitated.

"Well," he said uneasily, "I dunno as I'll look in on my pal just now. He's an odd cuss, sleeps most of the day, you know. I think I'll wait till the evening. Maybe I can get a bit to eat and a can of beer at a pub, where?"

Jennings felt irritated, for he had accompanied the stranger on the tramp uphill solely to witness the encounter. He might even, he had thought, see the famous charge of buckshot loosed at the presumptuous intruder. In the normal course, walks on the Downs were not at all in the artist's line. He preferred to hack picturesquely about the countryside, distributing hearty salutations to yokels as he trotted past them.

"Well, thanks for showing me the way," went on the stranger, "I'll be able to find it myself this evening. Is there a pub near here?"

"There's the Fox and Fancy at the bottom of the hill," said Jennings curtly. "Turn left before you reach the village."

Repeating his thanks, the bearded stranger turned back. Mr. Jennings went on to the Downs. As he had got so far, he might as well make a walk of it. Presently his feet were on the springy turf, and he quickened his pace. It was early for the full spate of flowers or butterflies which in late summer would liven the drab curves with an evanescent efflorescence. For mile after mile the hills undulated monotonously with an occasional copse like some vegetable waif abandoned in a great arboreal migration. Up above, the clouds scudded, hurried by the east wind. Towards all this familiar landscape Mr. Jennings felt the same proprietorial air that a tailor might feel towards a roll of material lying on his shelves. Flow many yards of this knobbly hill-land, with its soft depressions like marks of a giant modeler's fingers, he had snipped neatly off to put between the legs of horses! How often he had fitted an acre or two of this thin cloudy sky behind the haughty faces of M.F.H.'s, their pink coats carefully contrasted with the cold grey clouds behind them!

Sound stuff all of it, he thought. It seemed peculiarly appropriate that, on the brow of the Devil's Knoll across there, he could see a string from Mr. Billock's Hinton stables, cantering down a track marked out with gorse.

Then Mr. Jennings gave an exclamation of disgust. There, right in the foreground, was a young man seated languidly in front of an easel—young Marion! Painting!

Impelled by a contemptuous curiosity, Mr. Jennings strode on until he reached the amateur artist. Claude Marion looked round at the approaching steps and greeted him politely enough. The landowner was thin, with a sallow oval face and dark brown eyes inherited from his Italian grandmother, and fine arched eyebrows and a sensitive mouth coming from Heaven knows where, for all the Marion ancestors had been hard-riding, hard-drinking gentlemen. Today their portraits, all painted by the Jennings of their periods—looked down in disapproval from the walls of Marion Hall, on the strange parties of communists, poets, biologists, and other persons ignorant of horses, port, and farming, invited by their descendant.

"Good morning, *cher maître!*" said Claude Marion, continuing to paint. Mr. Jennings snorted. It was part of young Marion's sarcasm always to address the elder man in the tones of a humble disciple.

Then Mr. Jennings looked over his shoulder, and paled. It was positively outrageous! He felt all the indignation of the tailor already referred to, as if some young urchin had seized his most useful roll of material and dragged it through the mud. Marion was painting the Downs, but good Heavens! what was he doing with them? Those pleasant green undulations had become jagged brown rocks. They glittered with a morbid steel-blue light. Great chasms cleft the skyline, and the sky itself, that clear spring sky, looked like a bowlful of melted thunder and lightning poured indiscriminately upon the scene.

"And what," asked Mr. Jennings stung beyond endurance, "if I may venture to ask, are those apples doing in the foreground?" He pointed with his stick. "Here, this huge bunch hanging down from the top left-hand corner. I don't see any apples!"

"It's my signature tune, *cher maître*," said Claude Marion, rising and wiping his hands on a rag. "You always have a horse in your pictures, why shouldn't I—in my humbler way—have an apple in mine?"

"Well, I know I'm one of the Old Guard," began Jennings, "but I can't see the necessity for deliberate distortion, all this Neolithic business . . ."

"But you're a little Neolithic yourself, dear man," cooed Claude, slowly packing up his painting apparatus, "with your smelly tweeds and your beer-drinking, positively *primitive*."

"You know," he went on, as, his folding easel tucked under his arm, he stood beside Jennings, "I believe the stage is set for the revival of your school of Art. If you like to pay me a percentage on sales, I'm quite prepared to lead the Reaction. We might issue a little magazine 'jenningsart' with a small J and start an artistic colony here, all wearing smelly tweeds and gaiters."

"Unfortunately I happen to take my art seriously," said Mr. Jennings austerely.

"Really?" giggled Marion. "Lady Brutell said you told her you painted as other people played bridge, to occupy the time between the end and the beginning of the hunting season. Frightful liar, isn't she?"

Mr. Jennings blushed. Although Marion and he disliked each other cordially, Marion had an infuriating habit of seizing every opportunity of talking to him. Now for instance he had evidently resolved to accompany him all the way back to the village.

Jennings decided to change the subject. "Sorry to see

you've sold your hunters, Marion," he said brusquely, "death duties, I suppose."

"Something of the sort. And one has one's duties to oneself. If you were forced to choose, Jennings (which Heaven forefend), would you give up your hunter or your mistress?"

Mr. Jennings coughed. "The eventuality has never arisen, so I can't say."

"Oh, don't misunderstand me, I was only suggesting a hypothetical case. Dear me, what a lovely dandelion!" Claude Marion bent down to pick the flower. "Now, really, Jennings, I ask you, as a fellow artist, is there a more effective flower? And we call it a weed! When one thinks of the cheap vulgarity of roses, and those frightfully Fascist tulips, all standing in rows, one wants to simply denude one's garden and plant nothing but masses and masses of dandelions. Only my tenderness for old Bundling's feelings prevents my doing so. He'd probably resign his job, and then what would become of his hordes of children? Really, I often tell him it's time he thinned out his family." Marion bent his head confidentially towards Jennings. "Do you know, I'm thinking of doing a Venus in the Dandelions. Can't you see it? Perfect masses of dandelions in unbroken chrome with a very plastic nude, a Bushman nude, with just the subtlest suggestion of pure English womanhood about her, to offset the enormous haunches. Rather cynical, don't you think? Or don't you?"

Mr. Jennings, as always after an artistic conversation with Marion, felt his head swimming away from him. He evaded the question by waving his stick to Farmer Bunn, who was leaning against some wire fencing contemplating a herd of young bulls, a pipe in his mouth. Farmer Bunn gave a brief salutation to Jennings, whom he thought a well-meaning idiot, and a heartier one to Claude Marion, about whom he did not think at all, for a Marion was a Marion in

Little Whippering, and always had been, whatever he might say or do.

Claude Marion put down his painting tackle for a moment and leaning on the wire, looked at the bulls.

"What very *farouche* creatures, Bunn! Do look at that one over there with the black muzzle and the Clark Gable eyes! I really shudder to imagine what he can be thinking of. Don't you ever feel your personality *wilting* among all these primitive souls, with their dark mysterious lives?"

"I can't say I do, sir," said Farmer Bunn.

Mr. Jennings snorted. Fancy talking to a farmer like that! He prided himself he knew the tone of agricultural conversation.

Unfortunately he could not prod these animals with his stick, as the nearest was ten feet away, but he waved his thick stick in their direction. Then he gave an appraising grunt. "Fine beasts these, Bunn!"

Bunn removed his pipe from his mouth, and stared at Jennings, remaining dumb for two or three minutes from sheer astonishment. Then he spat reflectively.

"Fine beasts, Mr. Jennings? Why, they ain't worth a damn! I only keeps 'em for their manure and their company."

Marion giggled, and dug Jennings in the ribs.

"Remember that, Jennings! If we could say only half as much for some of the people in this world, it would be something."

Jennings did not reply, and at the crossroads he took the first opportunity of shaking off his companion.

"And that's the younger generation. My God!" he exclaimed stumping viciously towards the Fox and Fancy.

Humming gently to himself, Claude Marion walked on his way alone. It was already getting dark, and as he neared the village, he saw a stranger, a black-bearded man, quietly seated on a railing, apparently waiting, though for what, it was difficult to imagine. Perhaps he had a sweetheart among one of the village girls, and was keeping a tryst. In any case Claude Marion did not bother his head further about him, for his Venus among the Dandelions was taking shape already in his mind. Later he was to regret that lack of incuriosity.

What is more, he must have been the last person in the village to see the black-bearded stranger there, for after that he appears to have faded out of Little Whippering's ken. But not out of their minds. For it was, as it was later discovered, through his action that the village next day was set in a minor turmoil. The vicar detected the excitement in Miss Tipton's eyes as she hurried down the main street. "Whither away, so fast and so free?" he asked her. "Has anything untoward occurred?"

"Yes, sir, there's a telegram for the Miser from someone in Abingdon. Such a funny telegram, sir, it's put us all in a flutter. I'm taking it up myself for if I send the child goodness knows what he may say, something she oughtn't to hear, I'm sure! Mr. Gudgeon thinks there's something queer about the telegram, sir, but Mr. Padding says it's just what he always expected."

The vicar was not surprised at this committee meeting's report on the telegram. He knew it was a Little Whippering custom to save time by making public the contents of wires on their receipt. After all, they argued, if the matter were private, it would not be discussed in a telegram which, as everyone knows, is seen by the Post Office people. However, the vicar felt it his duty to make some remonstrance, however feeble, against the practice.

"I really don't think you should hand round a telegram in this way, Miss Tipton."

"But it's only among friends, sir. And it's that queer, sir. It says—"

The vicar raised his hand. "No, really, I don't think I

should become a party to this." He hesitated. "Yet, on the other hand, as everyone seems to have heard it, and no doubt my wife will have heard it by now . . . He lowered his hand.

Miss Tipton produced the envelope magically from her voluminous skirts.

"Yes, sir, you just have a peep at it. The flap's been pulled up once or twice, so it comes off easy enough."

"Dear, dear, this is making me a party to crime with a vengeance," said the vicar as Miss Tipton handed him the slip. Then suddenly the word *"dying"* caught his eye. If anyone was dying, thought the vicar, he had a professional interest in it. He took the telegram.

> O'LEARY,
> THE WILDERNESS, SOUTH FANCIFELL.
> AM DYING. COME AT ONCE TO 5, ETHELRED STREET, ABINGDON. HAVE GOOD NEWS FOR YOU. TUFFY SAMSON WAS KILLED IN A CAR ACCIDENT IN KADUNA SIX WEEKS AGO. WILL TELL YOU ALL ON ARRIVAL. COME QUICKLY—GEORGE CRUMBLES.

"Well, upon my soul," said the vicar. "This smacks of violence, or at least a strange lack of charity. 'Good news for you—Tuffy Samson killed.' "

He returned the slip, and Miss Tipton replaced it in its envelope with hands that quivered with excitement.

"Er—lick it well," said the vicar. "At present, it looks unconvincing even to a simpleton like myself. I trust he will not be violent, Miss Tipton. And if he is profane, well, you must be like the sailors of Odysseus; stop thine ears and make all haste from thence. I will wait at the bottom of the hill in case you want any assistance."

The vicar waited, and presently Miss Tipton came hurrying down the hill.

"Well, what did he say?"

"I'd not bemean myself by repeating it, sir," said Miss Tipton. "All the same, I oughter have stuck that flap down more carefully. To be called a nosey-parker at my age! I gave him a piece of my mind, sir, you can be sure, and then he calmed down a bit. Apologized in fact!"

"Apologized!" exclaimed the vicar. "You must have the tongue of Charity herself."

"Well, he had to soothe me down a bit, seeing as how he wanted me to take a message," answered Miss Tipton triumphantly. "He wants Harry Thompson to take him into Abingdon at once!"

"Well, well, upon my soul, this is exciting. It is not often our simple daily round is disturbed in this fashion. I don't know why it is, Miss Tipton, but somehow Tuffy Samson and George Crumbles—the very names suggest violence and crime. I see swarthy pirate faces with gleaming rings in their ears."

"Goodness me, sir, but you have got an imagination!"

"I have, Miss Tipton, I have. I sometimes think I ought to have had a more glamorous existence. Violence and adventure have a strange appeal to me. An Arctic explorer, now there's a life! Or a missionary riding through a dense jungle, with lions snapping at one's heels."

"Well, sir, I don't mind confessing I sometimes want a bit of romance myself. But I see it as cowboys, with six-shooters, tearing up and down mountains, with me on a great white horse, and the villain pounding away behind. And then just as he comes up to lay hands on me—"

"The hero leans down from a branch and snatches you out of the saddle," said the vicar, his eyes resting thoughtfully on Miss Tipton's eighteen stone or so. "Well, nothing is impossible to Providence.

"And we may be wronging Messrs. Tuffy and Crumbles. Let me see now, what other perfectly harmless explanations might there be? Suppose they were officials of some charity, and Tuffy was a philanthropist who had left the society a bequest in his will. I think even a Christian could describe that, in a telegram, without qualification, as good news."

Miss Tipton sniffed. "I hope I know Christian language when I hear it. He ain't no Christian. Well, I must be leaving you in case that dratted phone bell starts buzzing. Old Major Fawcett gets that annoyed you wouldn't believe, if he doesn't get his number directly he lifts his receiver. 'I'm not a Jack-in-a-Box,' I often feel like telling him, but it never pays to be rude."

"It doesn't," agreed the vicar, lifting his hat in farewell.

He walked back slowly muttering to himself: *"Am dying—Tuffy Samson hilled."*

Then he stopped in the road and apostrophized himself sternly. "Samuel Wykeham, Clerk in Holy Orders, you have given way to a most degrading curiosity. As a penance you will dismiss the subject altogether from your thoughts."

He forced himself to decide there and then the vexed question of who should fill the role of the Executioner in the "Mikado."

But somehow it suggested nothing but George Crumbles.

CHAPTER THREE
George Crumbles Dead

IT WAS getting dark when Harry Thompson drew up outside the Wilderness. There was a scrunch of tires on the gravel as he lugged back the hand brake with a sinewy right arm. His brick-red face beneath the battered uniform cap looked stolid enough, but behind it Harry Thompson's mind was seething with the parting injunctions of Gudgeon, Padding, Miss Tipton, and even, in a humble way, young Herbert.

Harry Thompson knew that he would be expected to bring back a detailed account of every incident on his drive to Abingdon and back, of every word said to him, and his replies, and any gestures or meaningful actions. Above all, they relied on him for a preciser description of the Miser's person than had been so far available to Little Whippering.

His report, he knew, would be the basis of all discussions in Little Whippering for at least a month. His accuracy was the more essential in that it was generally felt without being actually said that Harry Thompson had been unobservant on the previous occasion. He had recalled nothing of the drive from Abingdon Station to the Wilderness except the vague impression that the Miser was a middle-aged man, muffled up like.

Most people pictured the Miser in outdoor garb as a kind of mummy, with a head completely swathed in bandages except for two sinister eye-holes. In fact, however, the mystery man went no farther than wearing a muffler to cover the lower part of his face, as might any sufferer from asthma, and in addition, perhaps his hat was pulled unusually low down over his eyes. It was in this guise that Mr. O'Leary, amid furious barking from his dog, stepped out from the front door of the Wilderness.

"Good evening, sir!" said Harry Thompson, politely. He had turned on the roof light, and now stood holding the door of the landaulet open.

Mr. O'Leary gave an ill-tempered mumble. He stumbled into the car past Thompson with his head down and, with his back to him, switched off the roof light. Then he sat down.

Harry Thompson remained with the door open for a moment, debating whether to venture a further word of conversation, but something about the posture and impatient twitching of Mr. O'Leary decided him against this. He closed the door and jumped into the driver's seat, which was separated from Mr. O'Leary by a partition of glass.

"Come on, old girl," said Harry, as he reversed the car in jerks round the tricky drive.

"None of that, dang you!" he added, as the offside front wing scraped the gate. Then he bumped out along the track, turned down the hill, and once clear of the village, rushed along the white dusty road to Abingdon. No sound came from the passenger huddled in the center of the seat in the back. A melancholy whistle emerged from Harry's pursed lips as the ancient vehicle swayed and bumped along the rutty road.

Harry had expected No. 5, Ethelred Road to be a nursing home of some kind. To his surprise he found that Nos. 4, 5 and 6, Ethelred Road were all represented by the Ethelreda Hotel, and it was before the hotel therefore that he stopped.

"Wait till I come out!" mumbled O'Leary, his words muffled by his scarf. He hurried up the hotel steps.

Ten minutes passed. Then a porter flung himself down the steps. He ran up to Harry Thompson.

"Drive round to the police station as quick as you can," he cried, "and put a snap in it, son! Tell them a man's just done himself in."

"Crumbs!" said Harry, staggered at the dreadful possibilities this opened up.

Then he pressed the starter button, let in the clutch with a jerk, and leaped forward with a convulsive roar. As the car swayed round the corner awful visions suggested themselves. He imagined Mr. O'Leary prevailed upon to remove his muffler. At the sight of that ghastly face—for Little Whippering had long agreed it must be ghastly—the beholder had been driven mad and incontinently shot himself. By the time Harry Thompson reached the police station he was perspiring with excitement.

Sergeant Jobling heard his story without showing any emotion. Leaving a message for Inspector Gregson and the police surgeon to be rung up, he jumped into the car beside Harry Thompson and was whirled to the Ethelreda Hotel.

Harry accompanied him up the steps and into the reception hall. Here they were met by the manager, a thin man with large horn-rimmed spectacles whose eyes blinked nervously as he fussed round the sergeant.

"Absolutely inexplicable. The man had only just come . . ."

Sergeant Jobling did not make any comment or comforting remark, did not in fact commit himself in any way, but asked to be taken at once to the dead man. The manager led the way to the first floor, still talking nervously, and flung open the door of a large bedroom. Thompson pressed behind the policeman.

Sergeant Jobling stood on the threshold and stroked his large black moustache with one vast hand as he looked round the room. On the bed was stretched the body of a man, a black-bearded man. The livid and distorted features, and the deep red marks round the neck, showed that he had been strangled. In the chair facing them sat a figure which made Sergeant Jobling's eyebrows rise.

Only his eyes and the bridge of his nose were visible. The rest of his face was hidden by a silk scarf. He was wearing a hat, pulled well down on his forehead.

For the moment, however, the sergeant did not comment on this remarkable phenomenon. With Harry's frightened aid, he took the body off the bed, placed it prone on the floor, and began to apply artificial respiration.

"Not much hope," he explained to the manager, "but if he's only just been cut down I ought to try it till the doctor arrives."

The man in the muffler got up and went towards the door.

"Now then, sir," barked the sergeant, who in spite of his task, had apparently been keeping a wary eye on him. "Stay till the inspector comes, *if* you please!"

"Certainly," answered the other, in the indistinct tones, smothered by the muffler, to which Thompson was used, but which made Jobling look at him sharply. "I was only going to shut the door. We don't want the whole ruddy hotel staff watching us." Having closed the door, he sat down again.

Time passed. The sergeant's efforts with the Schaffer method were without result. Harry stood contemplating him with ox-like calm, but the manager, a bundle of nerves, prowled incessantly round the room.

The sinister person in the muffler was sitting in the most comfortable chair, apparently perfectly calm. But perhaps the veiling of his features masked his perturbation. Only once did he make a remark. When the sergeant rolled over the body to inspect the face for any signs of life, he gazed for a moment at the ghastly mask.

"Poor old George!" he murmured. "He's caught it proper."

The inspector and the police surgeon arrived together. Dr. Harringay gave a brief preliminary survey of the victim.

"No hope, I'm afraid, sergeant. Quite right to try, of course. Well, the spinal column is twisted but the cord can't have been severed for he has obviously died of asphyxiation. Died fairly recently, too, I should imagine. Lift him on to the bed, and I'll make a more detailed examination."

Inspector Gregson and Sergeant Jobling went outside the room for a moment, no doubt to confer. Directly they came back Gregson looked sharply at the person in the muffler. Inspector Gregson was an elderly man with a shapeless red face which seemed to puff out in strange places on his chin, at the sides of his nose, and above his eyes. In the middle of these volcanic contortions was set a pair of small hard, blue eyes. These hard blue eyes were fixed sharply on the stranger's face for about a minute. Then: "Before we talk together, sir," he said, "may I ask you to have the goodness to remove your hat and muffler?"

The stranger sat there without answering for a little. During that time the eyes of everyone in the room—even of the doctor—with one accord fastened themselves on that face, on that white silk muffler surmounted by an indistinct nose-bridge and two eyes deep in shadow. His chair, as the inspector had at once noticed, had its back to the light.

"I don't see what right you've got to ask me to do that," answered the man at last.

"Don't you?" said the inspector, his blue eyes glittering. "You don't, eh?"

"No. I don't."

"I see. Well, sir, I shouldn't take that attitude if I was you. It's true I can't here and now order you to take that scarf off your face. But the circumstances are rather suspicious, and it might be necessary to arrest you, and charge you with the murder of this person. Well, people don't wear mufflers in prison. Again, if we find that no suspicion attaches, you'll still be summoned to the Coroner's Court as a witness, and he'll order you to take that muffler off before you give evidence. If you refuse, it will be contempt of court. So unless you've some special reason, in which case you must state it, you'll kindly take off that disguise. You'll have to, sooner or later."

The man got up from the chair slowly. "Disguise! Come, that's a bit strong, isn't it? Still, if you insist!"

His hand went up to his head.

Harry Thompson gasped. Even Sergeant Jobling and Inspector Gregson showed signs of excitement.

With a twitch of his fingers, the man sent muffler and hat flying on the chair.

Before them stood a man with a bronzed sunburnt face, open and genial, but its thick lips and heavy jowls gave a brutal emphasis to what otherwise would have been a normal enough countenance. He was middle aged and cleanshaven, and his red hair was cropped, emphasizing the squareness of the skull. His eyes had a humorous twinkle in them, but at the moment they were wary.

The inspector let his breath out with a little hiss.

"Thank you, sir!" he said.

Then he turned to Harry Thompson and the manager. "Will you please wait for me downstairs?"

The two left the room, Harry Thompson with a final unbelieving backward glance at the stranger. Meanwhile the inspector sat down on the arm of a chair and swung one leg easily.

"Your name, if you please?"

"Sam O'Leary," said the other. "At present tenant of the Wilderness, Little Whippering."

"Did you know the dead man?"

"I did. Poor old George, I've known him ever since we was lads."

"Why are you here? And what happened?"

"Well, it's like this, inspector. I got a telegram from George saying he was dying, but had good news for me." The man unfolded a telegram, and handed it over. The inspector looked at it, and without any comment put it in his pocket.

"Well," went on O'Leary, "I reckoned George was in a hospital here, or something, so I was surprised to find he was at a hotel. But anyway they told me in the hall that he'd left a message for me to go straight up to his room. I went straight in and found no one here."

"No one here?"

"No, not a soul. That's funny, I thought, he's supposed to be a-dying and here he is slipped out for a quick one! But George was always one for a joke, so I made myself comfortable in a chair and waited. Well, after ten minutes I began to have a queer feeling, I dunno quite how to describe it, a sort of creepy-crawly feeling. Imagination, I tells myself. All the same I started to poke round cautious-like, and blessed if I didn't feel sure there was someone else in the room. It struck me that George was hiding and was going to pop out of a cupboard sudden-like. So I shouts, 'Hi, are you in here, George, you old . . . ?' There weren't no answer, so I looked in the cupboard. But there weren't nothing in there but a few clothes and a half-empty bottle of whisky. Then I pulled back the curtain in front of the wash basin there, and God strike me dead but there was poor old George, staring me in the face, hanging on a rope with his tongue stuck out, looking something awful, with his body just a-swinging gently to and fro, like as if he were doing it for a game. I whipped out my knife and cut him down and hollered for help, but it was too late."

"Only just too late," said the doctor looking up. "He can't have been dead long when you came in."

"Ay, that's the pity of it! If only I'd a-known at once! If only I'd guessed poor George was hanging there! Hang me if I know why he killed himself though!

It's my belief that it was some confounded joke of his that went too far, if you understand me. He only meant to pretend to hang himself like."

"I see. Well, that's possible." The inspector rubbed his chin thoughtfully. At present he wished to know a good deal more before he questioned O'Leary further. For all the man's sudden affectation of candor, the contrast to his previous furtiveness was too great. He felt sure there was something more behind the affair than the miscarriage of a practical joke.

"Well, Mr. O'Leary, that is all I want to know at the present, but I must ask you to be good enough to call tomorrow at the police station to answer a few more questions. As you will realize, I shall want to enquire into the things mentioned in this telegram."

"At your service, Inspector," said the man, with a wave of his hand. "Anything that will help to clear up poor old George's memory. He certainly acted a bit strange sometimes, but I never expected to see this."

Mr. O'Leary left the room, and it was noticeable that his muffler was now tied in a normal manner, beneath his chin.

As he passed out, he told Harry Thompson to meet him in the Brown Cow round the corner as soon as the inspector had finished with him.

Meanwhile, at a word from the inspector, Sergeant Jobling had slipped down after O'Leary, to see that he did not try to leave the district. Having seen him safely into the Brown Cow, the sergeant rang up the station from a call-office opposite the public house and ordered two plain-clothes men to be sent to take over his task. When they arrived he returned to his superior.

Meanwhile the inspector was questioning Harry. From him he got a lurid account of the Miser's arrival at Little Whippering two years before and his subsequent seclusion. He also ascertained that the period of Harry's wait outside the hotel agreed with O'Leary's own statement of the time he had been sitting in the dead man's room.

From the manager, Gregson learned that the dead man had turned up the previous night and had taken a room. He had had his meals sent up and had apparently spent most of his time gazing dreamily out of the window. He had only tasted the food, sending it away uneaten. He had signed the Register as George Crumbles, but for address had written "None."

He had given everyone the impression of being depressed or disagreeable. Thus, when Jim the boy who brought up his meal, had set it down on the table, he had heard the bearded man remark, in tones of abysmal melancholy, still gazing out of the window: "Gawd, what a town! What a climate!" And then, turning to the table: "And what a bleeding meal!"

"What do you make of it, Doctor?" said the inspector when his interrogation was finished. "Is it suicide?"

Dr. Harringay tapped his nose thoughtfully. "I don't really see how I can say. He was strangled with this cord, and violently too. Judging from the length of the rope, and the fact that he piled one stool on another, he took a fairly long drop, and he's not a lightweight. So the suicide hypothesis is reasonable enough, though I must say one suspects our sinister friend instinctively. If it was a suicide it was a neat job. The knot right under the left ear, you see, to jerk his head over. The jerk would have compressed his spinal cord so that he probably never struggled, but just hung limp and was soon asphyxiated."

"I see." The inspector began to make a careful tour of the room. "We'll check up on the fingerprints, of course, but a hotel bedroom is a pretty hopeless proposition from that point of view."

He turned out the contents of the wardrobe and ran through them. "Ready-made clothes. London tailor. G.C. in marking ink on the lining."

He examined the fatal rope carefully, and then sent for

the manager.

"Take this around among the servants and see if any of them identify it!"

Presently the manager returned.

"Yes, sir, the porter says the gentleman asked him last night to buy a length of stout cord to tie up his suitcase as the lock had broken, and this was it."

"Right!" The inspector fingered the cord thoughtfully, and then examined the man's empty suitcase. The lock was in perfect condition. Prowling round the room: "It does look like suicide, doesn't it?" he said. Then he stopped at the wash basin, of the built-in variety, and looked carefully into it.

"The taps ought to be good for fingerprints," he murmured. With a quick movement he put his two fingers down the plug hole, fingers which, the manager noticed, were surprisingly thin and long. They came up holding what looked like a bunch of wet fluff.

The inspector brought it to the light.

"Odd," he remarked, "a tuft of black hair!"

He went up to the corpse, and ran an exploratory finger through its beard and neatly brushed and parted hair.

"Doesn't look as if it's off *him,* but of course it may be," said the inspector doubtfully. "Trimming his hair perhaps."

"Perhaps the hair is from a previous occupant of the room," suggested the doctor.

"I expect so," answered the inspector. "However, you never know. It's dark at any rate."

He folded the hair up carefully in a piece of paper. Then he began to go through the dead man's pockets. In the trousers pocket he found a handkerchief marked G.C.; and in the outer pockets of the coat a driving license and a map of Abingdon and its environs. In the hip pocket of the trousers he found a revolver.

"Fully loaded," said the inspector with a whistle as he

peered into the cylinder. "That's odd! You'd have thought he'd have shot himself since he had a revolver."

Then he put his hand into the breast pocket and drew out a wallet. As he opened it two envelopes slipped out.

"Ah-h," said the inspector slowly. "Here's something addressed to the Coroner." The inspector took out the letter and read it.

"Dear Sir, —Being depressed and ill I have decided to make away with myself. I haven't been myself since I came back from Africa, what with the rain and the thoughts racing round and round in my head. I came here to give my old pal Spike O'Leary some good news and all I ask is that he should see me buried proper."

"Well, that seems clear enough!" The inspector examined the letter closely. "Do you see he wrote some other name instead of 'Spike O'Leary' and then carefully crossed it out?"

"Yes," said the doctor. "If they were such old pals it's odd he shouldn't be sure of the name. Overwrought, perhaps!"

"Perhaps," commented the inspector meaningly. "Ah, and now the other letter. Addressed to Spike O'Leary. He seems surer of the name this time."

"Good-bye, old man, I just can't stand it with the thoughts going round and round in my head. You'll understand. You'll be glad to hear Tuffy Samson was killed in a car accident as soon as he came out of jail. I saw his body myself. See I'm buried proper, that's all I ask."

"It certainly seems suicide," mused the inspector, "though there's a good deal to investigate between now and the inquest. This Tuffy Samson for instance. I think I'll just make sure these letters are genuine too."

The manager was sent to fetch the register and it also turned out that he had luckily kept a note which the visitor had pinned to his door, asking to be called early. The inspector compared the handwritings on these with the letters.

"Genuine all right," he pronounced. "All the same . . ."

He walked to the window, turned, and gazed thoughtfully at the dead man, his eyes pinpoints of distrust.

"All the same?" prompted the doctor.

"All the same," replied the inspector, and now his puffy face looked tense and energetic, "I should like to know why friend O'Leary, who's lived for two years indoors and never come out except at night, has a face as sunburnt as a man who's lived in the sun for months!"

Dr. Harringay gave a whistle. "By jove, you're right! It's odd, damned odd!"

CHAPTER FOUR
The Miser Much Alive

NEXT morning Mr. O'Leary without hat or muffler, and exhaling good humour, walked into Inspector Gregson's office in Wantage. He was prompt to time.

"Now, Inspector," he said heartily, "what can I do for you? Say the word, and O'Leary's your man."

Inspector Gregson leaned back in his chair and looked at Mr. O'Leary. There was no answering smile on his face. If the corners of his mouth twitched at all, it was in a grimace of contempt.

After a moment of this quiet scrutiny, the burly red-headed man seemed to lose something of his jollity. He shifted uneasily from one foot to the other.

"Sit down, Mr. O'Leary," said the inspector at last. "And the first question I'm going to ask you is, *are* you Mr. O'Leary?"

Mr. O'Leary's eyes transferred themselves warily from the inspector's face to the wall above his right shoulder.

"What makes you think I wouldn't be?" he asked cautiously.

The inspector took out Crumbles' letter to the coroner. "Your pal didn't seem sure of your name himself. You see he's crossed out the name he put first, and then written 'Spike O'Leary' over the top. Moreover I have learned that George Crumbles was in Little Whippering making inquiries about you a day or two previous to his death, and the name O'Leary meant nothing to him. He recognized you only by your manner of life. The deduction's obvious."

"I can see you're quick in the uptake, Inspector. That's a bit of what I call Sherlock Holmes. Well, between you and me and the gate-post, O'Leary *ain't* my name. Leastways George Crumbles always knew me as Spike Galloway, though I'm not saying I was born that."

"And why did you change your name, Mr. O'Leary?"

"Well, that'd be a long story."

"All the same I should like to hear it. Particularly if it has something to do with this Tuffy Samson. We want to know why George Crumbles thought you would be pleased at Tuffy Samson's death. Is it a part of your story?"

Mr. O'Leary slapped the desk in front of him with his open palm.

"You're a corker, Inspector. Right on the nail each time! Yes, it's all one story. And it's a long one. But you know all of us, except you coppers of course, have got a thing or two in our pasts we don't like making a palaver about. Well this story's about something of the kind. Just a bit of adventure, really, but folk in England mightn't understand it that way."

The inspector grunted understandingly.

"That isn't exactly a new experience for a policeman, Mr. O'Leary, and I don't think you will find us easily shocked. If you make a clean breast of everything you know of Crumbles, I promise in return to divulge nothing that isn't absolutely essential to clearing up the cause of death. At present it seems a clear case of suicide. All we require is further light on the motive for Crumbles' action, and then no doubt we'll let the matter drop."

The inspector offered O'Leary a cigarette. He took it, made himself comfortable in his chair, and cocking his head back stared thoughtfully at the ceiling.

"Well, there were three of us, down on our luck at Kano—that's in Nigeria—more'n twelve years ago—Tuffy Samson, George Crumbles, and myself. We got talking about how to make money, having met Tuffy casual like, and he told us he was in on a good thing. He'd learned from some drunken native where the treasure of the nigger kingdom of Balooma had been buried during a British punitive expedition. We'd continued to occupy the country, so the Royal family, who were in exile, had left the treasure hidden. Only the Guardian of the treasure knew where it was. Well, this drunk was one of the Guardians, only he'd got kicked out for making trouble, and there in Kano he'd sunk lower and lower the way a black can when he's cut off from his tribe and fetiches and so forth. Now Balooma wasn't far down the coast and Tuffy Samson's idea was that we should lift the treasure. Of course it was a risky business. First of all the local blacks would have it in for us if they knew. We reckoned we could make rings round them all night, but the Administration had been trying to find the treasure too. If they caught us pinching it we should be in for a term of gaol under some damnation law of theirs. If there wasn't one, they'd invent it.

"Any way Tuffy Samson knew where this treasure was buried. Of course he didn't tell us where it was at first. As it happened it was about fifty yards out from the shore of a sacred lake in Balooma, in the shallows. He'd have tried to go after it alone, only he was fairly new to Africa, and anyway couldn't raise the wind to hire bearers and so forth. Crumbles and I had a little cash between us, and so we agreed to fit out the expedition. The treasure was to be split four ways, George and I taking a part each, and Tuffy two parts.

"Then came the job of getting into Balooma, for of course we had to get permission from the Administration. Finally I got hold of some moth-eaten professor in Kano belonging to a German learned society, and kidded him we were great hunters who could bring him back some new beasts and bugs. We told him we'd seen the Devil Pig, which all the natives round that part of the world believe in, in Balooma and that it was a kind of pigmy rhinoceros. He got quite excited and soon got permission for a Zoological Expedition from the Administration. They stipulated that he must lead the Expedition, but that suited us, for we knew we could jolly the old fool along, and get him to go wherever we wanted.

"And so we started off. The Society paid part of our expenses and our bearers were all hung round with killing bottles, and snares, and cages, and butterfly nets, and God knows what. We told old mossyface we had seen the Devil Pig on the shores of the Sacred Lake.

"When we got there we stole out at night, pulled up the treasure—all thick gold and ivory and stuff—and filled eight boxes with it. The next day when the professor was out with half the carriers, browsing among the orchids and what-not, we loaded up the rest of the carriers with our treasure and beat it like stink out of Balooma.

"But somehow or other we were spotted. I don't know to

this day how it happened. I don't see how anyone can have guessed what was in our loads, for they were all corded and sealed. But the bush telegraph started going when we were hopping as fast as we could drive our carriers through the swamps at the mouth of the Nwama River. We'd arranged for an Arab fishing boat to hang round in the harbour there, to pick us up if we were successful. But those bloody drums! They're eerie enough when you don't understand them— *pink boom! pink-boom pink-boom pinkety-pinkety, boom boom!* that's the way they go all the time. When you know that they're sending a message calling for your blood it makes the sweat come out all over you. I saw those blasted blacks' lips moving as they tried to read the message. Presently one of them got it, then they all started jabbering together.

"I thought they'd turn on us at once, so we all got out our rifles and stood by. But they didn't even make an attempt to attack us. They just dropped their loads where they stood and beat it into the swamp as if they'd been carrying snakes. I tried to stop one, and he went as white as a black can go— and I tell you it's a nasty moldy color. You'd have thought he was afraid one touch of my hands would strike him dead. And so we were left alone, like three fools, and those bloody drums still going.

"Well, it was twenty miles still to the harbor, and we knew we couldn't hoick the loads all that way. We should have to run like hell to get away with our skins.

So we dumped the treasure in a spot where no one would think of looking for it, and then started to make ourselves scarce.

"We managed to get to the shore and be picked up by our Arab friend but when he found we hadn't got the treasure he threatened to put us ashore again. Then he said he would take us only on condition we told him where the treasure was. We knew what *that* meant. He'd come back and pinch it himself. We had a hell of an argument, and then stuck a gun in his stomach and told him to order the crew to up with the sail and shut up. So we got going, but two or three hours afterwards, on purpose I reckon, he ran us practically under the bows of a Balooma Administration gunboat. The johnny in charge spotted three white men on board and ordered us to heave to. Then we knew the game was up.".

Up to this point O'Leary had been telling his narrative with a fire and a freedom which argued either that it was the plain truth, or else had been frequently rehearsed. Now he hesitated visibly.

"It gets a bit complicated at this point," he said awkwardly. "You see we were tried and Crumbles and I had a bit of a quarrel with Tuffy. Crumbles and I were in favour of telling the Administration where the treasure was, so as to get away with a light sentence. Tuffy wasn't, like an obstinate fool. So he got sentenced to ten year's imprisonment while George and I got off with three months."

"And the Administration got the treasure?" asked Inspector Gregson.

"Yes, the Administration got the treasure," said O'Leary, an evasive look in his eyes. "Well, while we were in prison, we saw Tuffy. He was feeling sore. He tried to get us once with an iron bar when we were exercising. Traitors, he called us, and you wouldn't believe how wild the man was. You'd have thought he blamed it on to us that he was in prison at all. As they dragged him away he swore that directly he got out of prison he'd do us in even if he had to drag us out of hell. And the trouble was we knew Tuffy would keep his word. We knew one or two things in his past, you see. He used to boast when he was drunk that he'd shot a man who'd been rude to him once, and knifed another who'd been a bit too sharp for him in business. Tuffy was a pleasant-spoken sort of man to meet, but if you ever irritated him and saw the nasty look in his eyes, well, you took good care to keep out of his way in future.

"Of course a gust of temper is all right, it's soon over, but if a man has ten years to brood over it, a man like Tuffy, it's a different thing. So we were a bit nervous, George and I when we came out. I went back to England, but George hung around the West Coast, partly because he liked it, partly to keep an eye open for when Tuffy came out.

"There was the difference between our temperaments, you see George couldn't abear to think of a danger hanging around somewhere coming goodness knows when. He wanted to rush up to it and get it over, whatever happened. Contrariwise I reckon myself a prudent chap. I keep out of the way of trouble.

"Well, two years ago, Tuffy was due to come out of prison. And I started to take precautions. I changed my name, went to live in Little Whippering, which seemed about as peaceful a place as I could find, and kept my weather eye lifting for trouble. I was reckoning on his getting tired of looking for me, you see. With the trouble I'd taken to cover up my tracks it stood to reason that he'd never find me. I reckoned he'd try to bump off George first, I hoped George would get him first—for he was pretty smart— else if he got George first that he'd get hung for George's murder. And I was right. He must have gone after George, for you see two years passed and he must have been out on the West Coast all the time looking for George until he got killed in that car accident."

Mr. O'Leary looked at the inspector and winked confidentially. "Now that George's dead, I don't mind saying I'd be surprised if it *was* an accident. It was altogether too lucky from George's point of view. And happening in the same town as George too!"

"Your idea is that Crumbles murdered Samson?" asked Gregson quietly. "And afterward killed himself out of remorse?"

O'Leary shifted uneasily. "Well, I wouldn't say murdered exactly. I mean it ain't a nice word to use of a pal. But after all George was entitled to protect himself. Self-defence is legal, ain't it? And I reckon he attended to Tuffy. He was a clever little devil, George was, to give him his due. But he was moody, never contented with what he'd got, and it's just like him to worry hisself silly with a thing like that, which an ordinary man takes in his stride, as you might say."

"Well, I wouldn't have said it," said Inspector Gregson. "Not in this country at any rate. It may be different on the West Coast of Africa. However, thank you for your frankness, Mr. O'Leary. It is a very interesting story in itself, and certainly throws light on the deceased.

"I don't think I shall need to trouble you again, but it will be necessary to repeat a portion of your story at the inquest. How much I cannot say. That will depend on the coroner. You will find him very reasonable. As you doubtless know you need to say nothing that would tend to incriminate yourself. However that hardly arises, for your old offence in Balooma has been purged by your trial and imprisonment. Meanwhile you must not change your address without letting us know."

"That's all right, Inspector, I'm not proposing to leave Little Whippering for a bit. Now that I know Tuffy's dead I feel a sight more cheerful. Bless you, you might say I'm a new man."

After Mr. O'Leary's departure, Inspector Gregson remained lost in thought, studying his copious notes of O'Leary's strange and somewhat glamorous story.

Then he put a trunk call through to the Colonial Office. As a result of that telephone conversation (as the inspector would no doubt have expressed it in a court of law) he sent a telegram to an official in Nigeria . . .

~§~

That evening the public bar of the Marion Arms was exhaustively discussing the sensation provided by Harry Thompson who, for the moment, was the most important man in the village. There was not, of course, the slightest doubt of what had actually happened.

"He done him in," said Mr. Gudgeon, "the foul-mouthed old curmudgeon! There can't be a doubt of it. An' I'd like to know what the inspector means letting him come back here. Why any of us might be asflixeated in our beds."

"'E's a murderer," quavered Mr. Padding from the corner, "and I always knowed it."

He reflected with some annoyance that this had been his original theory, out of which he had been argued by Gudgeon. If only he had stuck to it he might now have been basking in all the glory of a successful prophet. As it was he did his best.

"I always knowed it, but naterly I didn't want to skeer the wimmen."

"Well, tell us what he's like, Harry," asked Mr. Bundling, wiping the froth off his beard. "I can't somehow picture un. Is he fierce-like?"

Harry scratched his head. "Well, he ain't anything particular, he looks ordinary enough, just like you or me."

"Who does?" said a voice.

Mr. O'Leary was standing in the doorway, a tanned square-jawed man in flannel trousers, a hat stuck on the back of his cropped head, and a disarming smile on his face.

"Good-evening, Harry! Good-evening, gentlemen."

No one in the room had looked on the countenance of Mr. O'Leary except Harry Thompson. Consequently they all, except Harry, returned the stranger's good-evening with an equable murmur, and prepared to continue their discussion. Harry himself was for a moment stricken dumb by the sudden appearance of the recluse. But he pulled himself together with an effort. At all costs the community must be warned of the murderer in their midst.

"Why, good-evening, Mr. O'Leary!" he said loudly. "We didn't think to see you here, Mr. O'Leary!"

There was a sudden awe-struck silence, then a volley of clinks as glasses and cans were hurriedly put down. Jaws opened in horror or surprise. Even Mr. O'Leary felt the sudden change in the social temperature.

"Surprised to see me, were you, gentlemen?" Mr. O'Leary laughed loudly and carelessly. "Well, I admit I've been a bit of a hermit as you might say. But I had my reasons. I had my reasons! It's all over now. And I'm going to make up for lost time. You watch me! I'm going to celebrate, and when Spike O'Leary says *celebrate* he means it. Yes, you sons of guns, I'll show you what we mean by celebration where *I* come from!"

"Where do you come from?" said Mr. Gudgeon argumenttatively.

"Where do I come from? That's a good 'un." Mr. O'Leary laughed again. "I come from a place where it's as hot as hell, as thirsty as the Sahara, and as smelly as the bilge of an Arab dhow."

Without waiting for comment on this cryptic remark Mr. O'Leary flung a handful of silver on the counter.

"Drinks all round!" he exclaimed to Mrs. Hippie, a little white-haired old lady dressed in rusty black. Mrs. Hippie looked at Mr. O'Leary, looked at the silver, and sniffed.

"Anything wrong with it, darling?" asked Mr. O'Leary, leaning one elbow on the counter with an expansive smile.

Mrs. Hippie jerked her head back indignantly.

"That's as may be, and my name's Mrs. Hippie."

"Lor', you don't half shrivel a man up, do you?" said Mr. O'Leary, the focus of a tense silence, which, however, he showed no signs of noticing. "Well, I ain't easily 'urt. Don't forget to include one for yourself in the drinks, with my respecks!"

The company in the Marion Arms waited for someone to voice their sentiments. The duty clearly fell on Mr. Padding, as the oldest. He piped up bravely:

"Thanking you, but I don't want no drink!"

Mr. O'Leary swung round abruptly, causing the ancient nearly to topple off his seat. Mr. Padding supported his quivering hands on his stick, and stared up at the stranger defiantly.

"You don't want no drink!" repeated Mr. O'Leary slowly, and his voice was cold and tense. "Are you ill?"

"No, I ain't ill."

"Are you T.T.?"

At any other time this ludicrous question would have provided laughter from the assembled company. But as it was they gazed silently at Mr. Padding's trembling lips. His eyes still fixed by the reptilian gaze of the stranger, he answered in a strangled voice:

"No, I ain't T.T."

"Then is it because you object to my company?" roared Mr. O'Leary, suddenly seeming to expand to twice his normal size. "Say so, if it is! Say so by all means! Then we'll know where we are. Go on, it's quite simple. Just say, *I don't like your company!*"

Mr. O'Leary towered over the awestruck yokel, his fists swinging gently by his side, their freckled backs turned towards the other, who stared fascinated at the dense growth of red hair running up to the knuckles. Blue fire seemed to shoot out of Mr. O'Leary's eyes. Mr. Padding, justifying himself to his cronies afterwards, explained, "He 'ipnertized me, that's what 'appened. I meaned to tell un to get out of a respectable public, but something went clickety in my throat."

"Do you object to my company?" thundered Mr. O'Leary again.

"No!" exclaimed Mr. Padding at last, with a kind of squeak.

"Then you'll have a drink with me?"

"Yes."

"Here's what I call a pal," roared Mr. O'Leary patting him on the back with a wolfish grin. "Hearty! Matey! Up-and-coming! Forward with the beer for Old Jollywhiskers here, Mrs. Hippie, darling! And here's yours, Harry! Help yourself, everyone."

The rest of the company did not feel it incumbent on them to stand where Mr. Padding had given way. The drinks were accepted, but if they thought they were going to finish with Mr. O'Leary so simply, they were mistaken in their man.

"Hey, drink up, lads! What are you, a lot of sissies? Bless my soul, I thought Little Whippering had a name for beer drinking. Down with the stuff. Come on, I'll show you. Mrs. Hippie, a quart of beer!"

"A quart?" said Mrs. Hippie incredulously.

"Yes, a quart, dearie."

"We ain't got a quart tankard."

"Don't be awkward, angel-face. Shove it in anything. Bowl, basin, jug, flowerpot, or," with a wink, "even 'umbler utensils!"

Mrs. Hippie eventually returned with a brimming Toby Jug, which she placed on the counter with an expression as who should say, "I won't be answerable for the consequences."

"*Now* watch me, lads," said Mr. O'Leary. Taking a deep breath, he threw his head back, applied his mouth to the jug, and began to drink. He was watched in an awestruck silence until he waved the jug triumphantly upside down in the air to prove its emptiness, at the same time expelling his breath in a long sigh.

"That's the way to lap it up, lads, bless my soul! A quart between breaths. It's good for the lungs."

He banged the jug on the bar. "That's some good beer you've got there, sweetest. Bring me another pint, and a pint all round. Damnation take it, make it a quart all round! And a bottle of Scotch for the man who can drink his off without taking a breath!"

The bottle of Scotch was won by Harry. Panting, with popping eyes, he staggered slightly, when Mr. O'Leary clapped him on the back.

"There's a man for you! We could do with more lads like him in Britain today!"

It is impossible to drink beer continuously at a man's expense and continue to preserve a frigid attitude towards him, particularly a man with a dominating personality like Mr. O'Leary.

Mr. O'Leary, moreover, was assiduous in his attentions to the company. With Harry he was patronizing. To Mr. Gudgeon he was respectful. With Mr. Bundling he was matey. With Mr. Snugg courteous. Even Mrs. Hippie thawed after the fifth gin, and smiled when Mr. O'Leary asserted that she had the most fetching dimple he had ever seen, it made him feel young again.

Then Mr. O'Leary jumped up on the bar. "Come on, lads, a song," he said, waving a siphon, "I'll lead you."

Little Whippering had always been proud of its glees, and it seemed that Mr. O'Leary, sojourning in heathen lands, had learned a number of songs, some of them with strangely attractive catches. Presently even Mr. Padding was opening his toothless gums and joining in the ditties, gently waving his mug, while Mr. O'Leary roared encouragement and from time to time bestowed smacking kisses on Mrs. Hippie's hand or any other available portion of her venerable person.

One song in particular appealed to Little Whippering, and it was only next morning that it struck them, in the circumstances, as peculiarly ill-chosen. It recited the sufferings of one Ted, a parson's son, condemned to live in a tropical port. The ending was sung with tremendous gusto and imitative gesture by O'Leary:

> He said: "I've missed the bleeding boat!"
> *(Poor old Ted, the parson's son!)*
> He tied a rope around his throat.
> *(Poor old Ted, the parson's son!)*
>
> He jumped upon the nearest chair,
> (Poor *old Ted, the parson's son!)*
> He swung his feet into the air.
> *(Poor old Ted, the parson's son!)*
>
> He waved his ankles to and fro!
> *(Poor old Ted, the parson's son!)*
> He kicked and jerked like billyo!
> *(Poor old Ted, the parson's son!)*

When Mrs. Hippie for the last time called beseechingly, "Time, gentlemen, please," Mr. O'Leary appeared to be the only person in full possession of his faculties. It was a dark moonless night, and for more than an hour afterwards figures wavered uncertainly among the lanes, making encouraging noises to each other, seeking their dwelling places. Once there was an appalling objurgation, when Mr. Bundling was caught by the ditch as it pounced on him for the second time. He tripped headlong into it. He was helped out by Harry Thompson, who, by some extraordinary freak of nature, suddenly found himself in the ditch, being helped out by Mr. Bundling. This gave him a horrible uncertain feeling, as if he were not quite sure whether he were Harry Thompson or Mr. Bundling. One person, believed to be young Bunn, made no attempt to go home, but remained huddled up outside the Marion Arms.

Meanwhile the steps of Mr. O'Leary could be heard tapping loudly on the macadam surface of the lull, and then suddenly dying away as he turned off on the long track which led towards the Wilderness. Even when his footsteps had become inaudible, and for long afterwards, the strains of his loud melodious voice could be heard, floating over the thatched roofs of Little Whippering:

> He waved his ankles to and fro!
> *(Poor old Ted, the parson's son!)*
> He kicked and jerked, like billyo!
> *(Poor old Ted, the parson's son!)*

CHAPTER FIVE
The Vicar Shocked

INSPECTOR Gregson smoothed out the cable and read it aloud to his chief.

Gregson—Berkshire County Constabulary.
REF. YOUR COMMUNICATION ERNEST SAMSON KNOWN AS TUFFY KILLED IN CAR ACCIDENT THREE MONTHS AGO. DEATH BY MISADVENTURE. TWELVE YEARS EARLIER SAMSON WITH ACCOMPLICES CRUMBLES AND GALLOWAY FOUND GUILTY ROBBERY WITH VIOLENCE, DESECRATION OF LOCAL SHRINE, AND OBTAINING PERMITS UNDER FALSE PRETENCES BY EUROPEAN COURT AT LORANGO, BALOOMA. CRUMBLES AND GALLOWAY GOT LIGHT SENTENCES, SAMSON GOT TEN YEARS, AND AFTER RELEASE WAS IMMEDIATELY CONCERNED IN BANK ROBBERY AT LAGOS AND GOT FURTHER SENTENCE. CRUMBLES FIRST CAME TO NIGERIA TWELVE YEARS AGO.
MacPHERSON, Nigerian Police.

Gregson looked up at his chief.

"That seems clear enough. It confirms O'Leary's story. He is the Galloway mentioned in the cable. It's a discreditable story at the best in any case, and doesn't seem the kind a man would make up. It's obvious that Crumbles and O'Leary played a despicable trick on Samson. I fancy if we got the whole record of the case we'd find that they not only gave away the hiding place of the treasure, but also threw all the blame on him. They may even have pleaded that they were ignorant of the object of the expedition. O'Leary seemed ashamed of that part of the story, so I fancy my guess is right. In any case it all explains O'Leary's terror of Samson.

"I suppose Crumbles and O'Leary kept in touch with each other throughout the ten years. Probably they promised to warn each other. Otherwise it's difficult to see how Crumbles managed to hit on the very village O'Leary was hiding in.

"Well, we've got to assume that Crumbles is the sort of man who would kill himself in this rather theatrical way, out of remorse for doing in Tuffy. It's a tall order. First of all he sounds far too tough a character for that. Secondly we don't know that he did kill Tuffy . . . The finding was 'Death by Misadventure.'" Gregson sighed dismally. "I suppose I ought to send over for the record . . ."

The chief smiled quizzically at Gregson. "I gather from all this that you're not at all sure that it is suicide?"

"No, sir, I'm not."

"But, man, why not, in the name of goodness? You've got evidence of preparation for suicide. You've got his last letters. And you've got an explanation. What more do you want?"

"I don't like O'Leary's sunburn!" burst out the inspector, "It isn't natural. And I don't like his manner. He's too damn pleased with himself about something."

"Tuffy's death."

"No, it isn't only that. If it was, it would be just sheer relief. But he's got the look of a man who's just brought off a damned good deal thanks to his own cleverness."

The chief shook his head reprovingly.

"Gregson, you're getting fanciful in your old age. Sunburn, indeed! Perhaps he has one of those ultraviolet lamps."

"Yes, perhaps." The inspector grinned mirthlessly. Then he pulled a twist of paper out of his pocket and unwrapped it, producing a tuft of hair.

"Look at that!"

"Ginger hair," said the chief, examining it carefully. "Rather dirty."

"It's ginger *now*," said Gregson, "but it wasn't when I found it. It was dark."

"Dyed?"

Gregson nodded. "I think so. The manager can't remember any red-haired men's having occupied Crumbles' room. My opinion is that it's O'Leary's hair."

"O'Leary's? But why should he want to dye his hair?"

"For the same reason as he sometimes wore a muffler, to disguise himself."

"Why both?"

"Well, sometimes the muffler would attract attention. O'Leary's red-headed, and without a hat and muffler his most conspicuous feature would be his red hair. Red hair's a thing everyone notices. Assume for argument's sake that to disguise himself at some time he dyes it. Now you can't get hair-dye off instantaneously. So supposing O'Leary wanted to get back to normality quickly, what would he do? Why, crop his hair down to the skull, to show the red roots."

"I don't quite see why there should be any red roots."

"Well, hair grows all the time, so a week after you've dyed it, it's its natural colour for a millimeter or so at the base. Cutting it short, therefore, restores its natural colour. Now it's obvious at a glance that O'Leary has had his hair cropped. Very recently. Perhaps in the last day or two. On top of that there's this tuft of dyed hair."

The chief constable whistled.

"That's odd, certainly! But why should he disguise himself? What do you think happened?"

"It seems to me O'Leary must have visited Crumbles before his death. Either that morning, or the evening before. He would have been hatless, with dark hair, and perhaps wearing glasses. Then, at some later time, he cropped his head in Crumbles' room, and tried to get rid of the dyed hair. But some of it got trapped in the basin. Of course we can't say whether he visited Crumbles in disguise so as not to be known by him, or simply to escape outside observation, but I feel sure that O'Leary saw Crumbles before he drove into Abingdon with Harry Thompson. In fact if he cropped his hair in Crumbles' bedroom, this must have been at some earlier time, for he could hardly have done it in the ten minutes between his arrival and his discovery of the dead body."

"It's a great deal to build on a tuft of hair."

"That's not all. O'Leary also made a thorough search of Crumbles' room. I found his fingerprints everywhere. Whether he found what he wanted, of course, I don't know, but the search certainly took more than ten minutes."

The chief constable perked up at the mention of fingerprints.

"Ah, now we're getting down to something."

"Another thing," went on the inspector. "Take the wire sent by Crumbles to O'Leary. Apart from the oddness of the wording, why was it ever sent at all? We have evidence from several people at Little Whippering that Crumbles went to Little Whippering two or three days previously to call on O'Leary. Why, if he saw O'Leary then, didn't he give him the good news? Why all this business about wanting to give a dying message? It all links up with my belief that there is something fishy about that wire. I don't believe it means what it says. I believe that Crumbles and O'Leary had met at least once, if not twice, before it was ever sent. Probably once in Little Whippering at the Wilderness and once in Abingdon at the hotel."

"Have you got the original of that wire?"

"Yes, sir, the Post Office sent it over to me this morning. It's in Crumbles' writing all right, and the assistant remembers his sending it. No, I don't suggest Crumbles didn't send it, but I think it was either a blind or a code."

"Yes, but after all, Gregson," interposed the chief, "you can't get away from the evidence about Crumbles' depresssion! Here you are, in your notebook: 'He wouldn't eat anything, but pushed the food gloomily aside.' After all, appetite is a pretty good sign! No one commits suicide on a full stomach, so they say."

"Oh, do they!" answered Gregson triumphantly, "well, then, I've found that Crumbles did have a full stomach. Although he pretended not to touch his meals at the Ethelreda Hotel, he twice went out to the station hotel and had a good blow-out."

"Are you certain?" exclaimed the chief constable incredulously.

"Positive! The waiter remembers a man who had on a light fawn coat with a fur collar—a black-bearded man. Well, black beards are uncommon, and fawn coats with fur collars less frequent still. Crumbles had both."

"In other words, Gregson, you've already quite made up your mind that this suicide is fishy," said the chief with a grin. "Otherwise you wouldn't have gone round everywhere enquiring after Crumbles' movements. Well, have it your own way! What do you want me to do?"

"Just as you like, sir," said Gregson humbly. "All I say is, there's something fishy here. If you ask me, this man O'Leary's been leading a double life. He's been pretending to be a sort of hermit, but all the time he's been gallivanting about, probably in disguise with his hair dyed. Hence the sunburn. There's something fishy about friend Crumbles too. A man who pretends to be fasting out of melancholy, and then goes and has a blow-out at the nearest restaurant! On top of that Crumbles and O'Leary meet once in Little Whippering and again in Abingdon, and yet Crumbles sends a wire asking O'Leary to come to Abingdon, as if they hadn't met for twelve years. Then Crumbles has got a fully loaded revolver in his pocket, and yet, instead of choosing a quick method like that, he prefers to hang himself.

Directly he's dead, O'Leary, who must have known about Tuffy's death at least two days earlier, when Crumbles called on him in Little Whippering, suddenly perks up, as if he'd cleverly turned the tables on everyone.

"There's a good deal wrong here, sir, as you'll admit. My own guess is that the both of them were playing a game, and either something went wrong, or else O'Leary double-crossed the other. A game within a game you might say. Of course it may still be suicide for all that. But if it is, let's have the true story. We haven't got it yet, by a long chalk."

"Yes, it certainly sounds odd, though no doubt there's some simple explanation. There generally is. What do you want me to do, Gregson? For I can see you want something by the look in your eye."

"Well, sir, I think we ought to go to the C.I.D."

"Really. At this stage?"

"Yes, sir. Those London chaps always say, when we do call them in, that of course it's really too late, all the clues are stale, but they'll do their best. So win or lose, they get the credit. Not that I blame them, I'd do the same myself. And they're smart lads, I'll give them that, but if we're going to call them in at all, we ought to do it now, I say. We needn't tell the press we've done it yet, sir."

"But is there anything we can't tackle locally?"

"Yes, sir, there's a lot. First of all I want to get a line on what this fellow O'Leary was doing before he came here. Where was he living? Where did he pick up the money to live on? He may be a London burglar for all we know. And where was Crumbles staying before he came here? It's an odd thing, sir, but there were practically no small personal possessions on him such as you'd expect, only a suitcase of clothes. He must have a trunkful of stuff somewhere. All that's C.I.D. routine. Then I want to get reports about the Treasure Trial and Samson's death cabled out here. That's a C.I.D. job. Those foreign chaps don't take much notice of us country fossils."

"All right," said his chief. "You probably know best, though all this Scotland Yard business annoys me. It's these damned detective story writers. Anyone would think there'd never been a murderer that the C.I.D. hadn't discovered." Grunting to himself, he made a note on his pad.

"And while you're about it, sir," put in Inspector Gregson. "May I suggest you ask for Inspector Campbell—Archibald Campbell I think it is? He's a smart boy, and easy to work with. You remember he was down here on that bank robbery."

"Archibald Campbell," wrote the chief with a grin. "Another Scot, eh? How you do hang together! I suppose you two will get together and discuss us godless Berkshire yokels for hours."

"I wouldna' waste ma time on sich havers," said the inspector primly, with a stage Scottish accent. "Discussing Southrons indeed! There wouldna' be ony end to that."

"Well," smiled the chief, getting up and going to the sideboard, "I think you can find something worth discussing here. Scottish too! Say when! You like it pretty strong, I know."

"I don't mind if I do," said Inspector Gregson.

~§~

The vicar looked up from his letters timidly. "Oh, my love, I don't know whether I have told you or not, but Mr. Jones is arriving today."

Mrs. Wykeham glared at him sharply. "Mr. Jones? Who is he? And what is he coming for? Tea?"

The vicar rubbed his hands together and smiled nervously.

"No, Pattie, dearest, to stay, of course."

"What, to stay the night?"

"No, my love, to stay—er—permanently."

Mrs. Wykeham put down the coffee pot and stared at her husband. She was a large woman, with an imperious nose. Two lines running from the nostrils down the inner edges of the cheeks and on to a double chin made her look rather like a bulldog.

"Samuel!" she said solemnly. "What've you done now?"

The Rev. Samuel wiped his mouth with his napkin to hide his agitation. Then he beat his forehead feebly with his fist.

"Dear me, my love! I do believe I forgot to tell you."

"What is it this time? And whatever it is, tell me *quickly*," said Mrs. Wykeham, beginning to quiver with annoyance. "I can't bear the suspense. Have you been gambling?"

For some reason unexpected bad news and gambling had become inevitably associated in Mrs. Wykeham's extreme youth, and now whenever one happened, the other also popped into her mind.

"No, darling, on the contrary! Don't you remember, some time ago, when we found the dilapidations so heavy, we decided we couldn't keep up this big house alone? And so we decided to take boarders!"

"I remember nothing of the kind!" exclaimed Mrs. Wykeham, shutting her mouth firmly. "Boarders indeed! As if I should agree!"

"But you must remember," wailed the vicar, feeling the ground trembling under his feet. "You were sitting there, just as you are now, and I picked up my coffee cup like this, and putting down the bill from Higgs the builders, I said quite distinctly, 'Pattie, my love, we must take in paying guests or, to use their grosser but older name, boarders'! You, I am sure, agreed. And from that moment I started to look out for them.

"In fact," blurted out Mr. Wykeham, everything coming with a rush, as it does so often when one embarks on a confession, "I advertised for one!"

"You advertised for one?" breathed Mrs. Wykeham, unable to let go the coffee pot, which appeared to be the only steady thing in a shifting world. "You *advertised!* Go on, Samuel. Tell me everything."

"But surely you remember," wailed the vicar for the third time, licking his dry lips.

"I tell you, I do not, Samuel!"

"I remember," interposed Psyche, Mr. Wykeham's only child, a girl of sixteen. "Only it was me you said it to, not mother. Mother was out of the room. You asked me what I thought of the idea. And I said it would be top-hole if you could get someone who could dance."

Mr. Wykeham beat his forehead again violently. "*Now* I remember. Of course, Pattie, will you ever forgive me? My terrible absent-mindedness! Having mentioned it to Psyche, I thought, as the result of the association of ideas, which is the foundation of human psychology, that I had mentioned it also to you, and got your approval. And dear me, he's coming today."

"Samuel, don't *flutter*," said Mrs. Wykeham, composing her hands resignedly before her vast bosom. "I suppose I shall have to forgive you, as I usually do. If you spent a little less time with your nose in those adventure books with all those pictures of savages, hardly decent I call it, and gave more time to ordinary things, this wouldn't happen, but there, what's the use of talking?"

Mrs. Wykeham patted her hair. "Let's know the worst by all means. Who is he?"

"Can he dance?" asked Psyche eagerly. "And is he good-looking?"

"Well, I can hardly say," said Mr. Wykeham evasively.

"SAMUEL!" asked Mrs. Wykeham in her most terrible voice. "Have you *seen* this person?"

"I can't say I have, my dear," confessed the vicar miserably.

"But don't worry," he added. "He was at Oxford, one of the better colleges. I am sure he is quite all right. He has a good scholastic record. And his batting average appears to have been distinctly good, at any rate during his last year. He will be an asset to our local team. After all," rattled on the vicar, feeling that he was navigating a difficult passage with skill, "he is certain to be a gentleman. At the worst he will have good manners. He enclosed a testimonial from his tutor about his character. 'Cheerful, intelligent, and diligent.' Even if I had seen him, it could tell me no more. You know how short-sighted I am. Don't keep jumping up and down, Psyche. What is it you want to know?"

"If he's from Oxford, will he be as wet as young Marion? Because if so it will be rather stinking."

"Psyche, Psyche, where did you pick up such expressions! And at your age you should refer to him as Mr. Marion. As for what you mean by *wet*—"

"You'd better not ask her," said Mrs. Wykcham wisely. "But one thing I must know, Samuel. Is he a *FOREIGNER?* For really I would have to think twice before I could permit a Frenchman to stay here."

"No, he can't be a foreigner. Not with the name of Jones. N. Jones, he signs himself. And now I come to think of it, he mentions, among other things, that he is a British subject.

He would be Welsh, of course, Joneses always are."

"Well, I only hope so," said Mrs. Wykcham darkly.

"I am sure it will be all right," answered the Rev. Samuel. Although he had got the confession off his chest, he did not seem cheerful. Mrs. Wykeham regarded him anxiously.

"In my advertisement I stipulated that we would only take University graduates," he went on. "In both cases the University is quite sound."

"In both cases?" exclaimed Mrs. Wykeham, "did I hear you say *both?*"

"Er, yes, my darling, I did make use of the dual number. You needn't trouble your pretty head about the second arrival, however. He is not due here for another week. He is coming from America."

"From America!" groaned Mrs. Wykeham.

"My angel pet, would you be so kind as not to repeat the final phrase of my sentence? I find it so distracting. You see, I am so used to preaching, where no one ever dreams of making any remark at all. Except that once when Mr. Bundling absent-mindedly said, 'Hear, hear,' and as the text was 'Blessed is he that hath his quiver full,' he no doubt felt called upon for an opinion. As it is, my head is swimming with all this business, I hardly know where I am. Ah, yes, the person from America. A Dr. Ridge. A very learned man, judging by his degrees, and although we know that not all American universities are—well, this is difficult. I have heard of the seat of learning that has honoured this gentleman. Harvard by name, and really I am quite delighted at the prospect of having someone who cares for scholarship here.

"The only thing is," added the vicar, staring at the letter thoughtfully and pulling his upper lip, "I am beginning to wonder if the doctor is quite—well, I hardly know how to put it, but he has some extraordinary ideas."

Mrs. Wykeham, thanks to considerable experience, had

managed to get the general drift of the vicar's vague ramblings.

"Do you mean to say that the man's a lunatic?" she asked with brutal simplicity. "It only needed that! A madman, and a Frenchman under my roof and a murderer up at the Wilderness. Good Heavens!"

"My dear, as I said, I feel sure that Mr. Jones is not French. As for the American, I am no doubt being unjust to him. I am quite unfamiliar with American academic expressions. Dr. Ridge writes to me on notepaper headed 'First Themistocles Berkshire Anthropological Expedition.' "

"Themistocles! Anthropological!" exclaimed Mrs. Wykeham. "Why the man must be positively dangerous !"

"Oh, what fun, Mother!" exclaimed Psyche. "Do you think it will be like that lovely film we saw about the man who murdered hundreds and hundreds of children!"

"Be quiet, Psyche! If I'd known what that film was like we'd never have gone to it. What is all this about, Samuel? This Themistocles business?"

"Well, my dear, it is not quite so odd as it sounds. Themistocles happens to be the name of the university where Dr. Ridge is pursuing his post graduate researches. Anthropological usually connotes research into primitive culture in England, but of course that is a specialized meaning. No doubt over the water it is used in a wider way. Even so, the letter itself is odd."

"Let me see it," said Mrs. Wykeham. She read it out slowly:

"Reverend sir,

"Thank your, for your letter of the 15th instant. I am glad to hear that you will be able to fix me for the period in question. The terms you mention are very reasonable. As to references, Professor Valinoff of Kings (University of London), or Dr. Hope-Smith, of Cambridge, both know my work.

"I may bring a Miss Philberry with me."

"Indeed," muttered Mrs. Wykeham, "you will do nothing of the sort. At least this place will be kept respectable."

"But this depends on whether the funds of the expedition cam afford to finance two workers. In any case I should warn you well in advance should she accompany me. If you are pressed for room, we could occupy the one bedroom."

"The beast!" exclaimed Mrs. Wykeham. "Does he realize what a vicarage is?"

"I am expecting great things of this expedition and hope the natives will be friendly. Meanwhile, I am learning the language.

"Yours faithfully,
"V. RIDGE, Ph.D."

"Natives, language!" exclaimed Mrs. Wykeham. "What on earth does he mean by the final sentence?"

"I think, my dear," said the vicar mildly, "that Dr. Ridge must be pulling my leg. Mr. Vansteem, over at the Elms, is fond of chaffing me in such a way that one never knows whether he is in earnest or not, so I think it must be an American characteristic."

"Well, we'll see, but I warn you," said Mrs. Wykeham masterfully, "that if there's the slightest thing wrong about either Mr. Jones or Dr. Ridge, out they go at once!"

"Yes, my pet," answered the vicar mildly.

The vicar was always mild, and Mrs. Wykeman was always masterful, which gave people the impression that Mr. Wykeham was henpecked. Nothing could be farther from the truth. In his mild fussy way, Mr. Wykeham always did exactly what he liked, while Mrs. Wykeham toiled panting after him, putting down her foot or drawing the line repeatedly, without any effect, except possibly the harmless one of consoling herself.

Such states of affairs are common. Indeed the psychologist will recognize that they are the rule rather than the exception. The really henpecked husband is the blustering bully with a meek timorous wife who, by skillful sapping and well-organized non-cooperation, always gets precisely what she wants, and leaves him beating the air.

"All the same," thought Mr. Wykeham, walking downstairs to the peace of his library, "it will be a little awkward if this Jones person turns out to be what dear old Toby used to call 'not the clean potato.' Such an expressive term! But it is hardly possible. After all, Balliol is surely Balliol, even in these unregenerate times."

The vicar settled down to a comfortable reading of "Ten Years Among the Head-hunters." He had just reached a thrilling incident, when he heard his wife's startled voice outside.

"Samuel. Come at once."

He put down the book with a sigh.

"And drawing his knife across my throat, the Dyak said," he repeated, memorizing the final sentence until he could pick the book up again.

Then he opened the door. "What is it, Pattie, my darling poppet, whatever is the matter? You look quite scared!"

Mrs. Wykeham tottered feebly to a chair. "Samuel!" she moaned. "Go downstairs, at once. I can't face it. Mr. Jones has come. Oh, dear, oh, dear, oh, dear!"

Trembling slightly the vicar hastened down the stairs. The front door was open. There, lounging casually against the door post and clad in an immaculate flannel suit, was a negro.

For one moment Mr. Wykeham thought he was back among the head-hunting Dyaks, then he pulled himself together with an effort. "Mr. Jones?" he faltered.

The negro smiled, showing a dazzling array of perfect

teeth.

"Yes, Neptune Jones. I say, Vicar, what a perfectly charming old-world village this is, isn't it?"

"Er, yes. Oh, yes! Delightful. Er—you must excuse my wife," fluttered the vicar. "She is liable to faint suddenly. Yes. Yes. Most distressing. At any moment. Er, come in, will you?"

So arrived the vicar's first paying guest.

CHAPTER SIX
Yet Another Body?

INSPECTOR Archibald Campbell was thirty-five years old. He was methodical, and although he had never startled his Department by any brilliant feats of intuition, he could be relied upon not to miss any obvious clues, and to keep hammering away at a case until all the rough edges had vanished.

He was the graduate of a Scottish University, who had come south to find a niche for himself. A chance acquaintance with a superintendent of the C.I.D. had suggested that there might be opportunities in criminal investigation for his combination of practical commonsense and mental tidiness. He had soon attracted attention by a scheme evolved in cooperation with the big car dealers, for keeping a better check on the stolen motor-car industry. He had been noticed as a clever youngster and had been able to prove his soundness in a number of other departments. Hence a fairly rapid promotion. But this would be his first connection with sudden death.

"Not that I think it's at all likely to be murder, Campbell," remarked his chief. "As far as I can see it's a plain case of suicide. The only thing is that there's some dirty business mixed up with it, as there so often is. Old Gregson wants to clear that up. You can't blame him, of course. So do your best to get a good line on the whole thing, even though there won't be any bouquets going."

Campbell also, as the train hammered along the Great Western track, was of opinion that there was not likely to be much in it. It was a commonplace of police work that suicides always looked fishy, always caused endless trouble, and always ended up by being—well, just suicides.

"It stands to reason, that a suicide must be absolutely potty," thought Campbell, serenely confident, out of the glow of health and the zest of a change of scene, that it was good to be alive. "So you can't apply any of the ordinary criteria to them."

At Abingdon he saw Gregson's familiar countenance flaming ruggedly beside the ticket collector, and the two men greeted each other with the restrained cordiality of Scots in exile.

They made a contrast, a contrast so acute that it was difficult to believe they belonged to the same profession. Gregson was large, clumsily built, and added to his awkwardness by wearing clothes which hung around him like a rhinoceros's hide. Above this was that formidable face, with its fiery contortions, bald dome, and fringe of silvery hair.

Campbell's slight but broad-shouldered figure was as usual clothed in a well-fitting suit which gave him a touch of the dapper, an elegance regarding which he had often been teased by his colleagues. It resulted in rather more than his fair share of allocations to nightclub round-ups. Campbell had a pleasant face, disarming rather than good-looking. In any case it had not been improved by an unregulated enthusiasm for boxing. A broken nose was one of the results. Even when feeling cheerful, Campbell looked serious. On serious occasions he appeared preternaturally solemn. But when he did laugh his merriment was prodigious. As a colleague said once: "Campbell doesn't often see a joke, but, my God, when he does!"

Gregson took Campbell round to the chief's private house and, sitting in his library, the three men discussed the situation.

"Gregson's crime," the chief called it good-humouredly, disclaiming any responsibility for bringing Campbell down. "If you ask me, all Gregson's wanted is someone to roll his r's with over a glass of whisky."

"I don't think he would bring me all the way down for that, sir," answered Campbell seriously, after carefully considering this suggestion against the professional honour of his colleague.

"Well, we'll see. Gregson, give Inspector Campbell an outline of the case."

Gregson did so, from time to time handing the C.I.D. man relevant documents and reports. Campbell made no comment, and only occasionally asked a question.

At the end of the story he remained for some time in silence, thinking. His first hasty reaction had been to agree with the verdict of his own and Gregson's chief. But soon, even at second-hand, he began to get a whiff of the sinister peculiarities of O'Leary's character, which had really been the governing motive for Gregson's doubts.

Then Gregson's discoveries—the tuft of hair, the fingerprints proving an exhaustive search by O'Leary of Crumbles' room, and the queer incident of the meals outside the hotel—combined to leave rough edges which offended his orderly mind.

"It's certainly odd. All the same," he said hesitantly, "I can't see any reason yet, to doubt that it's suicide. You've got an unstable criminal type in Crumbles, and there's no knowing what he mightn't do if his plans went wrong. It may be that remorse for having killed Samson had something to do with it, but I don't see how the report of the motor-car accident will help us. If it were really a faked-up accident, it would need a fresh inquiry on the spot to prove it. No, we've got to focus our attention on what happened here in England. First of all I'll get headquarters on to seeing where Crumbles stayed before he came to Abingdon. If he came from London, as seems likely, there's probably a trunk of his knocking round at a cloakroom or a hotel. The shipping companies will help too. We can go through the recent sailings, for it's evident he was in Nigeria not less than three months ago.

"We'll also go into O'Leary's previous history. The solicitors who let the Wilderness should help us there. And I think we must see if we can't pick up some gossip in the village itself. If O'Leary really has been making expeditions under cover of pretending to be a hermit, surely someone must have spotted something suspicious. We all know villagers don't miss much."

"Yes, but the Wilderness is all by itself on the edge of the Downs. It would be easy for him to be picked up by a car on the other side without anyone's knowing. Even if he had been spotted walking over the Downs, they would just have thought of him as a stranger, never having seen his face, you see!"

"Well, we've got to take that chance. As for your famous sunburn, Gregson, why not be obvious, and ask him? Naturally he'll give us some excuse, but his face will be worth watching. And often a lie is more informative than the truth."

The phone bell rang, and after lifting the receiver the chief handed the instrument over to Gregson.

"For you."

Gregson put the receiver to his ear and heard the robust voice of Police-Constable Collop. His excitement was evident.

"Don't shout so loudly," exclaimed Gregson, as the earpiece jangled. "I can hear you all right!"

"Sorry, sir," said Collop, "seeing as how you were right over at Abingdon, I thought I'd better speak up. It's about O'Leary, sir. The William Bundling boy has seen him burying a corpse in his garden."

"What?" exclaimed Gregson. "Don't be a fool, man!"

"It's a fact," answered Collop stolidly. "Saw him with his own eyes, and the corpse too!"

"The child must be potty. When was this?"

"The night Crumbles hanged himself, sir. I've got the boy here and can bring him over, sir, if you like."

"Yes, do. Get Harry Thompson to run you over. I'll be round in my office in half an hour."

Gregson turned to Campbell apologetically.

"These villagers! Here's a child ready to swear he saw O'Leary burying a body in the garden. Absolute bosh, of course, but we'll have to see him and hear his story. You'd be amazed, Campbell, at the imagination of a villager!"

Gregson and Campbell returned to find Collop sitting solemnly beside the small figure of William Bundling. The boy was quivering with excitement.

Gregson smiled benevolently on him.

"Well, Tommy, what's this I hear? Tell me exactly what you saw. And don't make anything up. Here's Inspector Campbell from Scotland Yard. He'll see in a jiffy if you're not telling the truth."

William Bundling's eyes opened larger as he stared at Campbell.

"It's just as I'm telling you, mister. As I was acoming back from the Downs—"

"Snaring for rabbits, I wouldn't be surprised," remarked Collop heavily.

William Bundling ignored the interruption. "I saw a

lamp hoppiting about Wilderness garden. At first I were scared and then I heard a kind o' clanketing, as it might be someone turning of stones wi' a spade. So I crept up to the gate, and then I saw old Miser digging a grave for a corpus."

"Did you actually *see* this corpse?" asked Gregson.

"Yes, mister, with my own eyes I seed her. All cold and stiff and the eyes of it glooming in the light. It was all wrapped up in a cloth like but its arms was outside, and he dragged it by the arms and rolled her in the hole, and then he covered it up with dirt like fury."

Gregson rubbed his chin and looked significantly at Campbell.

"Whereabouts was this, Tommy?"

"In the front garden, mister, as it might be by a lump o' stone."

"That would be by the sundial," said Collop.

"I see. Right-ho, Collop! You were quite right to bring the child over."

When they were gone, Gregson looked thoughtful.

"There's no doubt the kid's seen *something*. But what the devil can it have been?"

"Well, it sounds like a body all right. A pretty graphic description, you know, for a kid. Those arms . . . Anyone missing?"

"Never a soul. The last thing I bargained for was another body. Crumbles is causing quite enough trouble as it is. Well, it's getting dark now. We'd better go over first thing tomorrow morning. I'll call round for you at your hotel."

"Right. I'm staying at the Ethelreda. In Crumbles' bedroom. The surroundings may give me an idea. Will you lend me that chart of the room showing the position of the fingerprints?"

~§~

"But after all, he's very well-spoken," said the vicar, "and he's a Christian. He told me so himself."

"A Christian," moaned Mrs. Wykeham. "What's that got to do with it? A negro and in my house! I tell you it made me feel quite creepy, seeing him sitting there at the end of the table eating toast."

"Why particularly eating toast?" asked the vicar curiously.

"The way he crunched it with those teeth of his, for all the world as if it was human bones."

"My love, my love, you are letting your imagination get the better of you. And to think how often you have knitted jumpers and run bazaars for the Church Missionary Society. And Neptune Jones is a very intelligent young man. I gather he is a chief or a prince or something in his native land. After all, all men are brothers, whatever the colour of their skins."

"I don't deny he's my brother. All I say is, I don't want him in my house."

"That, my lovekin, is hardly logical, if I may say so.

"And," added the vicar with unexpected guile, "he has a great admiration for you."

"Oh, has he, indeed," sniffed the vicar's wife. "I know those beasts with their harems." She hesitated. "What did he say about me, anyway?"

"He said you were a cow-hippopotamus, darling."

"Samuel, you allow me to be insulted in my own house by a savage!"

"But, my pet," explained the vicar hastily, "I understand that in Mr. Jones' country the hippopotamus is sacred, and is considered a symbol of maternal love. It was the highest possible compliment that he could pay you."

"Indeed! In any case, Samuel, have you forgotten that Dr. Ridge is arriving next week? He thinks he is coming to a respectable English country village. What will he say when he finds he is expected to live in a home for negroes?"

"Oh, I am sure he won't mind in the least," said the vicar lightly, "I understand that the Americans are a very democratic people. I am quite sure that they have no prejudices of that kind. Let me see, if I remember my history aright, they even fought a war to liberate the oppressed negroes of their states."

"Well, I only hope you are right. All the same, I should ask Mr. Vansteem. And if my wishes are to be respected, Samuel, I must insist that you get rid of Mr. Jones at the earliest possible opportunity."

"Your wishes are always respected, my love," answered her husband meekly, "all the same it is quite impossible for me even to mention the departure to Mr. Jones at the present moment. Apart from the fact that he is a Christian and a member of my own University, we are playing Great Whippering next week, and it is essential we have all the sound batsmen we can muster. In any case he is a most interesting young man. You have no idea of the way they hunt elephants in his country. Upon my word, it almost made me wish I were a savage myself. I can picture myself worming my way through the depths of the jungle and then springing up with a yell—"

"Oh, well, if he's starting to talk like that," said Mrs. Wykeham resignedly, "I suppose he'll be here forever. I should like to know what the villagers think of it, that's all."

~§~

The villagers, however, took it with remarkable calm.

"Another furriner," said Mr. Padding, "so they says. Up at the vicarage. A black one this time."

"A black one, hey? Well, how would that be? These Londoners are a proper caution," replied young Sawyer. "What will they be a-doing next!"

"He ain't no Londoner. He's a converted heathen from Afrikker."

"Ar."

"Same as we had that jumble sale for. And if you ask me, we bin done. What's the use of jumble sales for black men that drive round in their cars like Christians? It ain't natural!"

"You're right there, Silas Padding. That ain't natural."

"All the same, they do say he plays cricket like a Christian."

"Ah, we could do with un then. We're playing Great Whippering next week, and I'll lay a black man will be useful in the fighting arter. And what may the vicar's missis think of him? A heathen in the house with all that silver of hers?"

"They do say she doesn't hold with it. Young Ann up at the vicarage heard her creating something fierce."

"I'll be bound she did, you mark my words."

Meanwhile the vicar, not unstung by his wife's Parthian shaft, had made a point, on his next walk, of calling in at the Elms, to have a talk with Mr. Vansteem.

Mr. Vansteem was a tall white-haired American who had lived in Little Whippering now for ten years, and. who combined the peaceful cultivation of roses with a connoisseur's knowledge of ecclesiastical brasses, on which he had written several monographs. The vicar, sometimes a little torn and harried by the strenuous cares of village life, found Vansteem's peculiar blend of mildness and acerbity tonic, and often sought it.

Mr. Vansteem listened to his story without comment.

"So you see," concluded the vicar, "I have come to ask your advice. Is this American doctor likely to mind having a negro as a fellow boarder? I can't think it likely of your great free country, but in view of my wife's remarks I feel I ought to put the case to you. Do you think, when Dr. Ridge finds he has to share our hospitality with a negro, he will be likely to say anything wounding to the young man's feelings?"

"What part of the States does this Dr. Ridge come from?" asked Mr. Vansteem curiously.

The vicar took out Dr. Ridge's letter, and looked at the address.

"It appears to be Georgia."

A slight twinkle appeared in Mr. Vansteem's eyes.

"Oh, no, I don't think he'll say anything," he said.

"Oh, well, that is a great relief. Not that I thought it was at all likely, but still it is so easy to be tactless."

"He won't say anything," repeated Mr. Vansteem slowly, as if he had not heard the vicar's answer. The twinkle in his eyes had spread to his mouth, "I guess he'll just up and shoot him."

The vicar began to flutter. "Oh, dear, Mr. Vansteem. You are jesting surely? Do you really think he would shoot him? Oh, dear, my wife was right! I should never have put that unfortunate advertisement in. What do you advise me to do?"

"I should cable Dr. Ridge something short and snappy. *'Sorry cannot fix you, negro',*" suggested Mr. Vansteem.

"Unfortunately he will have sailed by now, and I don't know what boat he is coming on. What a most unfortunate situation. Do you really think he would go so far as to shoot Neptune?"

"Oh, well, things may have changed since the N.R.A.," said Mr. Vansteem helpfully, "but I wouldn't count on it if I were you."

"This is most awkward. I shall have to warn Mr. Jones to keep out of the way. I can't possibly have shooting in the drawing room. My wife would never tolerate it, with all her silver about. We shall have to break the news to Dr. Ridge gently. I count on you, Mr. Vansteem! You must find some excuse for disarming him tactfully outside the vicarage!"

"No, sir," said Mr. Vansteem with a delighted grin. "I

wouldn't interfere with a delicate matter like this, not for a million dollars. If it were just an ordinary case of murder, now that's plain sailing. But when it's blacks, no, sir, not Hamilton Vansteem!"

"I don't think you are treating this matter with the seriousness it deserves," complained the vicar, at last detecting the twinkle in Mr. Vansteem's eyes. "It will be most annoying if, after I have virtually guaranteed this scholar a pleasant English home during his stay here, he finds himself unable to remain under our roof."

"Well, I shouldn't worry, Vicar. If he does find himself unable to stay with you, I can fix him up here. That is, always providing he's not another negro."

"Good heavens!" exclaimed the vicar in alarm. "Such a possibility never entered my head! How more than rash I have been."

"On the contrary, it seems to me that would solve the question. That is if African and American negroes mix. I don't know."

"Well at least you have prepared me for the worst," said the vicar. "Nothing can surprise me now. Let us turn to a more cheerful subject. Have you heard the extraordinary story of the man who hanged himself in Abingdon? I should explain I have only heard it at fourth hand, from my wife, who heard it from Miss Tipton, who heard it from Harry Thompson, so it may not be accurate in all its details."

Mr. Vansteem was only human. The two spent an enjoyable hour discussing the possibilities of the case.

"Although I am sure," concluded the vicar, "that Mr. O'Leary is a very worthy man. After all it does not follow that because a man is given to blasphemy he is a murderer. Still, I fear he has a violent nature, which reminds me, I must get back to prepare my sermon. It will be on the text 'Strong drink is raging.' I am not a Puritan, Mr. Vansteem, but there appears to have been an orgy last night led by this person O'Leary, whom I should never before have suspected of conviviality. I am informed that many of them were so intoxicated they went back to the wrong cottages. As you can imagine, I feel it is my duty to stop that kind of thing! It might have the most regrettable consequences."

"It certainly might," agreed Mr. Vansteem, "particularly if they happened to be married."

"Er—yes. Er—quite. Most awkward . . . A little wine for the stomach's sake certainly," said the vicar, holding up to the light the excellent sherry which Mr. Vansteem had poured out for him.

"I will go further," said the vicar, as he sipped it slowly, "enough may be taken to induce a feeling of benevolence. After all, charity is charity, even if it comes out of a bottle. Though possibly that opinion is bad theology. I shan't refer to it in my sermon. Regard it as *obiter dictum* not *ex cathedra*. But the line must be drawn somewhere. Firmly. Thank you, I think I will have another, and then I must take myself off. The line, as I say, must be drawn. Liberty, yes. Licence, no."

The vicar walked slowly back, across the Common, over the stile, and up the poplar-lined path to the vicarage. The air was balmy, and the vicar, taking off his hat, let the breeze caress his iron-grey locks.

"After all," thought the vicar, feeling a gentle glow in his soul, "'the labouring hind hath little to rejoice.' I think the harm of overindulgence in alcohol is exaggerated. Perhaps it would be more fitting if I repeated my old Missionary sermon on the text, 'Go out into the highways and byways and compel them to come in.' As Mr. Jones has promised to attend the service, it will be peculiarly apt. That reminds me, I must ask him how on earth he came to be christened Neptune. Such a droll name!"

CHAPTER SEVEN
The Vicar Shocked Again

THE morning after William Bundling's revelation, the two policemen drove over in Gregson's car to the Wilderness. They pulled up some distance from the front gate, and before going in, cautiously surveyed the garden through the hedge.

"Good night!" exclaimed the Scotland Yard man. "Has there been an earthquake here?"

"It certainly looks like it," admitted Gregson.

The garden looked like a battlefield. The long-neglected flower beds were pitted with craters; the lawn had been torn up and trenches had been ploughed through the gravel paths. The basin of a concrete lily pond had been cracked, evidently with the sledge hammer that lay beside it. Several shrubs had been uprooted. Indeed the scene did not seem so much the result of an earthquake as of the efforts of a giant terrier which had had a glorious twenty-four hours' romp through the garden.

"Well, this is a bit odd," said Campbell, "if we are to believe William Bundling's evidence, it looks as if O'Leary has been burying corpses on a large scale!"

"Yes, I expect to find a whole school missing when I get back," replied Gregson smiling.

"Well, let's go in and see."

The two policemen went up the graveled path, picking their way among the *débris*. As they neared the door, they heard the rattle of a spade and a weary curse, coming from the back of the cottage. They turned their steps towards the sound. O'Leary was digging a flower bed, with a kind of stolid resignation, varied occasionally by a curse. He dug for some time before he realized the presence of the policemen behind him. Then he turned round suddenly. His expression of irritation vanished, and his face assumed a look of wary good-humour.

"Why, Inspector Gregson, this is a pleasure! You needn't have put yourself out though. I could have come over any time. Or is it what you might call a social call? I see you've brought friends."

"Yes, this is a colleague of mine, Inspector Campbell."

"You seem to have been busy, Mr. O'Leary," said Campbell gravely.

"Yes, sir. I let things get behind-hand you see. Then I thought to myself. 'Damnation, here's summer coming round again and not a flower to be seen! It's time you did something about it, O'Leary, my boy!' I said, and without another word I got my spade. And here I am, as hot as the hobs of hell, confound it!"

He mopped his scarlet forehead and grinned.

"Well, the garden certainly was neglected," said Gregson, without an answering smile. "What are you planting?"

"I've not come to the planting yet. It's making the ground ready I am now. Getting the soil nice and clean, as you might say."

Inspector Gregson's eyes wandered to the ploughed-up gravel paths and the demolished lily pond.

"You're going to have some beds in rather awkward places. Still, I suppose you know best."

O'Leary's face took on an appearance of preternatural stupidity.

"Yes, Inspector, that's me all over. I rush into a thing like a bull in a china shop, and before I know where I am, I've done more harm than good. That lily pond now. Don't say another word! I know it's not right. I oughter have left it alone. I just blinded in and rooted it up without thinking about it."

"We can't all be experts," said Gregson heavily, who was an expert gardener himself.

He looked at O'Leary's blistered hands.

"If I may say so, that's not the way to dig. You're giving yourself twice the trouble you need, and a pain in your back as well."

"Surely there's only one way of digging?" said O'Leary, beginning to turn over the earth again.

"Yes, the right way, and that's not it. Allow me."

O'Leary, somewhat mystified, surrendered his spade to the inspector, who tucked it under his arm, and slowly and deliberately walked to the front garden, followed by Campbell and O'Leary.

Without hesitating, the inspector walked up to the freshly dug bed under the sundial, planted his spade with a firm gesture, and began digging rapidly and dexterously.

"Hey!" said O'Leary, "I've just dug that."

"All the better," replied Gregson placidly.

An odd expression passed over O'Leary's face. He laid his hand on the spade as if to take it back.

"Look here, why did you go straight to this particular spot?"

Gregson surveyed him through steely eyes.

"And why not?"

Gently but firmly detaching the spade from O'Leary's huge hairy hand, he resumed his digging.

O'Leary accepted the situation and moved back a pace.

"For all the world like an old terrier going at a bone," he muttered. Indeed the inspector did present a likeness to a fat and elderly fox terrier rummaging eagerly after a buried smell.

Campbell, watching O'Leary's face, felt certain that, whatever emotions he might be feeling, acute fear was not one of them. Consequently he felt a twinge of sheer surprise when Gregson's spade laid bare a portion of bloodstained canvas. The bundle was long and heavy. A few more strokes of the spade completely uncovered it, and he helped Gregson to haul it out of the hole.

"Dear me!" said O'Leary with a queer smile. "Looks like a body. Folk seems careless with their corpses this part of the world."

Gregson pulled sharply at the canvas cover and revealed the corpse. It was a large mastiff dog.

It had been shot through the head.

O'Leary roared with laughter at the policemen's disgusted faces.

"It was too good a joke to spoil, gents! Still I congratulate you on your policework. There seems to have been a little slip-up somewhere, that's all.

"But I suppose," he added, staring at Campbell, "that even Scotland Yard makes mistakes sometimes. Poor old Congo here had been ill for some time, moaning and dragging his hindquarters behind him. Then he started snapping at me when I fed him. So I put a bullet through him. If you hear of anyone in the village who's got a nice watch-dog for sale, you might let me know."

Gregson accepted his defeat gracefully.

"Yes, of course I will, Mr. O'Leary. Well, at any rate you've had a lesson in digging!"

He began to cover up the dead dog.

Meanwhile Campbell, who had been strolling round the garden inspecting the ruin, came back to O'Leary again.

"I'm afraid I'm going to ask you a personal question, Mr. O'Leary," he said slowly, "but then we C.I.D. men are fond of personal questions."

Mr. O'Leary indicated that he was all attention.

"That's some very fine sunburn on your face. How did you get it? I understand that you never went out of the house during the two years before Crumbles' death."

O'Leary smiled affably.

"Well, that's a funny way to put it, I must say. Anyone would think it was poor George's death that made me sit up and take nourishment as you might say. But no doubt having come down fresh, you don't know the ins and outs of the case. It was my hearing of Samson's death that made me a different man. Which is hardly surprising, seeing as how he'd sworn to kill me, and Tuffy was the man to keep his word."

"Quite," said Campbell. "I understand that, but the sunburn, now?"

"Don't you worry about that, mister! You wait here half a tick and I'll show you how I got that sunburn."

O'Leary hurried back into the house, leaving Campbell staring at Gregson in some surprise.

"Well, I've struck some odd criminals, but he'll be the oddest. Do you think the explanation is that he's just mad?"

Gregson rubbed his chin thoughtfully.

"It certainly makes one think, but here he is coming back again, and good lord with a basin of water!"

O'Leary gravely put down the basin. A rag and a piece of soap were floating in the water. He picked up the rag, soaked it, and rubbed vigorously at his chin. Then he rinsed his face. The two policemen saw a large white patch where he had rubbed his chin.

Campbell picked up the rag, it was covered with some brownish dye, rubbed off O'Leary's face.

"Pure vanity, gents!" said O'Leary, with a prodigious sigh. "Promise me you won't tell the girls? Yes, it's all done with sunburn dye. Handsome men are slightly sunburnt, what, what? You see I looked at my face in the mirror, white as a cheese, and I said: 'O'Leary, old boy, this won't do. No nice girl loves a walking corpse. You gotter spruce yourself up.' And this's the result."

"Well, I must admit that clears up the puzzle," said Gregson ruefully.

Meanwhile Campbell leaning against the sundial on which the basin of water had been placed, had his attention caught by some specks of dirt in the bottom of the basin. They glittered slightly. O'Leary's back was to him, and he carefully put in his finger and scooped up the specks. Taking out his wallet, he wiped them off his finger into the interior of an old envelope. The action was not noticed either by Gregson or O'Leary.

"Well, this is a nice place you've got, Mr. O'Leary!" went on Gregson, with dangerous affability. "Where would you have been before you came here?"

"Africa," said O'Leary shortly.

"I mean after that?"

"Various places."

"Such as?"

"London."

"Ah, what part now?"

"Various parts," said O'Leary slowly. "Which in particular is *my* business, I think. And what I says, gents, is, what does it matter? Tuffy's dead, ain't he? And George has killed himself, hasn't he? You're not denying *that,* I suppose?"

"No, we're not denying that. At present," said Gregson, gently.

"Then what do you want to come bothering me, axing a lot of questions? I spoke out straight, didn't I? I told you I'd been in stir out in Africa. Well, what about it? Plenty of better men than me has got into trouble, but it don't follow that wherever they go they gotter be treated suspicious. I ain't on ticket o' leave. So police or no police, gents, I'm asking you to keep your noses out of my cottage. If you want to dig up my dogs, well and good! But when it comes fishing about asking this and that and where have I been, I says, why? That's all. Just, why?"

"A sound question, O'Leary, and not easy to answer. As you say, why? These questions will probably be asked at the inquest."

"Oh, will they? And suppose I refuse to answer them?" O'Leary's affability had quite worn off, and he appeared to be working himself up into a state of righteous truculence.

"That's all what comes of my trying to help you coppers. Instead of being awkward-like, I tells everything, good or bad, and all I gets is a lot of narsty questions. Where have I been? What parts? It fair makes me sick! That's the sort of thing we're taxed to death for, I suppose—to be bullied and badgered by a lot of silly slops. Phew!"

Mr. O'Leary walked into his house with measured steps, and slammed the door. The two policemen went thoughtfully down the lane to the car.

"What do you make of it, Campbell?" sighed Gregson. "We seem to have made precious fools of ourselves, with our corpses and our sunburn."

"I'm not so sure," answered Campbell slowly, "no, I'm more than ever inclined to think that Crumbles' suicide wasn't straight. O'Leary's up to some game, whatever it may be. Does anything strike you as queer about that dog?"

"I can't say it does. Except our own damned foolishness."

"Well, it sounds odd to me. O'Leary's trying to tell us the dog got rabid. But dogs don't just develop rabies, they catch it. And that mastiff was shut up in the house all the time."

"Well, where does that lead us?"

"Do you know what I think, Gregson? Someone else shot it!"

"Someone else! Who? and why?"

"Well, we've been going on the assumption that Crumbles and O'Leary were friendly. But supposing they weren't?

You remember Jennings said Crumbles wouldn't go into the Wilderness by daylight? Suppose Crumbles intended to rob O'Leary? Or even murder him? And suppose he found the place too difficult to break into and had to shoot the dog, and beat it? Perhaps the wire to O'Leary was just another device to lure O'Leary into his clutches?"

"And then?"

"Well, O'Leary guesses who has shot the dog, guesses what is behind the wire, goes over there in the morning in disguise and does Crumbles in. Then he gets back in time to go over there the second time, with Harry Thompson, having dropped the disguise; cropped his hair and so forth; and pretends to discover the suicide."

"But how do you explain Crumbles' letters ?"

"I can't at the moment," admitted Campbell, "but if I am right they were part of Crumbles' plot for murdering O'Leary, which miscarried. The faked sunburn bears this out. When O'Leary went over to call on Crumbles, in disguise with dyed hair, his face had its natural pallor. Then before his second visit, knowing that the police would ask him to take his muffler off, he painted his face with sunburn tan. This would completely transform his appearance and eliminate the risk that anyone in Abingdon who had seen him on his first visit might recognize him again."

"It's certainly a possibility," said Gregson thoughtfully, as they drove along the main road, "I wish we could discover some reason for Crumbles and O'Leary's being enemies. By all accounts they should be friends."

"Has O'Leary a banking account?" asked Campbell a moment later. "It would be interesting to know where his money comes from."

"He doesn't appear to have one. Not locally at any rate. And all his bills were paid with cash, through that ingenious trap door of his."

Seated again in Gregson's office, Campbell took out his

wallet and shot out the specks of dirt he had collected on to the desk.

"Hello, what's that?" asked Gregson.

"I don't know, yet. I got it from O'Leary's basin. It looks to me like metallic dust. The question is, what metal? It may be brass from the pump bearing. On the other hand—Well, we'll see."

Gregson looked puzzled.

"I don't see what you're after. Still I always believe in following a hunch."

Campbell put the dust carefully into a cellophane envelope, sealed it and put it in another envelope addressed to the C.I.D.

Meanwhile Gregson, leaning back at his desk with his eyes closed, was thinking. Then he sat up and opened them.

"There's one flaw in your theory, Campbell, it doesn't explain O'Leary's digging mania. Unless he really has developed a passion for flowers."

"I think that is unlikely. So that leaves us with two possibilities. One. He's looking for something. We can dismiss that, I think, for he's been at the Wilderness two years, so he wouldn't start so frantically now."

"He may only have just heard. By Jove, could *that* have been Crumbles' good news?"

"It's a possibility," admitted Campbell, "but it's more likely that he's hiding something. Something bulky."

"Dead dogs," muttered Gregson. "No more of that, thank you! Anyway why so many holes ?"

"Perhaps that's bluff. He may only have hidden the stuff, whatever it is, in one of them. I admit it's damned difficult to account for everything. The simplest way would be to suppose he's mad. He can't be quite sane, certainly; there's a queer look in his eyes. But I wouldn't say he was mad in that kind of way."

"Neither should I. A nasty customer. Thank the Lord we

don't get many of that kind in this part of the world. Africa is welcome to 'em."

~§~

"Plantains, plantains, plantains!" sighed the vicar, as he crawled on his knees across the immemorial turf of the vicarage lawn. "Did they have plantains in the Garden of Eden, I wonder? If so, the blissful peace of our ancestors' lot is surely exaggerated. I often think, if one may, without irreverence, that had there been lawns in Palestine, the parable of the Tares would have been the parable of the Plantains. *And going out to his lawn, he said, 'Some enemy hath done this.'* Come up, thou thing of naught! Dear me, what long roots they have!"

"Excuse me," said a clear feminine voice. Its tone suggested that the owner had been watching the vicar gently crawling over the lawn for a long time, with increasing impatience. As indeed she had.

"Are you the vicar?"

The vicar looked up and beamed.

The speaker was a girl of about thirty, with a slight slim figure and a strikingly beautiful face. Her eyes were grey and her mouth was firm. If any fault could have been found with her, it was that there was a certain self-confidence and calmness, betokening an independence, even a contempt for human trivialities and emotions. To many, however, this would prove an added attraction.

The vicar was human, and there were few pretty girls in Little Whippering. Certainly none so pretty as this. He beamed again, but paternally, of course. Then he got up from his hands and knees.

The stranger was wearing a simple, rather severely tailored costume.

The vicar now noticed that she had a suitcase in her

hand, and that Harry Thompson was hovering in the background.

"Yes, I am the vicar.

"These are really my gardener's clothes," he added simply, "and I need a bath."

The girl smiled. "You're liable to get mussed up gardening."

"I am not sure whether the real attraction of gardening is not the getting thoroughly dirty. None of us would confess it, of course," said the vicar, waving his trowel, "but we all love a rollic in the earth. We like to feel its primitive humours on our hands and skin!"

"Do you eat it?" asked the girl gravely.

The vicar recoiled.

"Eat it. Good Heavens, no, my dear child! Why should I?"

"I beg your pardon. I thought it might be a local custom. Geophagy is practiced among the Paramuiti Indians in Brazil, by certain phratries of the Sea Bongos, and by at least two Micronesian peoples."

"Really, how strange! It is preferable to anthropophagy, no doubt. But excuse me, may I ask who you are? I don't think you belong to my parish."

"I'm Virginia Ridge."

"Really," said the vicar vaguely, "what a pretty name! Well, my dear, can I do anything for you? Or have you come to look round our garden? The box hedges are rather fine, are they not? I clipped them myself."

"I've come to stay," said the girl patiently. "Didn't you get my letter?"

"To stay!" exclaimed the vicar startled. "Well, of course that's very nice but—er "

Suddenly enlightenment came to him.

"What did you say your name was?"

"Ridge, Virginia Ridge."

"Not," faltered the vicar, "not *Dr.* Ridge?"

"Why, yes. Didn't you expect me?"

"Of course," answered the vicar hastily, "that is to say, we didn't. I mean we expected you, but we didn't expect you to be like this."

The girl smiled. "I'm sorry. Don't I come up to expectations?"

"Oh, of course we don't mean that," fluttered the vicar.

"On the contrary," he added gallantly. "You exceeded them. To quite a considerable extent. The sex, you see. Not at all what we expected . . . However, of course we are delighted. And Psyche, my little girl, will be delighted too. And my wife—er—of course, she also will be delighted. Yes, of course. Let me take your suitcase."

The girl surrendered it.

"I hope I won't soil the handle," remarked the vicar. "My hands are really quite uncommonly dirty. I don't know what you will think of us, you know. Such a bad impression!"

"Oh, don't worry," replied Virginia Ridge seriously, "we field workers are trained to be shocked by nothing. The last expedition I went on, Miss Philberry and I walked into the chief's house, and found him naked, toasting a piece of human flesh in front of a fire."

"Good gracious me!" said the vicar, putting down the bag, the better to listen. "This is *most* interesting. You must tell me all about that. Everyone, positively everyone, seems to have adventures here except me. Little Whippering will seem a very quiet place after that. Yes, indeed, you won't see anything of that kind here! And of course Miss Philberry. Yes, that explains her. We were wondering . . . So you're not easily shocked?"

"I reckon I'm unshockable."

"That's excellent, my dear—I mean Doctor," said the vicar, rubbing his hands. "Really excellent."

He hesitated a moment. "Do you happen to have a firearm of any kind on you?"

The girl looked at him, momentarily startled, and then a flicker of amusement came into her eyes.

"Well, I believe I've got an old automatic tucked away in my trunk somewhere. Shall I get it out for you?"

"No, no, no. By all means, no!" exclaimed the vicar hastily. They walked a little farther up the path. "I must warn you, you have a fellow lodger."

"That's all right by me."

"An unusual man. Most unusual. He is more or less of royal blood. A minor royalty, so to speak."

"Say, that's interesting!"

"The only thing is that—well, he's *rather* dark."

"Do you mean he's a wop?"

"I don't quite know what a wop is. I should describe him as a negro."

"A negro!" exclaimed the girl mildly, without, to the vicar's relief, any signs of an explosion.

"Well, I never thought to meet one here. Where does he come from?"

"Africa," said the vicar vaguely.

"Yes, but what tribe does he belong to?"

"Let me see now," said the vicar thoughtfully, "it was West African. The Ngama people."

"Ah, yes. Black skin, straightish nose, above the normal height. Fetish-worshippers. Matrilineal, high civilization with a developed system of taboo. They practice hoe tillage with a certain amount of stock-raising. Polygynous of course, and addicted to cannibalism."

"Well, really!" said the vicar. "How on earth did you know that?"

"Part of my job," answered Virginia Ridge coolly. "But, say, have I been sold or something? Your villagers don't know their own language!"

"Their own language? I'm afraid I don't understand.

What precisely did you say to them?"

The girl spoke a few sentences in Berkshire dialect so broad that the vicar was unable to understand it.

"Where on earth did you pick that up ? It's positively startling!"

"At the Institute. Gramophone records. We field workers always learn the language before we go to a district. It's essential; interpreters are always misleading. Have I been sold or did they give me the wrong set of records?"

"It's perfectly good Berkshire," admitted the vicar, "but unfortunately, since the wireless and the talkies, Little Whippering doesn't speak dialect, except when it gets excited."

"What does it speak then?"

"The younger ones who go to the pictures use a variety of expressions which Mr. Vansteem tells me are American."

"Land sakes!" exclaimed the startled anthropologist.

"The older ones, who only listen-in, speak in a curious mincing way which I am told is now current at Oxford. It certainly wasn't in my time, but no doubt I am a back number. However, don't look so downcast, my dear lady. There are a good many old men and women in those dreadful cottages in Cat and Dog Lane who still speak dialect. Not only will they be delighted to speak to you, but you will have difficulty in getting away from them. Yes, indeed."

"I'm glad to hear it."

"And now we are on the subject, if it is not rude, may I ask why you have come to our village?"

"It's simple enough, Vicar. Anthropology is concerned with the study of backward peoples. Our museums and libraries are full of data about tribes no one has ever heard of. We know their religions, their morals, their beliefs, their customs, their diet, their superstitions, their relationship system, and the most *intimate* details of their life. We actually know more about them than we do about the equivalent customs of European villages, where life is also primitive, but which are rapidly dying out. It is the object of our Institute at Themistocles to obtain a record of them before it is too late. I am prospecting the ground for the First Expedition which is to start work in England. Your English universities have given me every encouragement and help. We selected Little Whippering on advice, as one of the most characteristic of English villages, and one that is likely to be soonest swallowed up."

"Well, really. We are perhaps a little backward here. But as for our religion, and beliefs, to say nothing of our morals, it is surely sufficient to say that they are of the Church of England as by Law Established."

"Are they?" said Virginia Ridge darkly. "You wait until I've done a month or two's work here."

CHAPTER EIGHT
Inspector Campbell Strikes Gold

"YOU remember that dirt in O'Leary's basin?" said Campbell to Gregson.

"Oh, yes. What happened to it? You were going to have it analyzed, weren't you."

"Yes. I have. Here's the report. It's gold dust."

"Gold dust!" exclaimed Gregson, momentarily staggered. "Why, good Lord, of all the impossible things!"

"Impossible, but very interesting. O'Leary washes his hands in water and leaves gold dust behind. It makes one wonder, doesn't it?"

"Gold dust," mused Gregson. "And of course Crumbles had just come back from Africa. From near the gold district. It suggests, doesn't it, that there was something behind Crumbles' visit besides Samson's death?"

"It does. And it also suggests a reason for O'Leary's sudden joy. And a motive for killing Crumbles, which we always lacked before."

"Have your people been able to get a line on Crumbles' movements in London?"

"Yes. I've just been speaking to Sergeant Finch on the phone. They're sending down a trunk which was left by a black-bearded man at Paddington Station cloakroom two days before Crumbles' death. It seems to have various small possessions of Crumbles' in it. Nothing of any importance; the bulk of it is clothes. They've also found two hotels where he stayed for about a week in each case. Finch tells me that he's ascertained that Crumbles came over on the *Cromlech Castle,* which arrived in London a month before Crumbles' death. And here's an interesting point. Crumbles' passage was booked *before* Tuffy Samson's death. So either the death was not the motive of Crumbles' coming over, or, if it was, Crumbles must have known beforehand that there was going to be an accident. In other words, it wasn't an accident."

Gregson permitted himself a quiet chuckle.

"Things are fitting into place, laddie."

"It looks promising," agreed Campbell. "I was afraid at one time I might have to go to Africa, but if we are on the right track, we ought to be able to solve it from this end. Let's put up a provisional hypothesis. Somehow or other Crumbles has got hold of some gold, part of it as we know in the form of dust. We can, I think, take it that he's got hold of it illicitly. Remember they pinched the Balooma treasure. (We'll send a cable to Nigeria to see if there have been any robberies lately.) Crumbles intends to go to England to celebrate with the proceeds, and perhaps to sell the stuff, but meanwhile the menace of Samson's revenge is hanging over his head. Well, he settles with Samson—or Providence settles with Samson, we can't say which yet. Then he comes to England. So far, so good. But why does he come straight to O'Leary?"

"Not straight. He waits a month."

"Yes. He waits a month. That certainly is interesting. But why does he come at all? I think we can assume all these men are as crooked as hell, so it's a question of what material advantage he gets."

"H'm." Gregson meditated a moment. "I can't see any."

"I don't know. There are several possibilities. The difficulty is to say which one is likely to be correct. We want one which can account for O'Leary's peculiar behavior. Suppose we assume that O'Leary's entitled to a share of Crumbles' gold. He may have provided the information which resulted in the haul. The obvious thing then would be for Crumbles to double-cross him. So we must assume that O'Leary has some means of enforcing his rights. It wouldn't be physical power, for O'Leary is evidently a coward. Look at the way he hid from the moment he expected Samson to be out of gaol. He must have had a moral hold over Crumbles. Probably O'Leary knew some secret which could get Crumbles into gaol. Perhaps he knew that Samson had been murdered, and could get Crumbles hanged for it."

"That sounds the most likely."

"Right. Let's assume it then. So Crumbles comes obediently to O'Leary to divvy up. But he doesn't want to divvy up. So he secretly explores other possibilities during his month in London and makes a plan. First of all he tries to catch O'Leary out at the Wilderness, but finds he's too well entrenched. So he tries to lure him to his hotel. But meanwhile, as we've previously decided, O'Leary's been too clever for him. He, in his turn, has been spying on Crumbles, only with more subtlety. He calls on Crumbles in disguise, and murders him, then hurries back to the village. We don't know how yet. Perhaps he got a lift from some passing motorist. Meanwhile the telegram Crumbles has sent to lure O'Leary to his death (and this would explain the loaded revolver in Crumbles' pocket) is going on its way at the very moment when the sender is swinging on the end of a rope. By the time it arrives, O'Leary has got rid of his disguise. He got rid of a part of it—the dark hair—as we know, in Crumbles' bedroom. And there too, in a long search, he either found the boodle, or else found a paper which told him where it was. O'Leary then, or later, brings it back to his house rejoicing, and buries it in his garden. Meanwhile he has acted the farce of going over with Harry Thompson to discover the death of the man he murdered."

"It still leaves one difficulty. How do you explain Crumbles' depression? And that business of getting the rope. And how do you explain the letter to the Coroner?"

"They were obviously part of Crumbles' original plan for murdering O'Leary. As it miscarried, we don't know what it is. But perhaps we can guess at it. I suggest that we would have found an unrecognizable corpse with its face blown to fragments, lying in Crumbles' bedroom, with the suicide letters to suggest it was Crumbles, and dressed in Crumbles' clothes. We should have never seen any more either of Crumbles and O'Leary again, and we should have assumed either that Crumbles had committed suicide or, failing that, that O'Leary had murdered him and had fled. In any case Crumbles would by then have been on the Continent."

"It certainly hangs together," admitted Gregson. "Let's call it our working hypothesis. What's our next step ?"

"Well, we must wait to see if there's any news from Nigeria of a gold robbery in that part of the world in the last few months. Then we must either search O'Leary's house officially, or, better still, one of us can have him over here for an interview while the other digs up the stuff in the garden. Once we've got the link between Crumbles and the gold, and the gold and O'Leary, I think we can call our case complete."

Campbell ticked off the points one by one. "We've got proof of O'Leary's disguise. Of O'Leary's search of Crumbles' room. Of his behavior before and after Crumbles' murder. We know O'Leary's criminal record. We're certain to discover a good deal more after arrest. I think it's a good case."

"Fair to middling," said Gregson without enthusiasm.

"There's one thing we ought to put in hand though, and that is an inquiry to find if Crumbles has been seen round here before he came here openly the day before his death. If my theory is right, he must have come down more than once to spy out the lie of the land before he concocted his little plot."

"Well, he's a reasonable easy man to identify. I'll see what we can do."

~§~

Tea on the vicarage lawn. The afternoon sunlight filtered through the trees and shimmered back from large pools on the lawn. There was a drowsy hum from the bees as they reaped where they had not sown. A wasp from time to time turned its attention to the well spread table which, to its annoyance, instantly blossomed with flipping handkerchiefs.

From behind the trees came the peaceful pat-pat of a decorously struck tennis ball. The vicar, conscious that he added the final decorative touch to so English a scene, leaned back in his chair with his panama pulled over his eyes. From under its shade he contemplated his wife, operating a massive silver teapot.

So far all was drowsy and harmoniously lazy. But Virginia Ridge, with a notebook on her knee, sitting bolt upright, looked altogether too cool and strenuous to blend with the scene. It became frankly exotic with Mr. Jones, whose black face gave a startling emphasis to his white tennis shirt and flannels.

Presently the patting ceased, and Claude Marion and Psyche came towards the tea.

"Beaten again," groaned Marion. "I never had a chance."

"If only you'd run about more, you'd beat me easily," said Psyche severely.

"Don't be so painfully obvious, my dear child. When you are old enough to be tactful—however it is too hot to explain anything. I feel so old today. A million years old! Not primeval but just ancient, jaded, with all the wisdom of the ages on my brow. My eyelids are a little weary."

"Have a cucumber sandwich," said Mrs. Wykeham.

"Perhaps that would be best. And how is the Anthropology going, Dr. Ridge?"

"Quite all right, thanks. I've spent the last few days measuring. Heads mostly."

"Indeed, and what conclusion have you come to?"

"Field workers don't come to conclusions. However, it's a dolicocephalous village. Unexpectedly so."

"Dear me, is dolicocephaly a new form of vice? Or a disease?" Marion sniggered.

"If you are really interested in the subject, I shall be glad to lend you a text book," said Dr. Ridge gravely.

Virginia's firm treatment of the conversation produced an awkward silence.

"Well," said the vicar brightly at last, "that reminds me! I have often meant to ask you, Mr. Jones, how you came to be called Neptune."

"It's the nearest equivalent of my native name, Nga-ma-Nwama," explained Mr. Jones with a grin.

"Oh, I think I understand. Nga-ma-Nwama is your god of the sea and you were named after him."

Mr. Jones shook his head.

"No, not named after him. I *am* the god of the sea."

"Dear me," said the vicar blankly. "Well."

There was another silence.

"Do us a miracle," pleaded Marion archly.

"I'm afraid I have no miraculous powers in an English vicarage, old chap," replied Mr. Jones with a flash of white teeth. "You need an African sun, you know. And blood. And tom-toms."

"Really, Jones, you're positively barbaric under your academic veneer. Is this all Alma Mater and the missionary have done for you? What *are* you doing here anyway?"

"Reading law," said Mr. Jones.

"Reading law! The African god reads law!" exclaimed Marion in disgust.

"It's rather necessary," pointed out Mr. Jones, "if we are to keep our ends up with the European gods."

"Why not go back to your native land? It must be so nice to be a god!"

"It has its disadvantages. There are so many things one mustn't do. I mustn't walk barefoot for instance. Or sleep when anybody else is in a room higher than my head. I'm generally carried when I leave my house in Africa. In case I stumble, you see. And of course they watch me carefully to see that I am not getting weak, as I get older."

"Really. Do they depose you?"

"No, they cut my throat."

There was an awkward silence.

The vicar smiled. "You're joking of course!"

Mr. Jones made no reply.

"But of course you're a Christian," said the vicar happily, "and don't believe any of that sort of thing?"

There was another awkward silence. Even Virginia Ridge, who had been filling up the time occupied by this desultory and, as she felt, entirely time-wasting conversation by running through her notebooks, looked up and felt it. She hastened to the vicar's assistance.

"I've got some very interesting notes here on your vegetation ceremonies," she said.

"My dear child," answered the vicar blandly, "what *are* you talking about?"

"Your May-Day fertility rites. Most interesting. It appears that after the villagers have made an effigy of the vegetation God—"

"Really!" protested the vicar.

"They call him Jack-of-May. He is taken round to the local farmers to make their fields fertile, and then kept to be put under the pulpit at the Harvest Festival. A most interesting survival. Its place under the pulpit is very significant. I fancy you are considered the risen spirit of vegetation, Vicar."

"Ah, Vicar!" exclaimed Marion. "You see the heathen is at your very gates."

"Oh, but surely—a harmless little custom!" protested the vicar. "I am sure it would be impossible to find a more Christian village than Little Whippering."

"Their views with regard to betrothal and marriage are also very interesting," went on Virginia, flicking over the pages. "They have a certain resemblance to the social tenets of the Wahina tribe, a Melanesian people. A case of convergence no doubt, unless one is a rabid diffusionist. It appears—"

"Please," interrupted the vicar. "Remember Psyche is here! I know perfectly what you are alluding to, Dr. Ridge, and I must admit there is a certain laxity about village beliefs in this respect . . . I have done my best . . . very deeply engrained . . . I beg of you . . ."

"Oh, that's nothing, Vicar. I should say they are positively repressed in Little Whippering compared to Huicha-Veltra."

"That may be. I still cannot approve."

"There are also some very interesting remains of ancestor worship," went on Dr. Ridge.

"Ancestor worship!" exclaimed the vicar.

"Yes. It appears that food is spread for the spirits of the dead on a table after the funeral. Only the older members of the community are aware of the significance of the custom. I also have some interesting notes on wart-charming, from old Mrs. Boggins, who is I understand an expert witch. The methods used are virtually those of the Northern Todas. By the way, talking about Mrs. Boggins, her maiden name is Boggins, and when she married a Fritton, she called herself Mrs. Boggins."

"Yes, many of the older women did not take their husbands' names. It is an old Little Whippering custom."

"A relic of a matrilineal system," said Dr. Ridge, writing in her notebook. "This is a real discovery! Little Whippering is more primitive than I thought!"

"I find this most unsettling," said the vicar, pressing his brow. "Really, my dear young lady, since you came to stay with us, I have begun to feel that I am living among savages. I even fear that one of these days I will find I have some savage habits myself."

"You have a few," said Dr. Ridge judicially. "A trace of fetish worship, for instance."

"Fetish worship! My dear girl, you can hardly expect me to take this seriously!"

"When you are giving a sermon, do you or do you not always fumble with a loose button in your pocket?"

The vicar blushed. "A purely nervous trick. I feel uncomfortable without it."

"A fetish. Your unconscious endows it with magic power. And do you or do you not always tap the left gate pillar with your stick when you come in to the house?"

"Dear me, how dreadfully observant you are. I suppose I

do. Pure habit!"

"Another fetish. You unconsciously evoke luck on the house. You also show traces of animism."

"Animism!"

"Yes, you go upstairs two at a time, always trying to finish on your left foot. I've noticed it. You act, in other words, as if the stairs were alive and had power to harm you."

"Good Heavens," said the vicar tapping his forehead feebly, "my place is in the African jungle. I beg your pardon, Jones. Nothing personal, of course."

"Quite all right, Vicar. I should be delighted to see you there at any time. No doubt you would like to see an African domestic interior."

"Certainly. Are you married?"

Mr. Jones' white teeth flashed. "I think I might say so. Yes, quite definitely."

At this point Mrs. Wykeham suddenly found her conversational depth. *"Quite definitely,* Mr. Jones? Do you mean you have more than one wife?"

"Yes."

"How many, may I ask?"

"About sixty last time I was in Africa. But there are sure to be more since. There always are," sighed Mr. Jones wearily.

Mrs. Wykeham turned a trifle pale. "Really, how can you? As a Christian!"

"Unfortunately it is essential, Mrs. Wykeham. You see as a point of royal etiquette I have to have exactly ten more wives than anyone else in my little kingdom. So I am absolutely at the mercy of my subjects in this respect. Of course from your missionary point of view, my chief wife is the only one that counts and the others are—"

"Handmaids," interposed the vicar hastily. "Quite! Psyche, will you run and fetch some more milk?"

The sun sank lower and lower. The midges massed themselves for a final assault on their human banquet; and, for the first time, the trees sighed. At first it was like a sigh of well-being. The sigh grew to a steady rustling. A cold evening wind was getting up. The vicar shivered slightly, and then, quite suddenly, he heard, prefaced by an odd preliminary rattle, a distant band strike up. It was so far away that only the drums—the big drum and the kettle drum—were audible:

Pink, pink, boom! Pinkety, pinkety, boom-boom! Pink. Pink. Boom.

Mr. Jones listened, his head cocked on one side, his eyes dark pools of fire in the setting sun. Dr. Ridge also listened, with a surprised air, her beautiful profile tense against the greening sky.

"Well, now, that's odd!" said the vicar. "Where can that band be? It doesn't sound like a march, but I suppose it's soldiers."

Pink—Pink—Boom! Pinkety, pinkety boom!

"How deliciously eerie!" said Marion with a shudder.

Mr. Jones got up.

"Excuse me," he said. "I think I'll go in and change."

Dr. Ridge followed his retreating back with a brow wrinkled in thought. She shivered.

"Are you cold, my dear?" asked the vicar.

"No. Just someone walking over my grave I guess. I have a kind of hunch something queer is going to happen here."

The vicar laughed. "Here? No, my dear young lady, nothing queer ever happens in Little Whippering!"

~§~

"I've got someone interesting coming this morning," said Gregson. "A man here who saw Crumbles two weeks before his death. That seems to confirm your theory."

"Who is he?"

"A jeweler in Wantage."

"Good Lord, that's interesting."

Mr. Farthingale had read the descriptions of the dead Crumbles, and he had further heard through his nephew, who was a friend of the chief constable's daughter, that enquiries were being made by the police locally about a black-bearded man. This, added to a curious incident that had occurred a fortnight or so ago, in the way of business, had caused him to do some hard thinking and eventually 'phone up Inspector Gregson.

"Yes, he came in just about a fortnight before I read about the dead man's being found at the Ethelreda," said Mr. Farthingale, caressing the inspector's desk with the tips of his fingers as one who might at any moment say, "Beautiful stuff! Look at the lights in it."

"He was a queer-spoken fellow, surly and common. That made me suspicious when he pulled out a gold bracelet, wrapped up in a piece of newspaper, and said he wanted to sell it."

"A gold bracelet!" exclaimed Campbell. "What kind?"

"Oh, terribly clumsy work," said Mr. Farthingale depreciatingly. "Dear me, yes, one can hardly call it jewelry. I explained to him that it was only worth its weight. Of course I felt a little suspicious, there was something odd in his manner; and I asked him tactfully where he'd got it? He said, in Africa, and that seemed likely, for it wasn't made by any European jeweler. Well, since we went off the gold standard, everyone's been bringing out their old gold, so I didn't make any more bones about it, but gave him the £40 it was worth. It was good solid stuff I must say. But I remembered it, what with the man's being queer and the goods being out of the way."

"Thanks, Mr. Farthingale. This has been most helpful. We are very grateful."

"Nothing to thank me for, Inspector. In my profession we're always glad to help the police."

Mr. Farthingale bowed himself out.

Gregson slapped the desk.

"My God, there's the proof. Crumbles *had* gold. And now O'Leary's got it. And Crumbles was in this neighbourhood before he called on O'Leary. Campbell, that's our missing link!"

"Yes, but I wish we could get a line on that gold," said Campbell, with Scottish caution. "We haven't had an answer to our wire to Nigeria yet. If only we could find where this gold comes from!"

"We'll find, laddie, don't you worry! Things have started to run our way," said Gregson, in happy ignorance.

CHAPTER NINE
Buff Orpington Dead

"WHAT is a tragedy?" asked Campbell, flinging himself into a chair in Gregson's office.

"Eh?" said Gregson looking up, a little distracted.

"A beautiful theory slain by an awkward fact," went on Campbell gloomily. "I have just been over to Little Whippering."

"What's the trouble?"

"O'Leary's in a blue funk again."

"I should think so," said Gregson with a smirk. "He knows we're closing up."

"No, it's not us he's afraid of. It's someone else. He's gone back to his old tricks. Never stirs out of his house; no more celebrations in the pub; interviews callers through the trap door; and he's bought an Alsatian from Farmer Bunn."

"But it's impossible!" exclaimed Gregson. "The only people he can be afraid of are Tuffy Samson and George Crumbles, and they're both dead."

"Well, he's afraid of ghosts, that's all."

"Well, bad news never comes alone," remarked Gregson consolingly. "Here's the answer to your Nigerian cable."

Campbell read it aloud slowly:—

"HAVE NO RECORD OF ANY RECENT ROBBERIES WHICH WOULD ACCOUNT FOR MATTER MENTIONED IN YOUR CABLE.
                                                        "MACPHERSON"

"Oh, damnation! Gregson, I'm beginning to feel the whole damn thing's unnatural. Do you know what else I found in Little Whippering?"

"I'll buy it."

"O'Leary's not paying his bills."

"Well, that's a common trouble."

"No, but it's serious. Gudgeon is only going to supply O'Leary with bread for another week, and then he's going to stop supplies. Miss Tipton won't send him any more groceries, and none of the farmers roundabout will let him have any milk. The bailiffs are likely to be in at any moment as a matter of fact, because old Grimble, the butcher, has already got a judgment. The man must be starving to death shut up in that wretched cottage of his, and yet he washes his hands in gold dust. It beats me, Gregson. Where have we slipped up?"

"Are you sure it's not shamming? It may just be a device to attract our attention."

"Well, if Bunn's right, it's so serious that O'Leary's taken to stealing chickens from him. He's no actual proof that it's O'Leary of course, but O'Leary's the nearest to his chicken-houses, and he used to supply O'Leary with poultry until he developed a habit of not paying. Also Bunn swears he saw some spots of blood leading from his field down the road to the Wilderness. Quite a Sherlock Holmes in his way is old Bunn. And he loathes O'Leary."

"Chicken-stealing! I say, that's rather a come-down from murder, isn't it?"

"Yes. Collop's on the job watching Bunn's fowl houses, but you know I've half a mind to try myself. Of course it may be only some tramp. But if it is O'Leary, and we jail him for theft, I think we'll be able to wring something interesting out of him."

Gregson's lips twitched sardonically.

"Well, we didn't call the C.I.D. in to guard our local fowl houses. However, if you want to . . . I still can't believe O'Leary isn't shamming. He always gives me the impression of a man who's acting all the time."

~§~

That night, therefore, Campbell found himself lying on his tummy in the grass keeping a careful eye on the long lines of diminutive dwellings in which Farmer Bunn's cherished Buff Orpingtons spent their nights. There should have been a moon, but it was almost completely hidden by the thick clouds that drifted slowly across the night sky.

"So much the better," thought Campbell. "O'Leary's more likely to try to replenish his larder."

There is something about lying flat on the ground in the country watching on a dark chilly night which unhinges even the most stolid mind. First the rustlings begin to obtrude on the silence. Disconnected footsteps flutter round one, resolve themselves into bits of paper or dry branches, then vanish abruptly. Then dim objects distend themselves, quiver and move. "Only the whitened end of Bunn's cow byre!" you tell yourself, but slowly it begins to swell, and shift, and presently . . . With a start you pull yourself together, and at that moment there is the sudden agonized cry of a rabbit caught by a weasel. By a purely reflex action, your skin suddenly contracts, and a cold shudder runs up your spine.

A puff of wind blows the cloud off the moon. For a few minutes everything is flooded with a clear, a blinding light. All your carefully identified blurs take on fresh shapes, and a moment later the light perishes, and your eyes, temporarily dazzled, see nothing but blankness and menace.

Campbell, though not particularly given to night fears, felt jumpy. He told himself that it was merely primitive instinct, and remembered having read somewhere that, in such circumstances, if a man climbs a tree, he at once feels safe, the inherited instincts of his apish ancestors being set at rest. But there were no trees near. He tried to think of something highly rational. His mind roamed from aeroplanes to philosophy, and just as he was musing vaguely on the Categorical Imperative, a cow coughed. The unearthly sound, resembling the cry of a damned soul, made him nearly leap out of his skin.

"What a damned fool I was to take this on!" thought Campbell, turning over from one sore hip to the other on his mackintosh.

Another hour passed.

"This must be getting on my nerves," muttered the detective to himself. "I could almost swear that shadow there is moving."

Campbell looked casually away from the shadow, and then looked at it again. It had moved another two or three paces. The detective pulled himself together, and made a resolute effort to focus his attention on reality. But the shadow moved again.

"My God, I believe it's human," said Campbell, straining

his eyes in the darkness to make out the vague outlines of the shadow.

It was beside a door now, and Campbell saw the door open. The door remained open. The shadow—or man if it was a man—made no attempt to go in. Campbell waited for the indignant squawking of a disturbed roost. But there was none.

Campbell took a tight grip of himself. Unless he was mistaken, he could hear a kind of buzz. It was a low penetrating note, that seemed to make the bones in his head tremble in sympathy. Was it the pounding of blood in his head? No, it was a distinct noise.

A hen, ruffling its feathers and staring about it as if it was still not quite awake, walked out of the door. It was bathed in the rays of the moon, filtered through the cloud. But the shadow merged in the shadow of the building.

Immediately the door closed, with a slam of wood meeting wood that Campbell seized on as a gratifying assurance of reality.

He strained his eyes to make out what the hen was doing. But it remained, even in the glimmer of light from the obscured moon, a mere blur. It was standing quite still. The buzz had stopped.

Then it began to move, jerkily, towards the shadow. The moon's light was less obscure now, and, even though the shadow was standing in the penumbra of the shed, Campbell could make out its outline distinctly. It was satisfyingly human. There were the arms, there were the legs. That was the head. Round the torso was wrapped tightly some black material.

But there was something horrible about the face. It was blank, featureless. Simply nothing. He caught a glint of eyes, but for the rest it might have been a blank wall of flesh.

Campbell, with an effort, transferred his eyes to the hen. It had walked right up to the man and now suddenly jumped in the air. It landed on a kind of mound, as it might be an upturned basin, in front of the shadow. It stood there quite still. Then suddenly, with a kind of ghastly busy-ness, the figure knelt down. There was a wild cry, which blended with the abrupt squawk of the fowl.

Campbell leapt forward, and covered the few yards between them in four bounds. He heard the quick intake of breath near him, and his hands closed round something solid, but infernally slippery, and damnably strong. Before he could gain enough knowledge of the shadow's anatomy to apply an effective grip, he found himself swung off his feet like a child and dashed full tilt against the fowl house. His head hit it with a resounding bang, and his field of vision flowed with melting colours.

Immediately the fowls set up a loud resentful squawking. Campbell took the count for about fifty seconds, and when he staggered to his feet with an aching head, all trace of the shadow seemed gone. He shone his torch on the ground. A decapitated fowl was evidence that he had not been dreaming.

Then he heard a rustle about two or three yards from him, and saw a figure move. His blood boiled with rage again and he flung himself on it.

The figure was however strangely soft and yielding. It emitted a feminine squeal. Campbell let go and shone his torch on it.

It was a girl. Even seen under the present conditions, recovering from a violent physical attack and blinking in the rays of a high-powered torch, it was a remarkably pretty girl.

"Good Heavens, what are you doing here?" he exclaimed.

"Would you mind switching off that thing?" said the girl. "I was doing the same as you were, I suppose, watching."

"Who are you? Where do you come from?"

"I am an American. My name is Virginia Ridge. I am an anthropological field worker. I am staying as a boarder with the vicar of Little Whippering. Who are you?"

"I am a police detective."

The moon came out, as if someone had pressed a switch. Campbell peered at the girl. She seemed perfectly calm and self-possessed.

"What on earth made you come here tonight?"

"Curiosity!" said the girl equably. "I'm interested in your local customs, and when I heard a hen-roost was being robbed, I thought I'd watch."

"What did you see?"

"The same as you saw, I suppose. Most interesting!"

Campbell passed a hand over his aching brow. The girl's coolness, in contrast to his own excitement, irritated him.

"Do you realize this is highly suspicious, your presence here? I'm not sure I oughtn't to take you into custody."

"Now then, captain, I've read something about English police methods. You can't do that, unless you bring a charge against me. And you can hardly get anyone to believe I came here to rob hen-roosts. You've got my name and my address, and I think I'll go back home. Goodnight, captain."

"I shall call in and see you tomorrow," threatened Campbell, feeling foolish, as they both walked towards the fence.

"Any time," said the girl with a laugh. "Would you mind holding this wire down while I get over?"

Rather sulkily, Campbell did so.

~§~

Campbell duly came round to the vicarage, and verified the fact that a Virginia Ridge was staying there. As he went down the garden path he heard a voice:

"Hey, captain!"

He turned and saw the girl. By the light of day she looked really beautiful, and Campbell remembered with contrition how violently he had struck her.

"I am a detective inspector," he confessed. "We don't have captains. You must excuse me for my roughness last night. I hadn't the remotest idea who you were until you cried out."

She looked at him curiously.

"You look quite mild! I imagined something huge and rough . . . My arms are black and blue."

Campbell hesitated and then thawed.

"Well, now that you see I'm quite harmless, won't you tell me why you were hanging round there?"

"I've told you the truth," she said with a smile. "Cross my heart. It was sheer curiosity. And you see I was rewarded."

"But what did you expect? What made you expect something?"

"Only that I'd heard chickens were being stolen. And where I come from, when we hear of hen-roosts being robbed, we always think of—" She paused.

"Of what?"

The girl smiled. "Oh, I don't know, it would sound silly to you I expect—And here comes Mr. Jones. He's promised to answer a questionnaire about his country's classificatory system."

"Good Lord, a black man!" exclaimed Campbell, as he saw Mr. Jones's amiable figure approaching.

"What's he doing down here?" he added suspiciously.

"Oh, he's just a negro student reading law."

"Oh, is he? Well, Miss Ridge, if you feel disposed at any later time to give me further information, I shall be glad to call on you. You can always send a message through Collop here."

With a curt nod, he was gone. He had an uneasy feeling, as soon as his back was turned, that Miss Ridge was laughing at him. It had been quite obvious that she understood perfectly the significance of last night's incident, and equally obvious that she did not propose to tell him. It was of course impossible to prove that Mr. Jones had been the chief actor in the scene. But he now felt certain that the mysterious man had been black, although it had not occurred to him at the time. That blank featureless face . . . Surely a white face would have been more distinct.

On the other hand, had the fowl-house affair anything to do with O'Leary? How could it? It was true that twelve years before O'Leary had been in Africa, and the man was a negro—

"But I shall go potty soon," muttered Campbell, "and start seeing Africa in everything."

For no particular reason, five minutes later, Campbell said aloud: "A damned pretty girl!"

Looking at his watch, Campbell saw that the Marion Arms would be open, and he turned in there for a drink. Mrs. Hippie already knew him and gave him a cheerful greeting.

He looked round. There were no strange faces in the private bar, only Jennings and Bunn, and as Campbell thoughtfully imbibed a glass of beer, he tried to sort out his puzzled impressions.

"We've got hold of the wrong end somehow," he thought. "I suppose if we keep teasing it, we'll see a glimpse of the right thread. I'm damned if I can see it now!"

Mrs. Hippie returned from serving the public bar, to smile amiably at the private.

"Seen any more of our friend O'Leary?" asked Campbell.

Mrs. Hippie bridled.

"No, indeed. And I'll be thankful to see the last of him, even if he doesn't pay for that last lot of drinks I sent up. I don't like those gentlemen who come in here and Create. They may be free with the drink, but what I says, sooner or later Creating gets you into trouble with the police—begging your pardon, sir—and then your license goes."

"So he used to create, did he?" said Campbell with a

smile.

"He did, sir, something awful. The row that used to go on some nights, you wouldn't believe. Well, he soon shot *his* bolt. 'Pay you any day now, Mrs. Hipple!' H'm, I've heard that story before. I can whistle for my money, I can see that."

Brooding darkly, Mrs. Hippie retired to the saloon.

The private and public bars were opposite one another, and were served from the same point, so that it was possible, during lulls, to hear anyone speaking loudly in one bar while in the other. In one such lull, Campbell heard a curious jabbering noise coming from the public bar. It sounded like the meaningless slobber of a lunatic, but as there were two voices, it could hardly be that.

He pushed aside one of the glass screens whereby the "privates" could conceal themselves from the contaminating gaze of the "publics," and stared into the public bar.

The jabbering was coming from two men in the corner. One was—Campbell suppressed an exclamation of astonishment—a negro. In contrast to Mr. Jones' black elegance, he was a very seedy-looking negro, bald and dressed in a ragged and shiny blue serge suit. One cheek bore a reddish scar. He was talking to a dapper young gentleman with a tanned face and neat toothbrush moustache, wearing flannel trousers and a tweed coat. This young man in the intervals between his ejecting a spirit of incomprehensibility, sucked stolidly at his pipe. The queerly assorted couple talked on for about five minutes, and then the Englishman got up and went out abruptly.

Campbell strolled casually out of his own door, and was in time to see the young man jump into a sports two-seater and drive off. Campbell made a note of the number, and then went back into the bar. Ten minutes later the negro got to his feet, picked up a peddler's tray from the seat beside him, sighed, and walked out. Campbell saw him trudging up the street. He followed him for about half an hour, but the man did nothing but go from door to door trying to sell his wares. He seemed *bona fide* enough, if rather unexpected in a Berkshire village.

Campbell saw his carefully reared pile of hypotheses beginning to totter.

"But at least all this proves there is something fishy about this business," he thought. "Fishy—why it positively stinks! What is it that girl knows and I don't?"

He jumped irritably into his car and pressed the starting button. A hen shot out from under the car, startled by the noise. Miss Tipton emerged from the Post Office and after a word of reproof to the hen, popped back again. Mr. Padding leaned against the pump and regarded him thoughtfully, then spat.

What could have been more peaceful, more rural? Yet Campbell, in spite of his matter-of-fact temperament, suddenly had the feeling of something hot and livid, something like an evil influence borne on the wind, without any visible change, infecting the drowsy village with some insidious disease. He could almost smell it in the air . . .

"Pshaw," he said, and shot up the main road.

Mr. Padding straightened himself, steadied himself on his unassisted feet, and limped, painfully, away. The bush telegraph was about to acquaint Little Whippering with the arrival and departure of the policeman from London.

~§~

Campbell told Gregson his findings to date, and the local man found himself completely unable to integrate the remarkable experiences of his colleague.

"We've never had anything like tins before in Berkshire!" he grunted. "What do you make of it?"

"Damned if I know. This girl guesses something. Did I

tell you she was very pretty, by the way?"

"Yes, you did."

"Well, she knows something. She couldn't have been there last night by accident. And there's some important link between O'Leary and Africa—and Crumbles as well, no doubt—that we haven't got. It may not be Jones. There's that young fellow I saw, obviously a Colonial, talking to the nigger in the Marion Arms. It looks as if somebody—probably several people—are after that gold. That's why O'Leary got the wind up."

"Do you suggest the same lot killed Crumbles?"

"They may have done. Wait a bit though, I should say no. Otherwise O'Leary would have got the wind up earlier. If you ask me, O'Leary settled with Crumbles himself, and thought he'd scooped the pool. Then suddenly he discovered he was in for other troubles as well. Hence his funk."

"Wait a bit, laddie. Not too fast! What can these men be after, if O'Leary's so broke he can't even pay his tradesmen's bills?"

"That's the point. O'Leary hasn't got it. But he's looking for it!"

"Looking for it?"

"Yes. That explains his frantic digging. He wasn't bluffing, he was looking for the stuff. And he can't find it. No doubt he reckoned on finding it quickly and beating it from Little Whippering. But he can't. And meanwhile he's run out of cash. And he also knows someone else is round looking for it too."

"But why the devil hasn't he found it before, if it was hidden in his own garden?"

"Well, there are two possibilities. First of all Crumbles may have hidden it there when O'Leary was away. The time he shot the dog."

"But why?"

"That's what we've got to find out. Either he may have

arranged with O'Leary to do so, or else he may have reckoned on murdering O'Leary at once and becoming the next tenant of the Wilderness. The other possibility is that it has been hidden there some time before O'Leary took the place, that this was why he took it, but that for some reason he has been searching for it *indoors*. Then Crumbles comes home, having found exactly *where* it is hidden, and lets on to O'Leary that it's actually hidden in the garden. No doubt Crumbles refuses to reveal the actual spot, intending to bag the lion's share. Perhaps he goes to get it when he shoots the dog. In any case, he gives O'Leary a hint of its whereabouts, who promptly murders him, thinking he can find it now that he knows it's buried in the garden. But he still can't find it."

"Well, the first theory is the best. That Crumbles hid it in the garden himself. For we know Crumbles was selling gold to Farthingale a month before."

"Um, yes. That may not be the same lot of gold though. It may just have happened that Crumbles had a gold bracelet which he'd brought back with him. After all, so far as we know, the stuff is gold dust, not bracelets."

"Yes, and that's another point. If O'Leary doesn't know where this hypothetical stuff is, how does he come to have his hands covered in gold dust?"

Campbell grinned.

"Well, that's where I think we're one up on O'Leary. It gives me a suspicion, only a suspicion, but still . . . However, I won't run the risk of being laughed at until I've got some kind of confirmation . . . I think the sooner I have a go at searching O'Leary's house, the better. If you agree, perhaps you can fetch him over on some excuse tomorrow? I'll pop in and search the place. You'd better get me out a search warrant in case anything goes wrong."

"Right-ho. I'll send a police car over and we'll put him through a reasonably convincing interview. Got a set of skeleton keys?"

"Yes, thanks." Campbell got up and put on his hat.

"Well, I'll leave you, and moon around and do a little heavy thinking."

"O.K. Oh, I say, Campbell!"

The policeman halted at the door. Gregson's rugged features had assumed an expression of exaggerated innocence.

"That girl you saw up at the vicarage at Little Whippering. Did you say she was pretty?"

"Urcha!" replied Detective-Inspector Campbell.

CHAPTER TEN
Mr. Jones Drops a Catch

EARLY the next morning Inspector Gregson arrived with a car and, after a parley through the grille, the tenant of the Wilderness was persuaded to accompany him back to the station. Gregson was able to see that O'Leary's nervousness was not acted. The man was as jumpy as a cat who knows a dog is in the vicinity. Indeed he seemed actually pleased to be sitting beside a policeman in the comparative security of a police car.

As they were pulling out of Little Whippering in to the main road, Gregson heard O'Leary mutter something and, looking up, was startled to see him almost as white as a ghost. His artificial sunburn—for he was still "tanned"—was crusted on his skin like lichen.

Gregson looked out of the back of the window to see what had scared O'Leary but he could see nothing, except a man who looked like a tramp, sitting by the side of the road in the distance. The tramp's back was towards them, and in another moment a bend in the road had hidden him from sight. Gregson hesitated for a moment, considering whether to order the driver to turn back and have a look at the man, but in the end he said nothing. A moment later O'Leary had recovered his composure.

They reached the office.

"Now," said Gregson, settling himself back in his chair. "We should like you to be so good as to make us a more detailed statement as to your movements on the day of Crumbles' suicide..."

Inspector Gregson was "holding him."

~§~

Meanwhile, Inspector Campbell was walking carefully round the garden of the Wilderness carrying a suitcase. He peered carefully in every window. He was followed from room to room by a furious Alsatian. At every window man and beast regarded each other in unfriendly manner from either side of the pane of glass.

Campbell did not at present want to go into the house. Having satisfied himself that it was empty he opened the suitcase, and took out a queer-looking steel contraption. It consisted of a pair of curved jaws which, as he held the apparatus up to inspect it, were closed. He fastened the end of a reel of fine cord to a ring on the jaws and pulled at the cord experimentally. The jaws expanded, actuated by a simple system of levers to which the cord was attached. Fully open, the jaws had a spread of several feet. Campbell seemed satisfied.

He put the apparatus on one side. He started to tap the compacted gravel and earth round the base of the house with the sledge hammer which had been used to crack the concrete bed of the lily pond. After about ten minutes of this probing, he came upon a patch which, to his keen ear, seemed to give out a hollow sound.

Campbell began to dig. With the dexterity of a surgeon, he shaved off the moss-coloured top layer of earth and put it carefully on one side so that later it could be replaced. Then he went on digging, piling the earth some distance away. Presently his spade struck something metallic.

A few minutes' more digging exposed a steel cover, such as is used for manholes. He lifted it and found himself, as he had expected, gazing down into the well which supplied the Wilderness with fresh water. The water was tapped by a suction pipe connecting with the pump in the kitchen.

Campbell went to fetch his steel grab and reel of cord and took out from his suitcase a coil of rope. He attached this to the grab and lowered it, keeping the jaws as wide open as the width of the well would permit by means of a steady strain on the fine cord. He fished about for a little and then released the cord and tugged.

Campbell smiled. "Feels like a bite!"

It was a fairly heavy weight, for Campbell panted and strained as he hauled in the last few feet and brought his prize ashore. It was a cylindrical metal container, two feet high, and about a foot in diameter, discoloured and weedy. By tapping sharply on the lid with the hammer, Campbell managed at last to loosen it and screw it off. The container was quite watertight for the contents were perfectly dry.

The main item was a table or stool. Only its carved ivory legs were visible. The rest was hidden by a confused muddle of gold, jewelry, weapons, and chains. The stool or table had evidently been thrust into the cylinder inverted, and the ornaments then stuffed hastily into the recess so formed.

Campbell carefully replaced the cap, put the container on one side and lowered the grab again. A few minutes' fishing resulted in another catch. But this time the cylinder was damaged. There was a dent in the side and the seam had started, leaving a perceptible gap. Campbell fished in the gap with a twig and, as he expected, the twig came out glittering with metallic dust. He screwed the cap off with considerable difficulty. The contents included a few skin bags—evidently containing gold dust—and some startling golden masks, with staring white enameled eyes and full barbaric lips, their cruel aquiline noses jutting out abruptly from under ape-like brows—ridges.

Campbell put this cylinder with the other, and fished again. Again he got a catch, but this time he changed his mind, for he slacked off the grab jaws and brought the tackle to the surface without his prize. Then he began carefully to lower the booty he had already brought up back into the well again. He replaced the manhole cover, and carefully covered it with earth, finishing off the smoothed top with the original moss-covered surface so that all traces of his excavation had disappeared.

Then he carefully packed up the implements, hid the suitcase in the bushes and stood for a few minutes thinking.

His guess had been justified. The stuff had been buried in the well, a clever hiding place. Some of the gold dust from the leaky container had been sucked up by the pump and discharged into O'Leary's basin. It was ironical that O'Leary had been using water that had lapped the very booty for which he was searching so frantically, that had even brought him glittering fragments of it, had he only eyes sharp enough to see them.

Apart from this confirmation of the fact that O'Leary had not himself known where the booty was, his discovery raised a much more important point. The moss-covered state of the earth above the well and the condition of the containers themselves showed that the hoard must have been sunk long anterior to the coming of Crumbles on the scene. Probably before the coming of O'Leary to Little Whippering.

Thus the whole affair began to take on a new complexion. Campbell perceived that the suicide of Crumbles must be only a comparatively late link in a long chain of events which had started when some unknown person had buried all that gold and ivory in the Wilderness garden.

Could it have been done by the first owner? He was, Campbell recollected, a retired sailor. A sailor was a traveler, and one glance at the carving on the ivory and the moulding of the soft thick gold had been sufficient to tell Campbell, ignorant though he was of art, that the stuff was African.

And now the latest chapter? What was O'Leary so desperately afraid of? Not merely of his losing to someone else the prize he could not find himself. It was of something more dangerous, of that Campbell was certain.

He gave up his unprofitable speculations and turned his attention to the Alsatian. Carefully unwrapping a juicy chop which he had brought with him for the purpose, he posted it through the letter box. There was a furious barking and scrabbling and Campbell retired to a distance to encourage the dog to give its attention to the meal.

He returned in ten minutes, and opened the door with his keys. The Alsatian was in a coma, stretched out beside the half-chewed bone. He picked the dog up carefully and locked it in an upstairs bedroom. In about half an hour it would wake, O'Leary would doubtless assume that it had wandered into the bedroom and locked itself in. By that time Campbell would be far away.

The state of the cottage made Campbell gasp. O'Leary had been searching it in the same wild manner as the garden. Floors had been torn up, wallpapers stripped, and in many rooms pieces of furniture had been hacked to pieces. A thick mantle of dust lay on everything except where it had been disturbed by O'Leary's operations. The walls had been gouged in several places, evidently while testing for secret passages. In two cases the chimney pieces had been prised bodily from the wall.

Campbell smiled, picturing the faces of Gorringe and Organ, solicitors, when they should inspect the scene.

"A bit eccentric we are told," they had said to Sergeant Finch, "but a nice quiet tenant as far as we are concerned. No trouble at all."

As to the rest, there seemed little trace of O'Leary's personality. The furniture had been taken over from the dead owner, and there seemed nothing that appeared to belong to the tenant. The drawers were empty of personal papers.

Campbell surveyed the gigantic disorder of the rooms and looked at his watch. Time was getting on. He had found the main object of his visit and O'Leary would be returning shortly, unless he went down to the village and phoned Gregson to keep him at Abingdon longer. But it did not seem worthwhile, as there was little he could expect to find in this disorder!

He paused in the act of replacing his watch in his pocket. His keen ears had caught a suspicious sound. Someone was cautiously scrabbling at the lock of the front door. Campbell had carefully closed it after him and he was, therefore, surprised when he heard it opening slowly. Then there was stealthy padding footsteps in the hall.

So someone else was sufficiently interested in O'Leary to provide himself with lock-picking apparatus!

Campbell heard the unknown go from one room to the other. The detective was in an upstairs bedroom and he now went quietly on to the landing.

Then, as the stranger started to climb the stairs, he flattened himself into a recess where he would be unseen.

The steps came slowly up the stairs, then on to the landing, then halted. Campbell stepped out quickly from his hiding place, at the same time cutting off the intruder's retreat.

"What are you doing here?" he said sharply.

The man wheeled round with a startled expression. Campbell himself was a little surprised to find that it was the same young man whom he had seen in the Marion Arms talking in some lingo to the negro peddler with the cheek scars.

By now the young man had recovered himself.

He smiled quizzically, eyeing Campbell with a certain wary good humour.

"I believe this is what is known as a fair-cop," he admitted, "but come to that, what are *you* doing here?"

"I happen to be a police officer in execution of my duty," said Campbell, taking out his search warrant.

The young man cocked an eye at the document and grew more thoughtful still.

"Well, that's awkward, isn't it?"

"Why are you here?" went on Campbell.

The young man shrugged his shoulders.

"Oh, I'm just taking a look round. Pure curiosity."

"I advise you to answer sensibly," the policeman warned him sternly. "Were you looking for one of your negro friends?"

The young man's face grew suddenly watchful.

"You know quite a lot, don't you? I'm afraid I can't add to your knowledge, however. I'm sorry I disturbed you and all that. Perhaps the best thing would be for me to trickle quietly home."

Campbell stretched an arm across the stairs. Meanwhile he mentally selected the place where he would plant his blow, if it came to a fight, as seemed likely, for there was a warning glint in the young man's blue eyes.

"On the contrary," he said, "unless you can give a proper explanation of your presence here, you will accompany me to the station on a charge of housebreaking."

As if by magic a revolver appeared in the young man's hand.

"Stand aside," he said coldly. "I can't afford to get mixed up in a charge of housebreaking now, sorry and all that, but this isn't a joke."

Campbell hesitated, wondering whether the young man would shoot if pushed. He decided he would, and therefore stood aside.

The stranger went down the stairs backwards, got as far as the front door, opened it still with his back to it, wheeled across the threshold and then vanished abruptly, slamming the door after him.

Campbell bounded down the stairs, flung open the door, and saw his quarry racing down the garden path. The young man cleared the gate with a good hurdling style, and Campbell heard as he did so the whirr of an engine being started. Evidently someone was waiting for him in a car. By the time Campbell got into the road, a green two-seater was hurtling down the hill and the fugitive had vanished.

"But I've already got his number," Campbell told himself, and he opened his notebook. Yes, there it was. A green two-seater. He hurried down to the village to phone Gregson to pull in the driver of a green two-seater, XYX 001—Charge housebreaking.

"Right-ho!" said Gregson. "O'Leary's just gone. He got a bit abusive towards the end, but we managed to hold him for the agreed time. Found anything?"

"Quite a lot," replied Campbell.

"Useful?"

"Quite exceptionally so."

~§~

"You seem very jumpy today, Mr. Jones," said Dr. Ridge. She was contemplating with disfavor the weary poached egg that constituted the vicarage breakfast.

"Yes, it is an important day for me," replied Mr. Jones prodding his own egg hopefully. But no blood came. All eggs at the vicarage were solid.

"Why, what is happening today, if one may ask?" asked

Dr. Ridge innocently, "everyone seems excited about something."

"I have to perform the most important task of my life," said Mr. Jones, showing the whites of his eyes.

"Mr. Jones is playing for Little Whippering," explained Mrs. Wykeham. "Have some more coffee, my dear? You aren't eating any breakfast."

"What are you playing?" asked Dr. Ridge. "Is it a ball game?"

"A ball game!" exclaimed the vicar putting down his paper. "Well, cricket is played with a ball, I suppose."

"Oh, cricket. I've heard of that!" said Virginia.

"She's heard of it," commented the vicar with a mild trace of sarcasm. "Well, well!"

"Do you play cricket?" asked the girl.

"Yes, I do," said the vicar benevolently beaming, "or rather did, before my eyes began to fail."

"Were you hot?"

"Oh, no, my dear, a complete second-rater," replied the vicar with the excessive modesty of the old Blue.

"Were you?" said Virginia Ridge, as yet unfamiliar with the modesty that is England's inverted vanity. "Perhaps you didn't take it seriously enough. That's the trouble with all your sport, I guess."

There was a dead silence after this pronouncement.

The vicar got up.

"I think I will go and take another look at the wicket," he said. "Bundling is a very good fellow, but he's not a cricketer. Dear me, no."

Presently through the French window they could see the vicar's long, lean figure hurry up the lane to Marion Park.

It was a good cricketing day, a clear sky, but not overwhelmingly hot, and the lovely cricket field of Marion Park, its wide expanse of ancient turf set in embosoming trees of equal age, was at its best.

The matches between the Whipperings could always be relied upon to be epic. They were followed by equally epic sessions at the Marion Arms where the humbler members of the team fought their battles over again, occasionally with somewhat sanguinary results. Even the gentlemen, dining together in Marion Hall afterwards, had been known in recent years to become a little acidulous, until the Marion port had had time to perform its calming office. In fairness to the gentlemen concerned, it must be admitted that there was some justification for this recent bitterness. Little Whippering, animated by Gudgeon, a formidable bowler of speed-at-any-price school, had suddenly developed a passion for leg theory. Last match they had practiced it with such fervor that four Great Whipperingites had been carried off the field.

This year fortunately the vicar, by virtue of his cloth, had been able to heal the leg theory controversy. It had raged during three seasons, and had bidden fair to break short this classic series which, according to Mr. Vansteem's researches, dated from the days of stoolball. Feelings—and in many cases persons—had been too wounded for Marion's intervention to heal the breach. Major Fawcett's hearty camaraderie had been equally vain; and it was generally acknowledged as a proof of the still vital power of Christianity in our rural districts, that the vicar, with the cooperation of the rector of Great Whippering (who had found a text in St. Paul which virtually forbade body-line bowling) had been able to persuade Little Whippering, not that the leg theory be specifically excluded—that would obviously have been impossible—but that the following compromise be adopted, namely:—

"That it is hereby understood and agreed, that while the captain's absolute discretion to set his field as he pleases is acknowledged, any bowling which can be held deliberately to be aimed at the person of the batsman, or results in an unusual percentage of injuries to the batting side, is to be considered unsportsmanlike."

Mr. Forgan, as a solicitor, considered the clause to be both nonsense and bad law, apparently an unusual combination. But with this exception, the compromise was accepted as satisfactory. Thus, this year, the Whipperings met on the Marion field under the happiest auspices. The vicar, naturally, was beaming, and Dr. Graham also looked carefree, since his professional assistance was not likely to be so frequently called on as in the days when Gudgeon, frowning like a devil, as he roared up the pitch, would discharge the ball at the body of the batsman was as near an approach to a throw as the complacency of the umpire could permit.

Mr. Vansteem was also there, and his compatriot had accompanied the vicar to the rural scene, hoping to detect some interesting survivals in this historic game.

Claude Marion, as the host, benevolently surveyed the scene from a deck chair, holding a sunshade to shield his sensitive features from the sun.

"I have no wish to compete with Mr. Jones!" he had muttered, on being taxed with softness by Psyche, who was the proud possessor of a handsome tan. "He has me beaten from the start."

"Did you play cricket, Mr. Marion?" asked Virginia.

"I did at one time, when I was in the public school or grub stage. I cannot admit to being outstandingly successful. On the field I was generally relegated to long stop. Although perhaps I did not stop a very high percentage of balls, at least I can flatter myself I waited for them with a certain amount of grace, which is more than can be said for old Bunn. He looks like a frog."

Virginia did her best to fight her increasing drowsiness as she watched the soothing scene.

"Say, why do they keep changing sides when they've just

got set?"

"It's not very logical, is it, when put in that way? It's just the custom of the country. It makes a break, you see."

Virginia wanted to ask more. But she was daunted by the ineffable weariness of her companion, who seemed barely able to murmur audibly the "Played, sir," that his duty as host demanded from time to time. Eventually she strolled away to join the vicar, who was scoring.

Great Whippering had won the toss and had elected to go in first. All the players were well known locally with the exception of Mr. Jones. The vicar, testing him out previously, had found him a sound bat and a brilliant fielder. He could snap up stuff in slips like a panther, and it was there, therefore, that he was stationed.

The game went on and the hours passed.

Meanwhile, a mile or so away, Inspector Campbell was searching Mr. O'Leary's abode and encountering the mysterious young man. It was tea-time before Mr. O'Leary was released from Inspector Gregson's clutches and had arrived home. Campbell had concealed himself in the bushes to watch his arrival.

He looked suspiciously round the garden, but went in without noticing the inspector's labours around the well.

Campbell now went down to the village again and this time in the course of a longer phone call told Gregson the result of his researches.

"It seems to me we know enough to take O'Leary into custody," he said. "If O'Leary is as frightened as he appears to be, he won't be sorry to be safely locked up in prison. Will you speak to your chief? And if he agrees, get out a warrant for his arrest and come down to me here? I'm going over to Marion Park to have a word with Jones, so meet me there. Any news of that car number?"

"We can't pick up the car, but we've found that it was garaged in Abingdon, and the garage fellow remembers the owner. Answers your description. He's been staying for the last week at the John Hotel."

"Oh, has he? What's his name and address in the visitors' book?"

Gregson laughed. "He's a young man with a sense of humour. According to the book, Watt's his name— A. Watt."

"And his address?"

"Ware!"

"The young puppy!" exclaimed Campbell, "wait till I get hold of him!"

Simmering irritably, Campbell walked down to Marion Park, and found the tail of the Great Whippering team, the bulk of which had been dismissed for the inglorious total of 101, being polished off by Little Whippering. Tea was just over, and the fielders had taken their places again, so Campbell had to wait to speak to Jones. Meanwhile he saw Virginia looking a little bored, and went up to her.

"Why hello, Inspector, fancy seeing you here!"

"For that matter, I hardly expected to see you. Or do you like cricket?"

"It seems a bit slow," ventured Virginia, anxious not to wound national pride.

"Yes, it's not really a game at all," said Campbell dourly. "It seems to me typical of the weaknesses in the English character; lazy, feckless, time-wasting!"

"Say, you're a bit of a knocker, aren't you?" said Virginia.

"I beg your pardon?"

"You don't think much of your home town, do you?"

"Good Heavens!" exclaimed Campbell in horror. "You surely don't think I'm English? I'm Scottish."

"Oh, I see," said Virginia, a little blankly. As a good field worker, she knew she should never show surprise at any answers to her questions. "Why did you come here then?"

"I wanted to have a word with Jones," he answered, looking at her sharply. She bore his scrutiny calmly and it was he who first withdrew his gaze and fixed it on the ebony countenance of Mr. Jones in the middle distance, waiting expectantly for a quick one to glance off Mr. Burnham's dashingly wielded blade. "How's he getting on?"

"I'm told he's doing quite well. The vicar told me he's made three catches, whatever that may mean in cricket. It seems to be something good."

"Well, he's dropped that one," said Campbell, with some satisfaction, as a red-hot one slipped through the negro's fingers. There was a groan from Little Whippering's partisans.

"Dear me," said the vicar wincing. "Of course we all make mistakes, but really—"

Worse was to follow. Mr. Burnham's tactics, aided by the devout stone-walling of his opposite number, the Great Whippering blacksmith, had brought Great Whippering's total up to 129 which, for Whippering cricket, was considered a sizeable total. The combination was showing signs of wearing down the patience of Little Whippering.

In these circumstances, an unlucky cut of Mr. Burnham's lobbed the ball—so it seemed—into Mr. Jones' very hands. But even as Mr. Gudgeon's triumphant *How's that?* rose into the air, the ball was seen to be lying at the feet of a palpably embarrassed Mr. Jones.

"Dear, dear, but this is tragic, really tragic!" exclaimed the vicar, looking more upset than Virginia had ever seen him.

"What can have happened to the lad? I fear he lacks stamina. Well, well, perhaps there is something in the superiority of the white races after all. Now if I were in Major Fawcett's place . . . Ah, good man! he's resetting the field. Jones won't do any more harm now."

Fortunately for the popularity of Africa in Little Whippering, Mr. Graham was dismissed two runs later by one of Harry Thompson's bucolic but effective yorkers. As the

Little Whippering team streamed off the field, the inspector called to Jones, who was passing within a few yards of him, but the negro took no notice. A little annoyed, the inspector went towards him, but, as he approached, Mr. Jones hurried off. Campbell quickened his stride. Jones did the same, and, to the inspector's annoyance, doubled round him and fairly fled into the pavilion.

"He doesn't seem anxious to see you," said Virginia when he returned discomfited.

"I don't know what his game is," answered Campbell crossly. "I'll catch him when he comes out."

Shortly afterwards Mr. Jones, resplendent in a blazer and cap, came out of the pavilion again. He passed near Campbell, but Virginia called out commandingly, "Mr. Jones!" With a startled flash of the whites of his eyes the negro came.

"Why did you run away from Inspector Campbell?" said the girl accusingly. "He won't do you any harm."

"I run away?" asked Mr. Jones displaying his white teeth. "I should never dream of such a thing! Delighted to do anything I can for you, Inspector."

"You weren't a moment ago."

Mr. Jones looked surprised, as far as his not very fluid features could express bewilderment.

"I really don't know what you are talking about, unless you're pulling my leg. If I didn't reply to a greeting of yours, it was pure inadvertence. My apologies, Inspector."

"Perhaps it was embarrassment at dropping that ball. The vicar nearly wept . . . What happened?"

"Oh, nothing," said Mr. Jones vaguely. "Just a little accident."

He waved his hand lightly, and it caught the girl's eye.

"Oh, I say, have you hurt your hand?" said Virginia. "No wonder you dropped the ball. You ought to explain to the vicar."

"Oh, it was nothing," mumbled Mr. Jones, looking down at the large bloodstain on his immaculate white trousers, and then at the damp patch in the palm of his hand. Taking out his handkerchief, he wound it round the fingers.

"What was it you wanted to know, Inspector?"

"What you were doing round Farmer Bunn's fowl houses at two o'clock in the morning on Thursday night?"

Mr. Jones glanced sharply at Virginia. Her face was blank.

Then he looked at the inspector.

"Confound his black face," thought the inspector, "what the devil is he thinking? Worse than a Chink!"

Jones grinned. "I'm afraid I haven't the faintest notion what you mean, Inspector. To the best of my knowledge and belief I was fast asleep in the vicarage at the time you mention."

"I see. May I ask what are you doing here in Little Whippering?"

"Really you are rather extraordinary, Inspector! Have I done anything to deserve these questions? I was recommended to this place as a quiet spot where I could catch up with some arrears of reading. I'm going in for my Bar Finals next year, you know."

Campbell looked at him woodenly.

"What part of Africa do you come from?"

"From Nigeria," replied Jones without hesitating.

Campbell was silent for a moment. Jones came from Nigeria; Tuffy was killed there; Crumbles had been living there. What was the web that bound them together?

It was an awkward position, for he felt certain that the influence he at present mentally bracketed together as the Anti-O'Leary Party—including the young man self-styled Watt, the scarred negro, and Mr. Jones—had so far committed no offences of any major importance. It was improbable that they had even been in the neighbourhood when Crumbles was killed. And this robbed his examination of Jones of some of its justification. Of course when they had O'Leary under lock and key, the whole truth might come out. Alternatively the Anti-O'Leary Party might quietly fade away.

"Are you staying here long, Mr. Jones?" he asked, with more politeness.

"No," said the other unexpectedly. "I find I have got to make a flying visit to Africa. It upsets my plans, but I shall be able to do plenty of reading on the boat."

"When do you leave?"

"Tonight!"

"Tonight!" So we've put the wind up you, have we? thought Campbell with some satisfaction.

He saw Gregson hovering in the distance and waved to him.

"Good-bye, Dr. Ridge. Good-bye, Mr. Jones!" He left them and walked over to his colleague.

"A shifty fellow," he said to Gregson. "He got a moment's fright and tried to dodge me, but then thought better of it. Couldn't get anything out of him though. He's going back to Africa tonight."

"Ay, and no doubt that's where Mr. Watt of Ware will be going to. There's been no hide nor hair of him seen round here. Well, jump in, laddie, we'll go up to the Wilderness and collect O'Leary and all this fabulous gold of yours. I've got the warrant in my pocket."

They drove quickly up the hill and parked the car outside the gate of the Wilderness.

"That hound's quiet," exclaimed Campbell as they went up the path. "Still woozy from that dose I gave it, I suppose. It must be more susceptible than I thought."

"Holy Moses!" Campbell had stopped short, his hand outstretched for the knocker.

Gregson followed his stare. "The well! Somebody's been

after that stuff!"

They both rushed to the gaping hole. Then Campbell went to the car and brought back the suitcase. He took out the grab together with the rest of the tackle and lowered the gadget into the well.

"My God! it's gone!" he exclaimed, after fishing round in silence for a few minutes.

He went to the front door and executed thunderous salvos on its panels. Then he waited.

There was no answer.

"What a double-dyed fool I am," exclaimed Campbell. "O'Leary's found the stuff and hopped it."

He knocked again, more violently. Through the wave of silence that flowed back afterwards came a faint booming sound that made Gregson cock his ear.

"What's that?"

Campbell listened. In the silence the trees, feeling the first cold breath of evening, shivered. Down at the bottom of the hill, from the cup of fertile land in which Little Whippering lay, came the thin high click of ball and bat, and an occasional shout.

But there was a sound deeper-throated than that, rudely insistent, like a threatening whisper in the silence of the summer air.

The Downs behind them slept in the sun, which lay on their shoulders like a cape. The silence of the Downs was alive with that prolonged faint buzz which is a blend of the voices of birds and insects and the wind. But more rhythmic than this natural noise of the Downs that has endured ever since primeval storms had scored their ancient brows to smooth curves, was this other noise, a crude barbaric booming. It was like the drums of a distant band, beating out clear and rhythmic above the faint slurring statement of the wind instruments.

Pink-pink-boom!   Pinkety-pinkety-boom!   Pink-pink-

BOOM!

"Well, that's odd," said Gregson. "It must be soldiers. But I've never heard a tune like that before."

Campbell shrugged his shoulders.

"It's hardly likely to be a band escorting O'Leary. Come on, we'd better go inside and see if he's left any message."

Getting out his *passe-partout,* Campbell opened the door. As he walked over the threshold, he stumbled over something. He looked down.

"My God, the dog's dead!"

Then, as the opened door released a warm ray of sunlight the length of the hall, both men stopped, speechless.

O'Leary was lying upside down on the lowest flight of the stairs. Or rather what had been O'Leary.

His face was as white as paper, and was contorted with an expression of utter horror, as if all the devils of hell were dragging him upstairs to perdition by the feet. His throat was cut from ear to ear. Indeed, as Campbell went nearer to touch the face, the head nearly rolled off the neck.

But more revolting, because of its touch of the farcical, was the unspeakable nudity of the skull. Every particle of the short red stubble had been shaved off.

"After death too," murmured Campbell, for several cuts, evidently made by a clumsily wielded razor, had not bled. It was like some appalling practical joke played by a lunatic to whom human life was a bad jest.

"He's not been dead more than an hour or two," said Campbell. "We'd better get Dr. Harringay on the phone. Or better still, Graham's down at the cricket field. Can you drive him up?"

Gregson went while Campbell roamed round the house without touching anything.

Dr. Graham examined the body carefully, and then got up. "The cause of death is obvious enough. Where was he killed?"

"Well, here I suppose. He couldn't have moved after that cut. And there's no sign of a struggle anywhere else."

"But look!" said the doctor patiently, holding up the corpse's almost transparent hand. Then suddenly the truth came to him.

"My God, he was killed *here!* His throat was cut while he was held as he is now, with his head low, and his feet up the stairs. So that when his throat was cut, all the blood ran out of him."

"But," asked Campbell, "if that's so, where's the blood?"

"Yes," said the doctor. "That's just it. Where is the blood? About eight pints I should judge, and all missing."

Campbell looked at the corpse with a scowl of disgust. Then he pressed his lips together.

"Well, this settles it, old chap. You'll have to take charge of investigations now."

"Why!" exclaimed Gregson incredulously. "You're not giving up—going back to London?"

Campbell smiled grimly.

"No. To Africa!"

II

WEST AFRICA

CHAPTER ELEVEN
Inspector Campbell Recapitulates

ON THE EVE of sailing for Nigeria, Campbell sat down and wrote a resume of the case to date. It was partly for the information of his London superiors, but also as an agreed basis on which Gregson could work, while Campbell, in Africa, ploughed the difficult furrow of an investigation in what, he now realized, would be the most troublesome case he had ever tackled.

"It seems to me (wrote Campbell) that we have been wrong in focusing all our attention on the incident which occurred in Balooma twelve years back. Naturally O'Leary emphasized its importance, but that, as we might have expected, was purposely to distract us. The hate stored up by that escapade was only one of the motives of the events in Little Whippering. It ended as a force when Tuffy Samson died in a motor crash in Nigeria (whether this was accident or murder on the part of Crumbles, is a side issue). The point is that it ended the importance of Balooma in the case. And even before that had happened, the main interest of O'Leary and Crumbles' lives was a valuable hoard buried in the Wilderness garden.

"Was this buried by the first owner of the Wilderness? Or after his death? Or after the tenancy of the building by O'Leary? That is a point which Gregson will have to settle, in my absence, by investigations. The executors, Messrs. Gorringe and Organ, may be able to help him. But judging by the state of the earth above the well, and the condition of the submerged containers, this treasure was buried before the arrival of O'Leary at the Wilderness.

"We now come to a second important point. Why did O'Leary come to the Winderness, of all places? Once there, why did he take such extravagant precautions to keep out intruders and to disguise himself? His own account is that fear of Tuffy Samson made him hide himself. He may have been afraid of Tuffy Samson, but personally I think this explanation is only partially correct.

"For two reasons. First of all because O'Leary went on hiding after the telegram came from Crumbles announcing Tuffy's death. It was not till after Crumbles' death that he threw off his disguise. The second reason, the even more convincing one, is that O'Leary went into hiding again after both Tuffy and Crumbles were dead, evidently as the result of seeing some person in the neighbourhood. Who that person was, we do not yet know. But we can be fairly sure that it was the person who ultimately killed O'Leary.

"What, therefore, was the *real* reason for O'Leary's coming to the Wilderness and that strange mode of life which earned him the nickname of the Miser?

"In my opinion he came to the Wilderness because he had found out that treasure was hidden there. His mode of life was adopted first of all to prevent anyone else's getting on the scent of the treasure, and secondly to prevent his being recognized. I am not quite sure why he minded recognition. Perhaps because he already feared his unknown enemy was on the trail. Perhaps he was afraid, that his mere tenancy of the Wilderness would give certain other parties, if they discovered O'Leary's identity with the Spike Galloway of Nigeria, the clue to the treasure.

"We now come to another difficulty. Why was O'Leary unable, during his two years of residence, to discover the treasure? Admittedly it was well hidden, but it is strange that, after completely gutting the interior of the Wilderness he did not try the garden at an early date.

"Again why didn't he lose patience at his lack of success?

"The only answer is that meanwhile he was sounding other quarters for a clue to the exact location of the treasure. I suggest in fact that he was working in with Crumbles who, in Nigeria, was trying other sources of information. I suggest further that Crumbles eventually got that information and— perhaps first settling accounts with Tuffy Samson—went post-haste to O'Leary to share the hoard with him.

"I am certain that long before sending that telegram Crumbles had met O'Leary. I think he met him in Little Whippering on the day he was seen by the vicar, Jennings, and Marion. I believe further that, there and then, he told him of the death of Tuffy Samson, if O'Leary did not already know it. But I suggest that at this meeting he was reticent as to the exact whereabouts of the treasure. We can imagine those two crooks, both aware that they would sell their own mothers for a five-pound note, fencing with each other, each mortally afraid of the other's double-crossing him.

"Therefore I think that this meeting was indeterminate. And I further believe that Crumbles was then already thinking how to outwit O'Leary and get the whole treasure for himself. I imagine that on one occasion he tried to steal it and was attacked by the dog, which he shot. And probably it was as a result of this O'Leary came to the conclusion that the only way to do business with Crumbles was to murder him. And I fancy also that by this time Crumbles had come to the same conclusion about O'Leary. But in this game O'Leary, with his nimbler wit, had an advantage. For whereas he suspected Crumbles' intention, I don't think Crumbles, intent on his own game, suspected O'Leary's.

"Now we come to the difficult events attending Crumbles' murder. Unfortunately just because Crumbles' murder plan miscarried, we shall never know what it was. But quite obviously it had been the result of careful thought. As we know, Crumbles was in Wantage as early as a month before the fatal day, spying out the land and incidentally paying his expenses by selling a gold trinket brought back from Nigeria.

"We now know of course that this bracelet had nothing to do with the buried hoard for at the time the earth above it was still undisturbed. In these days of high gold values it was quite reasonable for Crumbles to invest in such a thing in Nigeria and bring it home with him to realize in England at a profit. Except as evidence of Crumbles' movements, it is of no importance therefore.

"Crumbles' murder plan, whatever it was, had some connection with a faked suicide. Hence Crumbles' assumption of melancholia, the letters he prepared, and the cord he purchased. But it failed.

"For meanwhile O'Leary had (as I think) dyed his hair and gone over to Crumbles' hotel, and there murdered him, almost immediately after Crumbles had dispatched the wire which was to bring O'Leary into his trap.

"Why did Crumbles send this wire if he had already told O'Leary that Tuffy was dead? I think they had previously arranged to send the wire, as a plausible excuse for O'Leary's visit to Abingdon. Otherwise this visit, by a notorious hermit, might make the village suspicious. Knowing something about village Post Offices, they therefore agreed to send this wire.

"Why did O'Leary want to meet Crumbles in Abingdon at all? Probably because, after the dog episode, they preferred to meet on neutral ground.

"But as we have seen, before the wire got through to Little Whippering, O'Leary, in disguise, had murdered Crumbles. If my theory is correct, it is up to Gregson to find out, if he can, how and when a dark-haired pale-faced man got from Little Whippering to Abingdon in quick time—whether by car or bicycle—and how he slipped up to Crumbles' room without being noticed by the hotel porter.

"Having murdered Crumbles, O'Leary made a tour of his room in search of a clue to the treasure. I believe he found that clue. But he did not realize, until it was too late, that it was a false clue. That it had been purposely planted by Crumbles in case he was robbed or double-crossed.

"Rejoicing at his discovery of the clue, therefore, O'Leary cut off his dyed hair and washed it down the basin. Either then, or later, he covered his face with sunburn. Thus, it was a man completely altered in appearance who went back to Little Whippering, and Gregson must make inquiries therefore for the return to Little Whippering of a man with cropped red hair, and face pale or tanned, but probably tanned.

"Back once more at the Wilderness O'Leary waited for the telegram. It was duly brought him by Miss Tipton, whom he asked to inform Harry Thompson of his need of a car. Harry Thompson drove him into Abingdon and, as we know, he now pretended to discover the body of Crumbles.

"I need not recount the events of that day. As we know O'Leary soon dropped his misanthropy and started to celebrate his now undisputed possession of the treasure with a gorgeous blind.

"But O'Leary found he was celebrating too soon. Crumbles had been too clever for him. The clue, whatever it was, was a dummy one. Crumbles had kept the real clue either in his head or in a safe place. O'Leary dug madly all over the garden, without success. Meanwhile his stock of cash had started to run low. He got into debt. It is impossible to imagine a more exasperating position than O'Leary's. A fortune was buried somewhere in his cottage, yet at any moment he might have the bailiffs in, or even be evicted for non-payment of rent if he had not found it by quarter-day.

"His run of bad luck had only just started. Soon afterwards he saw something or heard something that made him realize that a fresh rival was after the treasure. Had he always known that? And had he hoped by murdering Crumbles to get a clear start of them? Or did he only later realize that someone, far more dangerous than Crumbles, was after the hoard? I am not sure in my mind which. The probability is that he had always dreaded these people (whom we will for the present call the African Gang), but that he hoped and believed he had a clear start of them.

"The African Gang brought an entirely new element into the situation. There is little Gregson can do here beyond making researches into the previous English history of Jones, of the young man with the moustache, and of the negro peddler. But personally I believe that all our information about them will come from Africa.

"Is it a purely criminal gang? Or a kind of secret society? Is the treasure a secondary motive, and is it rather a case of blood vengeance? The answer, I think, lies in Nigeria.

"Whatever the explanation is, it has to explain certain very horrible features. What was the significance of the queer ceremony I witnessed outside Farmer Bunn's poultry house? What was the meaning of the drumming we both heard in the Wilderness garden when O'Leary was lying dead? Why was the corpse drained of blood? Why was its head shaven? All these happenings are quite foreign to any ordinary murder in England. They introduce elements which open up various alarming possibilities.

"I am also puzzled by the American girl's attitude. While I do not think she has played any part in the murder, I feel she knows something we do not know. It might be as well to verify her previous history through our American liaison office.

"Gregson will also have to investigate, so far as he can, the movements of the suspected parties on the day of the murder. Our preliminary investigations on the following day seem to show that neither Jones nor the young man 'Watt' had any part in it. Jones was fielding in full view of Little Whippering at the time the murder was committed. The young man, or rather a car bearing his number and driven by a man answering to his description, was spotted, about the time the murder was committed, fifty miles away from Little Whippering, by a constable. It was then going hell for leather for Southampton. This is an alibi. By this time Mr. Watt is doubtless far away on the seas.

"For that matter, Jones too had completely disappeared by the time Gregson and myself went to the vicarage on the evening of the murder.

"It may be that during my absence in Africa these two men may be found, but even if they are, I do not see how we can charge them with anything. It seems more probable that the negro peddler with the scar is the guilty party. But we must allow for the possibility that the African Gang is a large one. Therefore Gregson will have to comb the neighborhood for any reports of strangers seen in the vicinity, particularly any black men.

"During my absence I have arranged that Gregson and I keep in close touch with each other by cable (Code B2.) and that my colleague at the Yard, Inspector Bernard Bray, be available for collaboration with Gregson or his chief at any time."

CHAPTER TWELVE
Reappearance of an Anthropologist

CAMPBELL was looking forward to his trip on the *Cromlech Castle*. He foresaw many days of pleasant idleness in which, free from routine cares, he could stretch himself mentally and physically, revolve the future conduct of his case, and enjoy a holiday.

It was of course against his national tradition to enjoy a period of pure idleness. He had therefore provided himself with a number of books on West Africa which would, he hoped, prepare him for his investigations into these unfamiliar regions.

His companions on the voyage were harmless without being interesting. Campbell placed in the first few meals, three missionaries, a nurse, a doctor, two vaguely administrative officials, the representatives of a firm of agricultural implement makers, a party of big game hunters, and several amiable and earnest youths who were probably going out for the first time. The others were hardened pioneers with numbers of acquaintances, places and jokes in common, none of which meant anything to Campbell.

Never mind, thought Campbell, from the haven of his deck-chair. The weather was fine. The Bay had been comparatively calm. He had the feeling, new to his industrious nature, that he would be quite content for the voyage to go on forever, the ship still to glide through blue or dark green seas without ever reaching land.

He let the book drop from his hands. He did not know whether he altogether approved of Colonial administration. There seemed an odd mingling of administrative with police functions, and some of the local practices that were tolerated, even encouraged, seemed to him very unsettling.

"Back home if I found a man had two wives," reflected Campbell, "I should charge him with bigamy at once. Here apparently, it's a regular thing among the population. Most unsettling."

"Good morning, Inspector!"

Campbell started, for he had carefully refrained from revealing his profession to the purser or anyone else. He had found, from sad experience, that a strange constraint, due to a kind of guilty conscience, overtakes even the most law-abiding of citizens when they find themselves in the company of a full-fledged police detective.

He looked round.

Lying in a deck-chair, separated from him by a few feet of gangway, was a girl. Her face was partly hidden by a book and still more by a large pair of tortoiseshell spectacles.

The girl put down the book, removed the spectacles, and revealed the features—altogether too beautiful for an anthropologist—of Virginia Ridge.

"Good Heavens!" exclaimed Campbell, momentarily staggered. All sorts of conjectures as to the reason for her presence on the ship flashed through his mind.

"Well, that's not a vurry flattering remark!" said Virginia in her soft throaty voice, with its entire absence of emotional complications.

"However," went on Virginia, "perhaps you're in disguise or something, and I oughtn't to see you."

And, resuming her tortoiseshell spectacles and picking up the book, she switched off her attention as one might pull down a blind.

"Not at all," said Campbell hastily, with an unusual

breach in his customary quiet and determined manner. He had noticed before that this girl had an odd ability to disconcert him and he put it down to her unusualness. Dash it all, you don't know whether to treat her as a professor or a pretty girl.

"Not at all," he repeated. "I was only surprised at the coincidence that we should be both going on the same boat. I wonder why I didn't see you before?"

Virginia Ridge put down the book again and regarded the gently heaving ocean with distaste. "I was ill," she said. "The least bit of sea makes me ill!"

"That's bad luck. Where are you bound for?" He told himself that the *Cromlech Castle* was going as far as Cape Town and that her presence on board might, after all, be pure coincidence.

"Molengi," she answered.

"Is that in Nigeria?"

She smiled. "No. It's a good deal farther down the Coast."

"May I ask you why you are coming out here? I thought you had settled in Little Whippering. Excuse me if I seem inquisitive."

"That's all right, Inspector. We field-workers get so used to asking questions about people's home life, how they address their relatives, and who they are proposing to marry, that we've just got no sense of privacy left at all. Well, I've finished my job in Little Whippering, and I'm going to do some field-work in Africa."

"I seem to remember your telling me that enough was known about Africa already!"

"Yes, but most of the field-workers have been men. The result is that everything we know is from the native man's point of view. We know little about the women's real beliefs, their secret societies and initiation ceremonies. Well, I've got a chance to do so at Molengi and I guess I'll bring back some interesting data. It's a matrilineal village, and I'm going to live there just like one of the native women. I expect to find that all we're told about native women being down-trodden and doing all the work is only what their menfolk say. The women probably run the whole show on the quiet just as they do where I come from."

"Very likely. But isn't it a bit dangerous?"

"Huh, I guess I can take care of myself," replied Dr. Ridge self-confidently.

"Yes, but after all," protested Campbell, "a woman, I mean—"

He found the sentence tailing off under the stare of her clear grey eyes.

"I'm all right. I'd best be keeping my hand in, all the same," she admitted. Opening a capacious bag that lay on the deck beside her, she pulled out what looked like a pistol.

"It's all right," she said, seeing Campbell's surprise. "It's only an air pistol. I've got an honest-to-goodness gun in my baggage, but I don't want to frighten the captain!"

The girl placed a target of cardboard on the railing, returned to her chair and fired, with a quick upward flick of her wrist which could hardly have given her time to aim. The target was neatly drilled through the centre.

She repeated the hit.

"By Jove, you're a dead shot!" exclaimed Campbell.

"Oh, that's not much," she answered. "Stand up."

Somewhat amazed at this peremptory command, Campbell obeyed.

"Don't put down your cigarette!" she added.

As she walked several paces away, her intention became clear.

"I say," protested Campbell. "Er—isn't it a bit risky?"

"There's nothing to be afraid of! I've shot the ash off my father's cigarette hundreds of times with real bullets. A li'l' slug won't hurt you, even if it does touch you."

Campbell was not quite sure whether this was a jest. Reflecting on the painful possibilities of a slug slap in his eyes, he turned sideways as commanded and waited. There was a faint pop. The ash on his cigarette was unmoved.

"Hard luck!" he said politely.

"Hard luck nothing!" she replied coldly. "You trembled."

"I did nothing of the sort."

"Well, you winced. Stand still, please, *quite* still."

There was another pop, and this time the ash vanished.

"Good Lord, that's neat."

"Oh, it's nothing much. I'll get my automatic out later and show you some more."

Campbell made a mental vow to avoid the occasion.

"Anyway, you see I can take care of myself!"

"You certainly can. I shouldn't like to do that myself, even with an air pistol," for Campbell happened to be a deadly shot with a revolver.

"Who on earth taught you? Or is it all part of the Ph.D. syllabus?"

"My father taught me," said Virginia simply. "When I was a kid. He was a police chief."

There was a silence. Campbell attempted to make conversation.

"What are you reading?" he asked.

" 'The Organization of the Classificatory System Among the Tribes of the Amazonian Delta.' Have you read it?"

"No," confessed Campbell.

There was another silence.

"Do you play deck tennis?" asked the detective.

"I do not," she answered severely, "nor do I believe in talking for the sake of talking. Conversation—except in the case of real dialectic—rarely proceeds along logical lines and at the best is apt to be desultory. However, if you really wish to talk, let us discuss something that really interests you."

Campbell was only human and this unprovoked attack

annoyed him.

"In that case," he said firmly, "I should like to discuss your eyes or your hair."

Dr. Ridge looked at him with a crushing stare. Then to his own surprise and her own, she began to blush. All attempts to suppress it failed. Jumping angrily to her feet. "A vaso-motor disturbance," she muttered, picked up her bag and book, and left the field to him.

"Well, that's a point to me for a change," reflected Campbell, sinking back into his chair and contemplating the smoothly sliding sea with a wholly novel feeling of elation.

He thought that he might have offended her, but apparently she had decided to assume that Campbell's remark had not been made. She greeted him with a bow next morning. She was leaning on the railing watching an albatross hover in the current of air diverted from the hull. It soared there like a part of the air, drawn by an invisible string behind the ship. He leaned on the railings beside her.

They talked.

Evidently she had decided to be more human. He guessed that the icy academic manner of the previous day was a pose or a joke. She even admitted that it was the glamour of her task, the lure of strange peoples, strange customs, and alien methods of thought that attracted her to her task. He confessed that, basically, the same adventitious glamour had attracted him to his own profession.

"So that we are really both incurably romantic persons."

"But I couldn't be a policeman," she said, "I should always be seeing the criminal's point of view."

"Oh, come," he remonstrated. "Right is right and wrong is wrong!"

"You wouldn't say that if you were an anthropologist. Among the Australian aborigines in the Northern Territory it is right to eat up your dead relatives. Among certain Brazilian tribes, it is entirely wrong to let anybody just die.

As soon as they look seriously ill you pop them in a large jar and bury them—otherwise their soul will escape and get lost. Among a number of tribes it is a dreadful calamity to look on your mother-in-law's face. A man who does it even accidentally takes to his bed and dies."

"Perhaps some peoples are wiser than we are," admitted Campbell, with a smile.

"It's all very well to joke!" said Virginia, "but supposing you were a police officer of these tribes. It would be your duty to see that dead relatives were properly finished off the plates, and sick people killed in time. You would perhaps have to arrest the man who looked at his mother-in-law."

"That's all very well in theory," he answered, "but I don't see how such a problem could really arise in my line of business."

"I'm not so sure!" said Virginia thoughtfully, "you may find yourself up against just that problem. And very soon too."

The sun had vanished. The sky, with the abruptness of low latitudes, had darkened almost in a second. Now the moon, in a black velvet sky, was flooding the rising sea with its brilliant light. Campbell, made sensitive by the glamour of the night, detected a special meaning in the tone in which Virginia had pronounced the last words. He turned his head. Her eyes were fixed on him.

"What is it you know about this affair?" he said. "It's no use your pretending you don't know something !"

"Nothing I can tell you," she said softly, her eyes turning back to the contemplation of the rushing waves lit by flashes of light from the portholes.

"In any case it's of no importance," she added hastily, as if regretting her confidence.

"Is your visit to Molengi connected with it?"

"Good heavens, no! I've told you that's purely anthropological."

She seemed to answer sincerely enough, and he let the matter slide out of his mind with an easiness that can only be explained by the situation and the temperature.

There was a silence. The ship seemed to rush still faster through the waves as the wind, blowing from ahead, tore off fragments of the bow wave and splashed their faces with it. Campbell felt exhilarated, almost intoxicated. Virginia, however, became more and more uncommunicative; even, he thought, a little cross. He looked at her, her face slightly raised as she stared at the moon, and said playfully, as the prelude to a compliment: "What a ghostly-blue your face looks in this moonlight!"

"So would yours," she replied coldly, "if you felt as ill as I do. This ghastly sea coming up! Oh, why were ships ever invented?"

Picking up her wrap, she disappeared below.

"At any rate," he told himself bitterly, "no one could accuse us of getting sentimental!"

Whether any impartial observer would have launched the accusation later, is doubtful. Ships are privileged in this respect, and at first Campbell and Virginia never reached a closer stage of intimacy than that involved in exchanging childhood reminiscences.

An old hand would have suggested danger even here, for it was obvious that they were spending a remarkable amount of time in each other's company; to the annoyance of many of the amiable youths going out Africa for the first time. They had all obviously hoped great things of Virginia.

Even the "Organization of the Classificatory System Among the Tribes of the Amazonian Delta" had not daunted them, but now it seemed too late. That ginger Scotsman was well ahead.

From childhood reminiscences they had proceeded to early love affairs. Virginia admitted shyly an early passion for a Professor of Logic at Harvard, in spite of his bald head.

Campbell confessed that he had once fallen desperately for a tennis champion, in spite of her sinewy legs. Both agreed that love is inexplicable.

And then came Lagos. Campbell felt a surprising sense of resentment at having to walk ashore and leave his pleasant shipboard life.

"Pure laziness, of course," he told himself firmly.

Virginia's cool firm hand remained in his for some time as they said good-bye.

"And so we may never meet again!" he said gloomily.

He had, however, taken the precaution of finding her home address. "Just in case," he had remarked vaguely.

"I'm not so sure," she answered, "I shouldn't be surprised if we met again in quite a short time. In fact, I think we're almost certain to."

She left him meditating this remark as he walked ashore down the gangway.

CHAPTER THIRTEEN
Confusion Twice Confounded

CAMPBELL was recalled to sober facts abruptly when he stepped ashore at Lagos. He went straight to a Captain Hollingsworth, to whom he had a letter of introduction. Hollingsworth, he understood, would in turn put him in touch with those police officials at Kaduna who would be best able to help him in his quest.

Hollingsworth, however, already had in his care a letter for Campbell from Gregson. It had been dispatched four days after Campbell had left England, had been sent by air mail as far as Khartoum and had then been brought, with the rest of the Administration mails, in an Air Force machine to Nigeria. The letter was interesting but none the less disconcerting for that.

Dear Campbell,

I am afraid there are serious holes in the theory you have built up. First of all, the treasure you found must have been hidden after *O'Leary's determination to buy the Wilderness, for the well in question was only installed a few days before O'Leary moved in. It was one of the improvements he insisted on, as hitherto all water had to he brought in buckets from a pump at the bottom of the garden. Naturally that did not appeal to O'Leary's fondness for privacy.*

Secondly, O'Leary's search of the inside of the cottage is comparatively recent. A builder whom I brought down to examine it says that he is certain all the floor-ripping, furniture breaking, etc. has been done within the last few days.

These two facts together show (a) that the stuff was hidden after O'Leary's tenancy (b) that he did not start to search for it at all until the arrival of Crumbles.

Here is another odd fact. Harry Thompson remembers O'Leary's first dog barking when he went to drive him to the Ethelreda Hotel. Consequently the mastiff cannot have been shot by Crumbles. Yet it must have been shot soon after Crumbles' death, for next day, as we know, he was burying it.

I am not as yet attempting to account for these odd facts as I feel your investigations may bring to light a good deal more that we shall have to fit into place. I am continuing enquiries on the lines laid down, but so far have found no trace of a previous visit by O'Leary to Crumbles on the morning of his death.

I have also been able to secure temporarily the gold bracelet which Farthingale bought from Crumbles. He sold it again to a firm of bullion dealers who fortunately had not melted it down by the time I got in touch with them, and I was therefore able to borrow it. I enclose drawings. They may possibly throw some light on the source of the original hoard, now that we know it is of more recent date than we believed.

Yours sincerely,
DUNCAN GREGSON.

"You look worried!" said Captain Hollingsworth cheerfully, as the other put down the letter. "Bad news ?"

"Damn bad," replied Campbell. He tossed Hollingsworth the drawings. "Do you recognize this piece of jewelry?"

Hollingsworth studied them critically, then took a book from his bookcase and skimmed through a few of the pictures.

"They're West African workmanship, all right," he said. "Probably Ashanti stuff, or perhaps Beni. But I'm not an expert, you know. If you really want a first-class opinion, you'd better see old Goring, the padre at St. David's, in Kaduna. He's written several monographs on native art."

Campbell, as he jogged slowly along the line to Kaduna, although disappointed in the news from Gregson, had an odd feeling of elation, a feeling that he was getting near the secret of the murders. It was not so much a matter of facts as of psychological atmosphere.

Here—under this blazing sun, with the sharp abrupt contrasts of thick vegetation, arid clearings, sunbaked native villages, and stately groups of European buildings—here he experienced a sense of primitive urges which might well result in such a strange chapter as that of the murder at Little Whippering.

He had always imagined Nigeria as a tiny red spot on the

map. Hollingsworth had told him proudly that it covered, including the Northern Provinces, 335,000 square miles, and that the population probably amounted to 20,000,000 souls. Of these only a few thousands it seemed were European. The country was a network of cultures. Not only the cultures of those weird negro empires of Beni and Yoruba, but also Arabian and Mohammedan influences in the north, and Christian and European in the south. Here then was a melting pot out of which strange mixtures could come, where seeds of unspeakable enmities might be sown.

Campbell got out at Kaduna and found that Thornhill, assistant chief of police at this capital of the Northern Provinces, had come to the station to meet him. They drove back to his office through a bewildering stream of black and brown figures of all sizes and expressions, dressed some in elaborate barbaric drapery, others in European clothes, others in odd blends of both.

Campbell sat down and told, as briefly as he could, his story.

"Yes, we knew Crumbles well!" replied Thornhill, a young man for his job according to English reckoning, but very confident and at home with it. "You see there are so few Europeans here that we know them inside out; we all dine, play cards, and drink together. Naturally though we always had a cautious eye on Crumbles, knowing his record. But he seemed to be playing straight. He owned several shops here, and we kept a close watch to see that he wasn't doing any illegal trading in spirits. He may have been, but if so we never found it out; and the probability was that he had reformed. He wasn't quite the ordinary crook, you know. I mean he was the type of adventurer who would look on pinching a native hoard of gold as perfectly good business, while he would shrink with horror from picking a European pocket."

"And how long had he been in Kaduna?"

"Oh, he moved up here from Lagos about eight years ago."

"Do you know anything about his previous history ?"

"We've got a good deal about him in our records," replied Thornhill.

He went out and presently returned with a file. "H'm, he'd been in Nigeria twelve years; must have been fond of the country, God knows why!"

"You say he owned several shops. How did he make that money?"

Thornhill flicked over the pages.

"He seems to have had plenty of it from the time he fetched up here twelve years ago. Otherwise we should have been less friendly. We don't encourage ex-gaol-birds with no money to nest here. Yes, here's a record of his depositing a bond of one thousand pounds in connection with a land purchase soon after his arrival."

Campbell felt surprised. How had Crumbles, almost immediately after the Balooma scandal, come into money? According to O'Leary's account, they ought to have been broke.

"Do you know why he left Kaduna recently?"

"No, it was damned mysterious. Everything was at sixes and sevens here until we got news of his death at Abingdon. Since then his executors have been carrying on. As a matter of fact there was a rumour that he was shaky and had done a bunk, he cleared out so quickly. But it turns out that he was quite sound financially."

Campbell thought this over. It fitted in with the idea already taking shape in his mind.

"Are you sure," he asked quietly, "that he didn't have a hand in the death of this fellow Samson? It's only a wild guess, but this sudden disappearance, leaving everything in disorder, is a bit suspicious."

Thornhill looked startled.

"Good Lord, what an extraordinary thing! Do you know, I've always felt there was something fishy about that man's death? There was nothing we could get hold of though. Why should you associate the two?"

"Surely you knew Crumbles and Samson were both involved in that Balooma conspiracy trial?"

"Yes, but that was twelve years ago. They would both have almost forgotten each other by now."

"Didn't you know that Samson considered Crumbles and Galloway had done the dirty on him, and swore to revenge himself? He even attacked them in prison!"

Thornhill pulled thoughtfully at his small moustache.

"No, old chap, I didn't realize that. Or I might have been a good deal more suspicious than I was. To tell you the truth, we never even connected the two, apart from knowing they were together in this old scandal. After all, Crumbles has been a respectable citizen for twelve years."

"Well, can you tell me anything about Tuffy's accident?"

Thornhill sent down for the dossier to refresh his memory. Then:

"Samson had not been in Kaduna for more than a fortnight when it happened. As you know his sentence in the Balooma case ended more than two years ago, but almost immediately he was involved in a bank robbery at Lagos. I imagine it was one of those things that are planned between convicts in prison. It was in Lagos he was imprisoned, for the Balooma Administration by arrangement send all their European convicts there.

"Well, he got two years for that robbery, and as you may imagine when he came out again we looked on him as a pretty hopeless character. However, he came to Kaduna, and apparently with a bit of money—no doubt the proceeds of the robbery. He was negotiating to buy something in Kaduna, he said, and it seemed quite above board. Then, late one night, he and his car were found completely smashed up. He had driven straight into the bank on a lonely road and was a thoroughly nasty mess. There was a fairish amount of alcohol in the stomach and we concluded he had been drunk and had crashed. No one saw the accident, or heard it for that matter!"

"Whose car was it?"

"It was a car he had hired a month earlier. He paid for it from week to week."

"And when did Crumbles leave Kaduna?"

"He left that day. Whether he left Nigeria that same day, we don't know, as we didn't follow up his movements. We had no reason to suspect any connection between the two incidents."

"But surely in view of their association . . ."

"So far as we knew there had been no association. When we first felt suspicious of the crash we went into Samson's movements during his month at Kaduna, but there was no suggestion that he had ever come into contact with Crumbles. He had not even ever been in' that part of the town. You must remember that here, on the one hand, was Crumbles, a steady respectable citizen. True there was a blot on his past, but many a good citizen has worse, and the general belief was that he had been more sinned against than sinning, that Samson had led him on the expedition without revealing its true object. That, we supposed, was why he got let off with such a light sentence. On the other hand we had Samson—a real criminal type. Why should they be associated? They had not seen each other for twelve years. We knew of no bad feeling between them. It was natural for Crumbles not to have anything to do with Samson. Certainly it never occurred to us for a moment that there could be any reason for Crumbles to wish Samson dead."

"Yes, I think I see," agreed Campbell, "there didn't seem any particular reason for linking them together. I suppose none of Samson's papers helped you at all?"

"None. We examined those in his wallet and his lodgings. There was nothing but harmless business letters and little personal possessions. All the same I always had a dim feeling that there was something queer about that death. It was such an amazingly thorough smash."

Campbell read the miscellaneous collection of documents in the dossier.

"I can tell from the dates that Crumbles must have sailed the morning after Samson's death. That is to say he must have left Kaduna by train for Lagos immediately after the death. His passage was already booked. We were in touch with the London offices of the line. Well, that's pretty significant, I'm afraid, Thornhill, that the probability is Samson was deliberately killed."

"Well, we all make mistakes!"

"Yes. But it's not often Providence does our job for us. Even down to the hanging by the neck until dead! It couldn't have been much quicker if there'd been a trial and sentence."

Already Campbell had had considerable food for thought, and he felt it would be necessary to digest it before he could see his investigations completely outlined. However, one possible line of attack suggested itself.

"I imagine Crumbles would have booked his passage here at Kaduna. If so, whom would he have done it through? Who is the Line's agent here?"

"You'd better see Gregory," answered Thornhill. "He's agent for pretty well everything in the travel line and a good deal else beside. He was a crony of Crumbles, so I should think Crumbles would have gone to him."

"Right-ho, I'll go along. I hope I can make use of your name?"

"Sure," said Thornhill with a grin. "Make use of anything here. But I think your own coupled with the name of

Scotland Yard as they say will carry still more weight. Particularly as you can give friend Gregory the low-down on his pal's grisly end. When I say pals, I don't mean they were particularly fond of each other, but they gave each other a good game of contract. That's a good deal here. So long."

As Thornhill predicted, Gregory was only too anxious to oblige Campbell. He was, if anything, a little disappointed at the simplicity of the other's request.

"Yes, Crumbles booked a passage with me," said Gregory, flipping through his books and giving a date about three weeks before Samson's death. "I was a bit surprised about it, but he said he had some business to fix up in England, and that he'd be back shortly."

"He didn't say what the business was?"

"No. He was always a bit uncommunicative."

"Would you have described him as a level-headed man? Strong minded?"

"No, I don't think I should," replied Gregory. "Rather the reverse, I should say. At any rate as regards his card playing. A bit inclined to lose his head in a difficult situation."

"Yes, that is what I should expect," said Campbell thoughtfully. "Did he strike you as being at all agitated when he booked his passage?"

"I can't say. I was down at Lagos then, and for about a week afterwards. He certainly struck me as a bit nervous later. To tell you the truth, I thought he was in a financial jam, but it doesn't seem to have been so, judging from his estate. I tell you what. My young assistant, who sold him the ticket, will be able to tell you if he behaved oddly at the time. But he didn't know Crumbles personally, so he wouldn't have noticed anything unless it was really marked."

"Oh, I don't think it's worth troubling about," said Campbell. "Still, if you don't mind . . ."

"Quite a pleasure," Gregory assured him, slipping out of his chair and waddling to the door. "Bert! Come here a moment!

"You must lunch with me afterwards," he added, "and tell me what happened in England. I always had a feeling poor old Crumbles would come to a bad end. He never would call up to his hand."

Bert proved to be one of the amiable youngsters such as had swarmed on Campbell's boat.

"You remember Crumbles' buying a ticket?" he was asked. "What state was he in?"

Bert looked puzzled. "Crumbles? I don't remember him for the moment."

"Yes. When I was away in Lagos. Littlish fellow. Hook nose. Short grey beard. Bushy eyebrows."

Campbell smiled. The hopelessness of the average man when it came to describing anyone was so familiar to him, that it now awoke no more than a mild paternal amusement. In the past, however, it had been a source of very acute irritation.

"I don't think I should describe him like that," the detective interrupted.

"How would you then?" said Gregory sharply.

"Largish. Ordinary height, but largish frame. His beard had a few grey hairs but it ought certainly to be described as black. And he wore it long. Again hook nose will give a wrong idea. The nose was broad and flat, with dilated nostrils, and a deep depression below the brows."

Gregory looked annoyed.

"I pride myself on my gift of describing people," he said, "and frankly I should never recognize Crumbles from your description. Remember I have known him for eight years, whereas you have only seen him dead!"

"Still, it's my business to know his appearance. I've simply given you the official description we used when inquiring concerning his movements."

Bert grinned.

"Well, sir, I recognize the guv'nor's description, but I don't recognize yours."

He looked through the stubs of his order book.

"Yes, here it is. Crumbles. *Cromlech Castle*. No, sir, you've got him wrong. A hook nose and a short grey beard, I remember."

Gregory was still puffing indignantly at the doubt thrown on the accuracy of his observation.

"There, you see! Well, I'm glad to know that Scotland Yard isn't infallible."

Campbell felt irritated at this, and being sure of his ground, he endeavoured to make Gregory see reason.

"There can't really be room for mistake in my description," he said, "as it happens, I have the medical report on the body here in my brief case."

Campbell read out the few phrases devoted to personal description.

"You're wrong," replied Gregory stubbornly shaking his head. "I know the man when he was alive. It stands to reason a man won't look the same after he's been hanged."

"Well, it won't change the colour of his beard," commented Campbell, a little tartly.

"Perhaps not. But look here, I've got the manager of my Lagos office staying at my place. It's just two streets away. Let's go there. Crumbles would have had to call in there to get his ticket. We only give a voucher here. Let's see what he says!"

It was obviously a point that could not be allowed to remain in doubt. Campbell walked slowly—Nigeria had already taught his zeal the virtues of indolence—to Gregory's house, and here the Lagos manager, Perrin, was invoked to decide the point.

"You remember old Crumbles? Sailed on the *Cromlech*? I sent a special message down to you with the voucher to see he got a decent berth, as he was a pal of mine."

"Crumbles . . . Crumbles? Oh, yes, I remember now."

"Can you describe him?"

Perrin wrinkled his brows in thought.

"Yes, I remember," he said at last. "A rather striking fellow. Red hair. Hefty frame. Blue eyes. Rather strong face. I should describe your pal as a tough customer."

"But the beard!" exclaimed Gregory staggered.

"Oh, there was no beard. He was clean shaven."

Campbell made no comment. He saw with crystal clearness that an amazing confusion in identities had occurred, and that it would be hopeless to attempt to sort them out without far more accurate information than mere description. Parrying, so far as he could, the curious questions of Gregory, he went straight to Thornhill. After giving him news of the new developments, he arranged for him to obtain from the police surgeon any marks of identification they might have noted on the body of Tuffy Samson.

As he expected, all the obvious distinguishing marks had been obliterated by the crash. The man's face had been pulped from the force of the head-on collision. He had been identified by his clothes and papers. None the less there were various marks—fillings in the teeth, the scar of an appendectomy—which would still be of assistance.

Thornhill got an order for the body to be exhumed in case the preservative used for the autopsy, despite the quick decomposition inevitable in a damp and tropical soil—might have saved further distinguishing marks. Fingerprints were the most likely.

Thornhill also dispatched a cable to his colleague at Gorango, Balooma, with a request to unearth from the files and transmit to him the fingerprints, photographs, and Bertillon measurements of Samson, Crumbles, and Galloway (*alias* O'Leary). Campbell meanwhile dispatched an urgent cable to Gregson.

BELIEVED CONFUSION IDENTITIES CRUMBLES
O'LEARY, OBTAIN LONDON END'S ACCOUNT
APPEARANCE CRUMBLES ON ARRIVAL PARTICULARLY
BEARD, HAIR, ALSO APPEARANCE O'LEARY BEFORE
TAKING WILDERNESS, PERHAPS SEEN BY SOLICITORS.
MEANWHILE SEND FINGERPRINTS, PHOTOGRAPHS
FROM CADAVERS O'LEARY, CRUMBLES BY AIR MAIL.

CAMPBELL.

Campbell found it difficult to possess his soul in patience until the arrival of the material from England. In the interim, however, the documents came from Balooma, and, together with such information about Samson's corpse as was already in his possession, showed Campbell that he was on the track of a masterly crime. Finally the news from England came.

First the cable—

CRUMBLES ON ARRIVAL ENGLAND, RED-HAIRED,
SHORT-BEARDED, BELIEVED GROWN ON VOYAGE.
MIDDLE STATURE, BROAD SHOULDERS, BLUE EYES.
O'LEARY SEEN BY SOLICITORS DECLARED TO BE
BLACKBEARDED, BROWN EYES, ORDINARY HEIGHT.
LARGISH FRAME. BROAD, FLAT NOSE DEPRESSED
BRIDGE GAVE IMPRESSION MENTALLY DISTURBED
PERSECUTION MANIA ANXIETY NEUROSIS BUT NOT NON
COMPOS. FINGERPRINTS, PHOTOGRAPHS FOLLOW.
ATTABOY.

GREGSON.

The photographs arriving, established the whole story beyond doubt. It needed some considerable thought before every piece fitted into place, but when the picture of what had occurred was completed, Campbell had a wholly aesthetic satisfaction in the result. Whereas every previous theory had left much unexplained and invoked various unknown movements, the story, as now revealed, tallied perfectly with the movements and psychologies of the actors. Campbell was able to embody the whole thing in a complete report which, dispatched to his chief, soothed an official soul somewhat outraged by the expenses of sending a man to Africa. In addition it gave the man that content- ment which comes to every detective who sees a tortuous problem well and truly solved. Thereafter his chief was wholeheartedly behind the African investigation.

CHAPTER FOURTEEN
What Really Happened

"THE fingerprints, photographs, Bertillon measurements, and descriptions by various witnesses (wrote Campbell) show beyond all doubt that it was not Tuffy Samson who was killed in the car accident; that the O'Leary we knew was not O'Leary at all; and that the man we believed to be Crumbles was not the real Crumbles. He in turn was different in identity from the Crumbles who came over on the *Cromlech Castle,* who, also, was not the genuine Crumbles. The whole episode is the outcome of a diabolic- ally ingenious murder plan which was, in fact, completely successful.

"When Tuffy Samson was released from gaol after the Balooma desecration trial, he was completely penniless. This hampered his main object in life—the result of long embittered brooding—to make away with Crumbles and Galloway *alias* O'Leary.

"In order to obtain some money, Samson carried out a

bank robbery he had undoubtedly planned while in prison at Lagos. He was caught and underwent another term of imprisonment, which only increased his rancour against his former associates.

"Apparently he had been able to conceal some of the proceeds of his robbery for when he next appears he has some money to spend. He goes at once to Kaduna and lives as a person of means.

"Meanwhile Crumbles is well aware of his danger. He is an excitable sort of person, always prone to rush hysterically into any danger rather than bear the suspense of waiting for it to materialize. He decides to take Tuffy for a car ride, kill him, and after drawing out all his money, fly to England. If the thing blows over, he will return. If not, he will go into hiding.

"What actually happened on the motor drive with Tuffy we shall never know, for the good reason that both men are dead. I imagine that Crumbles counted on shooting Tuffy while he was driving, and then faking a crash which would conceal a bullet wound. No doubt he hoped his previous lack of association with Tuffy and the fact that the crash took place in Tuffy's car, would keep him clear of suspicion. If not, he had his passage ready booked.

"Whatever happened, Tuffy struck first. Perhaps he had already guessed—for he was a subtle man—what Crumbles was up to. The doctor reported a considerable quantity of alcohol in Crumbles' stomach; and I suspect that, as is common with the excitable type, he took something to steady his nerves, and instead merely dulled his wits.

"Anyway, it was Crumbles who was left, at the end of that drive, dead. Doubtless Tuffy hit him over the head, changed clothes and papers with him, drove the car to a quiet spot, and then, engaging the gear and jumping out after opening the throttle to the full, left it to crash full tilt into the bank. Afterwards also it would have been a matter of ordinary prudence to make sure that the corpse was sufficiently battered as to be unrecognizable. But that it was Crumbles' corpse there can be no doubt, for it has been possible to compare the fingerprints with those taken from Crumbles after sentence at the Balooma trial.

"On going through his wallet, Tuffy doubtless found the voucher for Crumbles' berth on the *Cromlech Castle*. He at once saw what a magnificent opportunity this gave him, if only he could bluff others into believing that he was Crumbles. He left for Lagos that evening. No doubt he would like to have been able to touch Crumbles' cash as well, but as it was all banked, that was hopeless. On the morning when the local papers were reporting that one Tuffy Samson had been found dead in a car accident, the real Tuffy was sailing for England, under the name of Crumbles, having been fortunate enough to meet no one who knew the real Crumbles. The description of the Lagos travel agent may be recalled here. He described the pseudo-Crumbles as a broad-shouldered man with short red hair, blue eyes and a rather brutal face. This description is worth noting. It is the authentic description of Tuffy Samson. We shall come upon it again.

"Stretched out on a deck chair on the deck of the *Cromlech Castle,* Tuffy had ample time to reflect on his next move. Tuffy was a subtle man, but I do not think he was a very imaginative man, or he would not have made some of the mistakes he did. Lacking imagination therefore he made the usual error of the murderer, who always repeats the methods of his crime. He had murdered Crumbles, and got away with it, by exchanging personalities. Why not make another swap, this time with O'Leary? It was all the more easy as Crumbles was an embarrassing personality for him to be saddled with, anyway.

"It is obvious, however, that there must have been other reasons as well for Tuffy to have been able to plan so neatly the elimination of O'Leary. I think it is almost certain that O'Leary and Crumbles had kept up a correspondence. And it seems to me circumstantially proved that Tuffy found among Crumbles' papers a letter from O'Leary, not only giving his Little Whippering address, but also revealing that O'Leary had a hoard buried on his premises. O'Leary, as the solicitors who saw him confirm, was by this time a little mad. Not legally *non compos,* as they were careful to explain. But neurotic. A sufferer from anxiety neuroses. This explains his behaviour at Little Whippering. He was trying to flee the demons of his imagination by going to a lonely cottage in a lonely village and hiding from the face of man, with his carefully cherished hoard securely buried beneath his eyes.

"But to give him his due, they were not demons of pure imagination only. Also there was the tangible fear of Tuffy, ready to murder him directly he came out of gaol. There were other Avengers. That their vengeance was a very real thing was soon to be proved. And although O'Leary shut himself up, he did, contrary to village opinion, sometimes venture out. Thus from time to time he sold some gold ornaments which he had put aside from his hoard to pay current expenses. One of these bracelets we traced as having been sold by a black-bearded man with a flattish nose to Mr. Farthingale. This man answered the description of the *corpse* of Crumbles, but *he also answered the description of O'Leary when he visited the solicitors to rent the Wilderness.* In other words, all three people were one and the same—the real O'Leary. We have only known the false O'Leary.

"Meanwhile Tuffy—the pseudo-Crumbles—had been preparing himself to play the part of O'Leary. O'Leary, he knew, in his Galloway days had worn a beard, and therefore he started to grow one. It was well developed by the time the Cromlech—a slow intermediate ship— reached London.

"Tuffy now began to prepare for his coup in more detail. He secretly visited Little Whippering and its environs and got all the information he could about O'Leary. He must have managed to see O'Leary, perhaps pottering around the garden gathering wood, and so confirmed that he had a beard still, and noticed approximately how it was cut. He then returned to London, dyed his beard black and cut it to correspond, cut his hair short and put on a black wig, and sallied down to Abingdon for his final lightning stroke.

"We know how, in the brief time at his disposal, he gave the hotel manager the impression of a man suffering from acute depression, and how he prepared, and left, two letters to back up that opinion. They were of course written in the same hand that punctiliously signed the register, and took care to leave a note outside his door—so giving us poor fools the opportunity to 'verify' the handwriting of the suicide letters. On the morning his trap was ready for the springing, he sent O'Leary the one wire which, he knew, would ensure his coming to Abingdon. But he counted, knowing O'Leary's habits, on his continuing to hide his features. The cream of the jest was that the very fear which made O'Leary hide his features—his fear that he would be recognized as Spike Galloway and so be delivered into Tuffy Samson's hands or worse—was also the fear that enabled Tuffy to execute his vengeance.

"While the wire was in transit, Tuffy made his final preparations. He shaved off his dyed beard—hence the hairs we found trapped in the wash basin, which led us to wrong conjectures. Now when a sunburnt man like Tuffy has worn a beard for some time, it will leave, if it is shaved off, a white area of skin on the chin and lips, contrasting sharply with the tan of the nose and forehead. This whiteness as good as says to the observant eye: 'I had a beard which I have just shaved off.' Tuffy had anticipated this danger, however, for as soon as he had shaved off his beard, he toned the white patch with the imitation sunburn paint used by some women nowadays to heighten or imitate a natural tan. Either he failed to reflect that this also would arouse suspicion, owing to O'Leary's home-keeping habits or else (as is more probable) he foresaw how easy it would be to bluff his way out of the difficulty. And he did bluff his way out, very credibly, when Gregson and I taxed him with the inconsistency.

"His wig of course he merely removed and put in his pocket. No doubt he had taken off his own clothes and laid them by ready to put on the corpse—directly he had manufactured it. And he manufactured it with the utmost dexterity.

"As I picture the scene, Tuffy was hiding behind the door. As O'Leary walked in unsuspectingly, Tuffy threw the loop of rope over his head and garotted him before he could make a cry. It was skillfully done, for if he had strangled him with his bare hands, the marks of fingers would still have been detectable on the dead man's throat.

"Probably before the doomed man had ceased struggling, while he was still asphyxiating with the rope knotted tightly round his neck, he undressed him, put on O'Leary's clothes, and dressed the body in his own. Then he tied the rope to a hook and swung the corpse off the chair with enough violence to account for the strangulation—indeed he almost dislocated the neck.

"Doubtless he gave one last hasty glance round the room, but everything had been carefully prepared. So smoothly had the whole affair gone, that ten minutes after O'Leary walked into the room, Tuffy, now muffled up in O'Leary's clothes and precisely resembling him, was able to run down the stairs shouting that he had found his old pal George Crumbles dead.

"A man dead of strangulation is a nasty sight, with livid, distorted features. The manager—who in any case had only met Tuffy for a few minutes—gave one glance at the body, and, seeing the black beard and familiar clothes, without hesitation identified him as his guest. It is hardly fair to suggest he 'identified' him. It naturally never occurred to him, nor to anyone else, that it could be any other than his guest. The elaborate mystification of the false O'Leary's 'unveiling' however helped the illusion.

"We might perhaps have been able to suspect the truth from the fact that the false O'Leary's fingerprints were over everything in the bedroom, but instead of realizing that this was because the false O'Leary had in fact actually occupied the room under the name of Crumbles, we attributed it to a search hurriedly made as a visitor for a clue to the treasure buried in the garden.

"The false O'Leary went back to the Wilderness rejoicing. He had disposed of both his enemies; the world was at his feet; and he had undisputed possession of a cottage in which a small fortune was hidden. No wonder Tuffy came into the Marion Arms and celebrated. In any case he was a convivial soul, unlike the neurotic O'Leary, and in addition he had ample cause for rejoicing.

"As he opened the door of the Wilderness with a key taken from the dead man's pocket, O'Leary's dog sprang at him. The mastiff at any rate was not fooled. But Tuffy had been prepared for this, and at once shot him. The shot dog should have led us to suspect the change of identity.

"But now the false O'Leary began to discover the dead man's cunning. He had thought to find the hoard hidden in some obvious place—in a safe, or buried in the garden. But he could not find a trace of it. As we know, it was hidden in a rather cunning place, in the well. Days passed. Tuffy worked like a madman, digging up gardens wholesale, ripping up floors, tearing furniture to pieces, stripping walls. All in vain.

"And now a still more sinister colour tinged the picture.

The redoubtable and careful Tuffy began to have a taste of O'Leary's own fears. By a comic irony, the very hoard that he could not himself find was yet putting him into ghastly danger. The Avengers were after the false O'Leary too. Tuffy bought a dog, barricaded himself in, and continued his frantic search. Meanwhile the money he had got from the bank robbery had run out. A small fortune was hidden in the house, and yet he was being dunned and county- courted ! His very food supplies were cut off! The next step would be that, on quarter day, he would be unable to pay his rent, and would be evicted. The shades of O'Leary were harrying him with a vengeance.

"Then the reality of his fears, and of O'Leary's fears before him, were proved tragically. He was butchered in a horrible fashion. To find out how this was done is the next step in our investigation, and I firmly believe the threads are here in Nigeria, or at any rate not far from here. In any case, we have the satisfaction of having cleared up two murders— that of Crumbles, and that of O'Leary, *alias* Galloway. Their murderer is himself dead, and now it is for his killer we must look."

~§~

After he had completed the above report, Campbell remembered the Reverend Arthur Goring of St. David's. Taking with him the drawings of the gold bracelet, he went to the rectory.

The genial parson's eyes kindled with the ever ready enthusiasm of the hobbyist when he saw the drawings. He studied them meditatively, sucking at an empty pipe, and then went to a case full of strange figures.

"Ashanti proverb weights," he explained. "Each illustrates some Ashanti proverb, and also is—more or less—a standard weight. This bracelet is a very different type of thing. Of course these weights are all *cire perdu* stuff, whereas gold ornaments are beaten. Here's some Ashanti gold-work, still a big difference in treatment, you see. There is an element of naturalism that is absent in your bracelet. I should say there's a good deal of Islamic influence here."

"What does that mean?"

"That it's from somewhere farther north or more inland. Hollingsworth suggested Beni workmanship, did he? Dear me, quite ridiculous of course. Ashanti was a better guess."

Mr. Goring pulled out a cabinet and studied it thoughtfully, humming gently.

Then he turned to Campbell.

"This comes from Balooma. Here's an anklet with almost exactly the same motif."

"Oh," said Campbell, "it comes from Balooma, does it? By jove, so that's the explanation!"

CHAPTER FIFTEEN
A. Watt Again

THE Chief Commissioner for Balooma Territory, Colonel Max Wittington-Hopefull-Smythe, C.B., C.M.G., O.B.E., padded impatiently about his office in carpet slippers—an innocent habit of his. He was studying the guarded letter from Inspector Campbell which his assistant, young Dakin, had laid before him that morning. Dakin had put it down on his desk in discreet silence, but with a significant glance.

"Damn the fellow!" muttered the chief commissioner, pulling irritably at his moustache. "Why the devil can't these people at home let us alone?"

The chief commissioner has been described in *Boromori* the vernacular paper, as "the Father of this country and the nephew of the Earl of Hopefull." In actual fact he looked exactly like the peppery Colonel who has for so long been a mainstay of English humour. Not only was the chief commissioner aware of this resemblance, but he took some pains to five up to it. Only an occasional twinkle in his eyes betrayed the fact that behind this facade lurked an acute and subtle intelligence, an intelligence armed with an almost encyclopaedic knowledge of native customs and beliefs. Buried deeper still was an idealist's love for the country he had shaped out of the collapsing ruins of the Balooma Federation.

It had not been an easy task. The Balooma Federation consisted of a group of petty kings or chiefs, each with his own territory. They all owed fealty to the so-called Emperor of Balooma, by virtue of some fetishistic power in his family and regalia. In '09 several murky incidents where Balooma marched with French and British possessions had made necessary a punitive expedition. In its dispatch, Smythe, then a young district commissioner of Nigeria, had anticipated France by ten days. The whole Federation ultimately became a British protectorate, and so evolved into a British colony. It functioned under indirect rule. The British Government, represented by a chief commissioner, governed through the Emperor, who had considerable latitude in the disposal of revenues and justice.

All had been peaceful until the famous desecration, in which the equivalent of the Balooma Crown Jewels had been stolen by Samson, Crumbles, and Galloway.

The native mind is dark and mysterious, nowhere more so than in Balooma. In a way that will seem obvious to the native mind, it was to the Crown Jewels and their fetishistic power rather than to the Royal Family that the local chiefs owed their fealty. When they had been desecrated, the tie that had bound the Federation together had weakened.

There had been the trial. The desecrators had been punished. The treasure had been recovered and solemnly presented back to the Royal Family. Yet all the time something had been going on, deep down in the native mind. It had been like some neurosis paralyzing the whole kingdom. Behind every chief's stool had stood the sinister figure of his Queen-Mother, with her immense power, urging, threatening, fomenting trouble.

And trouble there had been abundantly. Rising after rising; ritual slayings; the whole place honeycombed with secret societies.

The chief commissioner, padding about in his carpet slippers, thought of young Duguid speared, Captain Garstang and six Hausa soldiers clubbed to death, poor old Climmins shot—only items in the ghastly death roll of the last twelve troubled years.

Well, at last, thought the chief commissioner, they had got the country more or less pacified, goodness knows how. The new Emperor was a sensible person, like his uncle the last Emperor.

(In Balooma property or rank never passes from father to son. It goes through the women, from the father to his sister's son. Only the woman can transmit the sacred blood-right.)

At last there was some reasonable prospect of peace and quiet.

They had even been able to open most of the provinces to tourists—for the first time for twelve years. And now an infernal muddling policeman wanted to go and rake up this sacrilege trial. A trial that had made Balooma a nation of whispering assassins! Which they had taken twelve years to forget!

Colonel Max Wittington-Hopefull-Smythe began to go purple with rage as he thought over the intrusion. His rages were famous. They were discussed reverently among his subordinates as if they were a crop of fine fruit. "Absolutely record fury" one would say to the other. "Bit his blotting pad!"

The chief commissioner looked at the letter again. "With a special letter from the Colonial Office too!"

he snorted. Seizing his heavy brass inkpot of Balooma workmanship he hurled it through the window with a kind of choking gasp. The action relieved him. Sitting back in his chair and mopping his brow, he rang for his secretary. A dark and earnest young man appeared.

"Hilton," the chief commissioner said, "I have just flung my inkpot out of the window."

"Quite, sir."

"Don't say quite, as if you were Godalmighty. Get it for me!"

"Yes, sir."

"And Hilton, when this fellow Campbell comes, shoot him!"

"Well, really sir—" began Hilton helplessly.

"Oh, well, perhaps you'd better not. The Colonial Office would never stop sending us memos about him if we did. Be nice to him and show him straight in to me."

"Not to Mr. Dakin, sir?"

"Good Heavens, no!" He mopped his brow. "Phew, no! You'd better warn Mr. Dakin when he comes. But don't let the fellow see he's unwelcome. The wisdom of the serpent, Hilton!"

"Quite, sir."

Hilton made an unobtrusive exit to retrieve the brass inkpot.

~§~

In these unpropitious circumstances Inspector Campbell went his unsuspecting way towards Government House, in Gorango, chief port and capital of Balooma Territory. Gorango was a somewhat smaller and shabbier edition of Kaduna. Hollingsworth, at Lagos, had told Campbell that the appearance of coastal Gorango bore no relation to the conditions he would have to encounter if he went up-country. Even the old up-country capital, still the residence of the Emperor, was no more than a large native village.

It was hot, very hot, and Campbell felt limp and in-effective as he climbed the massive steps of Government House. He asked for Mr. Dakin, as he had been told at Kaduna, but he was informed that Mr. Dakin was away sick. The chief commissioner would see him.

"Well, I hardly like to trouble the commissioner him-self," said Campbell.

"It's no trouble, Inspector. He is anxious to make your acquaintance."

"Well, that's very nice of him!" thought Campbell.

He felt skeptical, however, when he was shown into the commissioner's luxurious office. Peering above the desk was a figure with rugged face and bloodshot eyes, and the expression of a resentful walrus.

"Sit down, Inspector," said the walrus, extending a limp flipper. "Good passage?"

"Yes, thank you sir."

"Good hotel?"

"Excellent, sir."

"Good! Very good."

There was a silence.

The chief commissioner opened his mouth as if to speak, shut it, puffed formidably at his cigar, the puff lifting the white hairs of his moustache, and then gave a bellicose roar. At the same time he waved one flipper in the direction of the inspector's letter.

"What's all this precious nonsense, eh? Murders, trials, gold bracelets! What? Eh? What? What's it all about, eh?"

Campbell was startled by this onslaught. Why on earth did they tell me in Kaduna that Smythe was the cleverest official who ever came to Africa? he asked himself.

Campbell put on his most official voice and told him, as concisely as possible, the history of the Samson case to date. He looked keenly at the chief commissioner from time to time to see if he were following the story. The chief commissioner's eyes were quite expressionless, like two pools of stagnant water.

"Pshaw!" exclaimed the chief at length. He got up to his feet and padded the length of the room and back again. Then he shot out an accusing finger at Campbell.

"All this Box and Cox business is all very well. I suppose you're right if the fingerprints agree. Granted O'Leary became Samson and Samson became Crumbles and so on, but what's it got to do with us, eh? Why should a law-abiding place like Balooma be dragged into your Little Whippering atrocities?"

Campbell smiled. "Simply for this reason, sir. The motive for the final murder was the hoard buried in the garden of the Wilderness. I saw that hoard, and it was obviously African workmanship. O'Leary, at an earlier date, sold a bracelet, which I believe to be from the same hoard. Goring, at Kaduna, tells me the bracelet is undoubtedly of Balooma workmanship. The assumption I make is that the whole hoard came from Balooma. And what is more, I believe it to be in this country now."

"Rot. Absolute rot!" shouted the chief commissioner suddenly. "You're talking through your hat, young man, or your helmet, or your cap, whatever it is. It's nothing to do with us! We don't know anything about your confounded murder, see!"

He flung himself into a chair, which creaked at the assault, and glowered at the policeman.

Campbell felt annoyed.

"Am I to understand, sir, that you are not prepared to give me any support in this investigation?"

"My dear Inspector Campbell," cooed the chief commissioner in a voice whose insinuating sweetness was as unexpected as the previous outburst of rage. "Why should you suppose anything of the sort? We only exist to help you. Say what you want and it shall be done. You are recommended from the Colonial Office. No more need be said. You are looking pale, Inspector! It's the heat. I insist that you have a whisky and soda with me!"

Campbell thought it better for the moment to fall in with the other's change of manner without being in the slightest impressed by it. He accepted the drink, but returned with pertinacity to the charge.

"Naturally, sir, I have been wondering lately whether these recent events do not link up directly with the Balooma desecration trial."

The chief commissioner looked puzzled. He wrinkled his brows.

"Desecration trial? Was that before my time? *Desecration trial*, did you say?"

He clapped his hand to his forehead. "Oh, you don't mean that terribly ancient affair! Why, we had forgotten about it long ago. Dear me, yes, I remember now. Of course all your Box and Cox people were involved in it. But surely you are joking, Inspector. What could it have to do with Little Whippering?"

"That, sir, is why I am here," said Inspector Campbell, quiet determination behind his polite tone. "For, of course, the probability of the connection is obvious. If there are any facts connected with the trial that bear it out, but which never reached the public, you will be able to tell me them."

Campbell fixed his eyes sharply on the chief commissioner's stagnant pools. A gleam seemed to rise to their surface. Colonel Max Wittington-Hopefull-Smythe smiled.

"Well, let me see." He suddenly became a serious administrator. "Let me see. What exactly are you looking for?"

"Is it really the case that the treasure stolen was recovered by the Crown?"

The chief commissioner nodded.

"Crumbles and Galloway revealed its hiding place in the swamp. We accordingly retrieved it. We then handed it back to the old Emperor."

"And they still have it?"

"So far as we know, yes."

"Are you sure you recovered all of it?"

The other hesitated for a fraction of a second. "Presumably. Naturally I cannot say for certain. We never had the original inventory of the royal regalia. They were too afraid we might seize it ourselves to give us any information."

"But did the attitude of the Emperor suggest he had recovered everything?"

"He was very grateful."

"But I believe I am right, am I not, sir, in saying that there has been constant trouble in Balooma ever since that date?"

"Yes, that is so. And naturally. For the theft was considered a desecration, which robbed the national fetishes of their power."

"I see, sir. But today the country is quite peaceful?"

"That is so."

"You don't think that significant, in view of the events in Little Whippering? Doesn't it all link up? Naturally I do not pretend to know the native mind."

"I am glad to hear it, Inspector. If so, you are the first white man just arrived in this country not to suffer from that illusion. I am in the same position. After forty years in Africa I don't understand the native mind either. But I think you are trying to reason too logically. We have had some bad times. Well, it happens. Now we've a spot of peace. That happens too. In this game of administration you live from hand to mouth."

Campbell saw that the chief, with a patience doubtless learned at native *palavers,* was prepared to go on like this forever. Evidently he could look for no real guidance here. He tried another tack.

"I've not been able to get hold of the accounts of the trial, sir. One thing has always puzzled me. Why was there such a disproportion between the sentences of Tuffy Samson and his accomplices? Even allowing for their turning King's Evidence it seems inexplicable."

Here at any rate the chief would have to give a straight answer, for it was easy enough for Campbell to check his story from newspaper files.

"Crumbles and Galloway were only charged with robbery with violence, desecration of a native shrine, and obtaining permits under false pretenses," explained the other. "Samson was in addition charged with manslaughter."

"Manslaughter!"

"Yes, it should have been murder. But I regret to say that if it had been, in those unsettled days, with a European jury, he would have been acquitted. You see it was a native he killed. So we preferred the strongest charge we could. The native he killed was one of the Guardians of the treasure. I don't think Samson intended to kill him. He was only defending himself. But it happened while he was getting away with the treasure, and under our code, as under English law, manslaughter in the commission of a felony is murder. We would have charged all three men with it, except that Crumbles and Galloway swore they were some distance from the man when he was killed, and shouted to

Samson not to do it. Samson denied this, but Crumbles and Galloway confirmed each other's story and, incidentally, ensured Samson's conviction."

"Good Lord, no wonder Samson had such a grudge against his partners! What hounds they were!"

"They were not very estimable characters," agreed the chief commissioner.

There was an awkward silence, which the chief made no attempt to relieve. Campbell was trying to decide how far he should show the chief commissioner his determination to do his duty, however much it might interfere with the administration's desire to let sleeping dogs lie.

Campbell saw the chief commissioner's point of view clearly enough. None of the crimes had been committed inside his territory. Therefore, he saw no reason why the present peace should be threatened by stirring up memories of the twelve-year-old desecration trial. But equally Campbell was determined to bring Samson's murderer to justice. A barbarous murder had been committed. No matter that the victim was himself a murderer. Execution was the prerogative of the law of the land. Campbell, in his humble way, was the embodiment of the law. Moreover—human pique mingling with his ethical code—he felt determined not to be bluffed by the chief commissioner. He concluded there was nothing to be gained by trying to get help from someone who was obviously unwilling to give it.

He got up.

"Well, sir, thank you very much for your information. Naturally I have still to get my bearings here. I should like if I may to see the records of the trial."

"Certainly, Inspector." The chief pressed a bell. "Here, Hilton, give the inspector the verbatim of the desecration trial, will you?" He turned to Campbell.

"And if there's anything else you want, Inspector, don't hesitate to ask me. Or Hilton."

Campbell took his leave. The chief commissioner spent some time after his departure, lost in thought, staring at the battered inkpot in front of him. Then he gave a resigned sigh.

"I'm afraid we're going to have trouble with that young man!" he muttered prophetically.

~§~

During his short stay in Gorango, Campbell was the object of unremitting hospitality on the part of administrative officials. He was invited to cards, to drinks, to the clubs, to sail in the estuary, on shooting parties. He was shown objects of interest varying from ant hills to museums. But he found his hosts either extraordinarily ignorant or extraordinarily evasive about the objects of his inquiry. They all professed complete ignorance of what was happening "up-country."

Campbell himself strolled daily through the town, trying to decide whether it was possible to continue his investigations in the face of such an unpromising reception. He cursed his ignorance of the native language, which made all the black faces he saw so many meaningless masks instead of founts of useful information.

Was there really any secret society in Balooma, such as he had been told of by his friends in Kaduna? What had been the real effect on the native mind of the desecration trial? To these, and similar questions, he was unable to get any final answers. The interpreter provided him by the administration had proved a broken reed, assuring him that the questions he asked: "Would not be answered by any of the natives, sir. I regret to say that they are very secretive about matters of that kind." His white teeth had flashed in his black face in a way that reminded Campbell painfully of Mr. Jones' naive impudence.

None the less something else besides sheer obstinacy kept the inspector in Gorango. For he had suddenly noticed, two days after his arrival, that he was being shadowed—an odd experience for him. He was not being shadowed by Europeans or by educated natives but by the wild and dirty variety one saw even in Gorango. He could not identify any one of them. Indeed these shadows that always kept within a few hundred feet of him were always changing in identity. But they were always there, silent, watchful, menacing. Even when he went into European houses, he sometimes had an odd feeling, encountering the eyes of a native servant as he went through the garden, that even here his movements and speech were silently being taken note of.

"Well, I can look after myself," said Campbell grimly, taking care that his revolver was loaded and ready to hand. None the less it made him a little jumpy, and remembering what had befallen Samson, and the terror he had shown before his death, Campbell began to understand that he was up against a very real opposition. He thought at one time of complaining to the administration, but he realized they would only take it as an additional argument proving the nuisance caused by his investigations.

He had heard that the central market of Gorango was also the centre of the goldsmiths and coppersmiths for whom Balooma is famous. Here, any day, the most skilled members of this mystery could be seen plying their craft, which is regarded with superstitious fear by the Balooma black. Even the tools are supposed to be sacred, and it is believed that a goldsmith can bring death to any man by pointing his little hammer at him and giving it a menacing wave.

Campbell thought he would have a look at their wares in order to check if the hoard he had found in the well, whose general appearance was photographed on his mind, was of genuine Balooma workmanship, as Goring had pronounced the bracelet to be. He had learned by this time that the designs employed in native art were few and conventional. All had a double meaning, some several meanings, handed on through centuries of tradition; and therefore the quest was not' so hopeless as it sounded.

He strolled round the booths, where the black craftsmen worked with leisurely skill under the broiling sun. The heat came up from the pavement in waves. He had inspected several booths when his eye was arrested by a huge golden collar—as he supposed it to be—fashioned out of intertwined snakes. Each snake was biting its own tail and the other's head; and their eyes glittered with bright jewels. It was a striking design. The bracelet was of massive size; and he remembered in a flash that, coiled round one leg of the ivory stool from the well, he had seen a bracelet of just such a design.

He watched for some time the workman giving his steady patient touches to the work. It seemed strange to see the work going ahead like this on such a valuable object in an open market. But he had been told that the superstitious awe with which the goldsmith was regarded would prevent theft. The thief would expect to waste away and die or, as the native put it, "the gold would go to his stomach."

The man could apparently speak a few words of English, for when Campbell asked him how much the ornament would cost, he replied that it was not his. The gold had been provided by the customer and he was merely working it, as is usual with native goldsmiths, or for that matter any native smith. Campbell therefore asked him whom he was making it for. The man gabbled some name which was incomprehensible.

Could the man make one for him if he provided the metal? asked Campbell at a venture. The workman shook his head: No, it was a special design, a sacred design; so at least the detective gathered from his words.

Campbell felt this was a confirmation of his theory. The hoard sunk in the well had been of Balooma workmanship, and the designs, it now appeared, had some ritual significance.

As he was about to turn away, his eye was attracted by a polished steel mirror on the man's stand, not by the mirror itself, but by what he could see in it. Behind him—about fifty feet behind him—were two negroes, dressed in dirty white robes. They were evidently discussing him, for he saw one gesticulate repeatedly in his direction. What made him stiffen with attention was the sight of the European who was talking to them. Unless Campbell was dreaming, it was the young man he had seen in the public bar of the Marion Arms and again in the Wilderness. Mr. A. Watt of Ware.

Campbell continued to watch him. Presently the natives squatted down and the young man walked off. As he turned his back to Campbell, the inspector wheeled round and began to run after him. As he got within a few feet of him, one of the natives jumped up and uttered a warning cry. The young man whipped round. Campbell got a close view of his face. There could be no doubt. Campbell closed up to him and laid his hand on the man's shoulder.

"I want to have a talk with you."

The young man stared at him. "I say, who the devil are you?"

"You know well enough who I am," answered Campbell, transferring his grip to the arm.

"Look here, damn it, let go my arm." The young man made as though to break away.

"No, you don't," said Campbell. "Not this time. And you'd better not try using a revolver either. I'm armed."

"Whoever you are, you're making a mistake."

"No, I'm not, Mr. Watt of Ware," exclaimed Campbell bitterly.

The corner of the young man's mouth twitched, but he

answered.

"Good God, the man's mad, quite mad. Heat of course."

"I'm going to take you to the nearest police station to find out who you are," went on Campbell.

"Here, I say, you can't possibly do that."

"Oh, can't I?"

"Look here, I don't know who you think I am. But you'll only make a fool of yourself if you take me to a police station. I'm Dakin, the chief commissioner's personal secretary."

Campbell regarded him thoughtfully. He suddenly had an uneasy suspicion that the young man was speaking the truth.

"Look here, whoever you are," went on his captive. "You've evidently mistaken me for a confidence trickster. Never play cards, old boy. But if you do, look at the fellow more carefully! If you'll come along to Glory Hole you can identify me."

Campbell agreed. Glory Hole, as he had already learned, was the irreverent way in which junior officials were wont to speak of Government House. And here, Hilton, not without an ambiguous expression of discomfort or surprise, identified the young man as Leslie Charles Dakin, personal assistant to the chief.

"Well, for the matter of that I never thought you were A. Watt," commented Campbell. "Except in a metaphorical sense. Now I know who you really are, will you kindly tell me what you were doing speaking to a negro peddler in the Marion Arms six weeks ago?"

"The Marion Arms? It sounds a good spot, but where is it?"

"Little Whippering, Berkshire."

"But I say, old boy, I haven't left Balooma for the last nine months. Have I, Hilton?"

Hilton, thus invoked, hesitated, and then replied,

"Certainly not!"

"There, you see?"

"Yes, evidently there is some mistake."

"Or some misunderstanding," added Campbell slowly. "Sorry to have troubled you."

Campbell of course preferred to believe the evidence of his eyes rather than that of Mr. Hilton. He remembered, however, that the most insignificant movements of the most insignificant members of the Colonial Service were gazetted. Getting some copies of the local paper for the past few weeks he searched them. Yes, there under the "Official" section of the "Personal News" was the information:

LEAVE

MR. LESLIE CHARLES DAKIN, B.C.S., PERSONAL ASSISTANT TO HIS EXCELLENCY THE CHIEF COMMISSIONER, IS GRANTED SIX WEEKS LEAVE OF ABSENCE BEGINNING . . .

A little later, in the "Sailings," he saw a record of Mr. Dakin's name, and then of his return a few days ago.

What was the object of the lie? To conceal a secret mission of Dakin's? The idea of a secret mission, fantastic in any case, was rendered improbable by the fact that the thing was openly gazetted and that Dakin sailed under his own name.

On the other hand, what was the connection between his shadowers and Government House—for that it was to two of his shadowers Dakin had been speaking, Campbell felt certain. Was it conceivable that these sinister persons were in any way official? But no, the thought was absurd!

It was a biologist who opened his eyes to the next chapter of his search—Garrod, a tall thin man with a great mop of black bushy hair and a permanently pessimistic expression. He had just returned from spending four years alone in a hut up-country in Balooma trying to find out how *Formica hebetudiensis,* a species of large ant, found its way back to its nest at night. He had proved to his own satisfaction that it did so by means of the stars, and this apparently gave him a gloomy pleasure.

"Ghastly creatures, ants!" he would confide to Campbell over a glass of whisky, to which he was addicted. "We shall all be like them some day."

Campbell asked Garrod if he had seen the new Emperor.

"No," answered Garrod, "I did think of going up to Molengi for the Kwana Festival. But it's not my pigeon."

Molengi. The name struck a chord in Campbell's mind. Wasn't that where Virginia had talked of going? And suddenly all the suspicions in his mind revived.

"Where's Molengi?" he asked, "and what's the Kwana Festival?"

"Molengi's the native capital. Hardly any Europeans live there, though. It's nothing much more than a big kraal. But it's the Emperor's sacred residence. The Kwana is a yearly festival. It's a typical native idea. For one day everyone says what he likes. It's your duty then to tell your enemy (and your friends) exactly what you really think of them. Even slaves have to abuse their masters. The more they do it, the better luck the master will have during the year. It's quite a good idea really. As the native puts it, it 'gets the sin off one's soul.' But I'm not an anthropologist. Well, it's likely to be a pretty epic festival this year. You ought to see it!"

"Why?"

"It's my opinion, old boy, that they've got the Ivory Soul back! Of course there's no knowing. These devils are as close as oysters about it. But I happen to know the language, you see, and I've overheard one or two natives talking about it unbeknownst."

"What's the Ivory Soul?" asked Campbell curiously.

"Oh, good Lord, it would need an hour's lecture on the customs of Balooma and West Africa generally to explain it. It's a Great Fetish, but it's more than that. It's what made Balooma the Empire it is, or was."

"Is it a statue?"

"No, just a stool, such as every West African chief uses as a sign of honour. The equivalent of our Throne or Crown. But in Balooma a chief's stool is something more than a sign. It contains, in some symbolical way, his soul. When he is not sitting on it, he turns it on one side in case a spirit should sit on it and rob him of his soul. The stool, and the land and the chiefly power it carries with it, descend according to Balooma law from man to man, but through the female blood. When a great chief dies his soul is tied permanently to the stool by fetters; it is blackened; and offerings are made to it. It becomes a kind of shrine or god."

"I see. And whom does the Ivory Soul belong to?"

"To the Emperor. But it's more than a family stool. It was consecrated by a great witch doctor famous all over West Africa, who said that he would bind to it by fetters the soul of the whole Balooma nation. Every chief sent portions of his hair and blood to be fastened to it, in amulets. It is such a powerful fetish that no one not of royal blood would dare touch it. He would waste away. And even the Emperor himself dares not sit on it. He pretends to sit on it, held up by two slaves. Or perhaps he leans an elbow on it when he is seated on the ground."

The upturned legs of an ivory stool in a dripping container . . . Golden and sacred regalia . . . The image was vividly present in Campbell's mind.

"Do you know what's happened to the Ivory Soul?"

Garrod swirled his whisky in the glass.

"No, I don't. As I say, it's not my pigeon. For that matter I doubt if anyone does know. Ever since we conquered this country the Ivory Soul has been hidden. It's probably just as well. If we'd laid our hands on it, it would have been desecration. We know better now, of course, and wouldn't touch it. As long as it was in existence and respected, the chiefs obeyed the Emperor. As the Emperor obeyed us the Ivory Soul was the link by which Britain held Balooma. When there was that rumpus about the theft of the Royal treasure, everyone thought the Ivory Soul had been stolen too. But apparently it hadn't, for it wasn't among the treasure mentioned at the trial. On the other hand, lots of Europeans say that the Ivory Soul was stolen and that it's at the bottom of all the troubles Britain has had in Balooma during the last twelve years. They say the Ivory Soul is always at the back of all the troubles that ever are in Balooma. The fact remains, the natives are talking about the Ivory Soul again, and as I say, they seem to think it will come into the open again at Molengi. Have another of these damned whiskies? You may as well rot your guts like me. Did you know that even ants took stimulants?"

"I didn't. Wise ants. But will you excuse me, old boy? I want to pop round to Glory Hole."

At Glory Hole Campbell's request was passed from hand to hand until it came to the chief himself. He peremptorily demanded to see Campbell.

"What's this nonsense, eh? What do you want to go to Molengi for?"

"To see the Kwana Festival."

The chief grunted.

"We can't have all and sundry streaming up there to see a purely native festival. It unsettles them. They don't like it. I've given permits for three English people already. One of them a girl too. What's the good of it to you?"

Campbell hesitated. Then:

"I want to see the Ivory Soul," he said quietly.

"Oh," said the chief commissioner, leaning back in his chair. "Oh, damnation!"

He pulled a sheet out of his desk and scribbled his name on the bottom.

"There you are. And for the love of Mike don't do anything without consulting me."

"I won't," promised the detective.

CHAPTER SIXTEEN
The Dance of Loosened Hearts

CAMPBELL arrived at Molengi two days later, having covered the few miles from the plantation railhead to the village in an asthmatic Ford that had bounded from bump to bump of the deeply rutted track. During the rainy season the track was a swamp. During the rest of the year it was like rock. Campbell got the rock.

At the last moment Garrod had changed his mind and come with him.

"It's better than rotting my guts out with whisky," he had muttered. All the same, Campbell had heard a clinking from his suitcase as it was thrown in the back of the car.

They were to be the guests of the Resident, along with the more illustrious suite of the chief commissioner. They bumped their way to the Residency through a town, if it could be called a town, which was like nothing that Campbell had ever seen. There seemed miles and miles of whitewashed beplastered hovels, some of them adorned with rude designs—hands, snakes, poultry, apparently the first ornament that had come into the native craftsman's head. Here and there a gratuitous advertisement for some familiar English product revealed that the decorator had copied his decoration from some highly coloured advertisement page in a discarded magazine.

But most of the huts were plain mud and thatch, and beneath the hot sun rose a smell that Campbell was not likely to forget. Poultry, beasts, and people used the huts indiscriminately. Through the streets moved a mixed concourse of blacks—men, women, and children—singing, shouting and roaring with laughter. The Kwana Festival had already begun. As the car drew up outside the Residency, a band of native children started to sing a song which, Garrod told him, consisted of unprintable abuse of the white man and his habits, all part of the license of the festival.

They went inside. The Resident had already gone to the central square where, Garrod said, thousands of natives would turn up from all parts of Balooma. Meanwhile their luggage was carried in. A native servant brought long drinks to the two dusty men, which they consumed on the verandah.

They watched the people streaming into the town past the Residency. They came on foot, on cattle of all kinds, and a few in dilapidated motor-cars. Over thirty chiefs were expected, and a chiefly arrival could always be detected by the bustle, the gorgeous state umbrellas, the sword-bearers, the heavy ornaments, the slow walk of the chief himself, and the remarkable flow of language of his lively and usually ancient queen-mother.

The combination of black skins, bright Manchester cloths, brass and golden ornaments, and nodding umbrellas made an unforgettable spectacle. Chiefs were saluted and there was always an extra "hand" for any particularly famous fetish, as it came along in its great copper shrine, like a cooking pan, borne on the head of a priest, his face smeared a gruesome white, and shaded by an umbrella as big as a tent.

Suddenly Campbell stiffened with surprise. He had

heard a noise which evoked memories, memories of a peculiar kind. The noise was a thudding, a rhythmic thudding punctuated by a higher note, as of a metallic click. The two laced and interlaced with an irregular formless counterpoint.

Pink-pink-boom! Pinkety-pinkety-boom! Boom! Boom!

"What's that?" he asked.

"Only the talking drums," said Garrod indifferently.

"Talking drums. What do you mean?"

"Oh, drums to send messages with. They use them a lot in Balooma, particularly where the jungle's thick. Even the D.O.'s sometimes use them to communicate with each other."

"Good Lord, is it a sort of Morse?"

"No, much more primitive than that. These natives can't write, so they couldn't possibly send a message by a cipher like Morse. The drums actually talk."

"How do you mean, talk?"

"They mimic a human voice speaking Balooma. There's a small drum which makes the pinkety sound and a big one that makes the boom. Also a few metal gadgets fastened to them to make a kind of background of resonance. With these two sounds they imitate the intonation and syllables of the sentences they want to transmit. It's just as if we were to try to speak with drums instead of a larynx. Of course it's difficult to understand. Unless he's heard the message or word-group before, even a native finds it difficult to follow. But with set messages it works perfectly. It's easier to read than Morse, just like listening to somebody talking."

"I see. Curious. What are they playing now?"

"Can't read it. But it's sure to be one of the Festival hymns. Probably all abuse of the Emperor and the Government."

The stream of humanity into Molengi which had never ceased for twenty-four hours was dying down now. Soon the great central events of the Festival, the Procession and Dance, would take place.

Garrod and Campbell got to their feet, and in doing so they heard English voices inside the room behind them. There was nothing surprising in this, for the native servant who had brought them drinks had told them that their host had other guests. But Campbell was surprised that the voices seemed vaguely familiar. Surely he had heard both voices before. In Little Whippering.

The voices came nearer. Presently the two men came down the steps on to the verandah.

It was the vicar of Little Whippering. And Claude Marion.

The vicar recognized Campbell and gave a little cry of pleasure.

"Well, I never! How delightful! I haven't seen you, Inspector, since the day of our great match. Yes, indeed, that was a famous victory! And to think at the same time a diabolical murder was taking place. Have you found the murderer yet?"

"I am pretty near the end of the search," replied Campbell. "And what brings you here, Vicar?"

"The eternal lust after adventure, Inspector! Yes, indeed. Instead of Brighton you know. My summer holiday. Of course Pattie could not come. She went to stay with her mother and I—we—well—it was such an opportunity!"

"But why did you come here of all adventurous places?"

"Oh, we are guests of the Emperor. It turned out that Mr. Jones was the Emperor of Balooma. Most surprising, was it not? Or did you know it all the time?"

"I have known it for some time," answered Campbell slowly.

"Most remarkable! He has three hundred and twenty wives now, poor boy. Dear me, yes. It appears that one of the chiefs inherited the wives of a neighbour, and "It was a case of your wives, Bill's wives, my wives and I raise you ten," explained Claude Marion.

"Er, yes, something of the sort. I must say Jones seems a different man in his own surroundings."

"His wives, no doubt."

"Or the clothes he wears. He seems quite to have lost his Oxford manner. But there, what an adventurous life he has now! No wonder he has a commanding air. I lacked the courage to remind him of his dropped catch."

"Then I will," answered Campbell. "I've often thought of that dropped catch since. But tell me, Vicar, now you've seen life in the raw, what do you think of it?"

The vicar shook his head. "I've been very deeply disappointed!"

"Disappointed! Why?"

"Inspector, Molengi is exactly like Little Whippering! The natives have exactly the same manners and as far as I can say do exactly the same thing as the villagers. That is to say nothing. Nothing ever happens in Molengi. Nothing at all!"

"Oh, come," protested Marion, "we were nearly killed by that damned bongo or whatever it was yesterday. We had to run like hell."

"No faster than when I was chased by Farmer Bunn's bull last year," retorted the vicar. "And we didn't have to run so far. The bongo soon gave up the chase. I gather it is used to the native, who is rather indolent, and can't always be bothered to run away from lions, not in the very hot weather."

"I don't blame them!" said Marion, mopping his brow.

"Well, there it is, Inspector. I am most disappointed. Africa is not in the least like the books. There's one tiling I wish someone would tell me. Why, when I ask these natives anything, do they answer, *Hama-gwa-hoti-plumo*, as near as I can make out?"

Garrod smiled. "It's Baloomese for: *The circumstances are as it may happen that they are.* Translating literally."

The vicar nodded. "In other words: *That's as may be.* Yes, that's what they always say in Little Whippering, too. I thought the expressions on their faces were familiar. And why, when I tell them anything, do they say: *Ganda-nani Garanda nani?*"

"It means: *You have said it, o man.*"

"In Little Whippering it's: *So you say.* The same expression. Dear me, how small the world is! I fear I have been taken in by my travel books. Are all human beings the same, Mr. Garrod?"

"Yes, Vicar, just the same. Just the same as ants for that matter."

"Ants? Really, now you do surprise me! Well, I suggest we go down to the square. I trust the Festival is quite suitable for my cloth? Bearing in mind that I am on holiday?"

"Oh, quite all right, Vicar," said Garrod. "The songs are a bit free, but they're all in Balooma."

"Oh, that's all right. The songs the Little Whippering villagers sing are not always—well—they have a bucolic frankness. I believe in being all things to all men, as the Apostle so conveniently recommended. Shall we get on our way then? Dear me, are you really going to lug that great easel with you, Marion?"

"Certainly," replied Marion, "that's what I came out to Africa for."

"You paint, then?" asked Garrod. A fatuous question, in view of the fact that Marion was carrying an easel, a paint box, and a set of brushes, while his whites were already spattered with paint in one or two places.

"Yes. When I heard the vicar was going to Africa, I suddenly had a blinding vision. I decided I would become the Gauguin of Balooma. Do you realize Gauguin is positively the only painter who has ever dared tackle the tropics? And yet think of the opportunities."

Marion waved an excited hand: "Think of the skies! the verdure! The violent fiery blooms! The huge torsos of the men! The marvelously plastic rolls of fat of the women! The dusky skins! I tell you when the vicar mentioned Balooma, at one flash I saw all my canvases, all of them hanging in a row. The critics were staggering round the gallery blinded. I mean it literally. They had to be led down Bond Street back to their newspaper offices by messenger boys. And to complete the picture Jennings, in his foul smelly plus fours, was blowing his brains out through sheer chagrin on the doorstep. Well, you can imagine! I said to myself: Claude, to hell with your complexion. Some sacrifice must be made to art. And here I am, sore, blistered, mosquito bitten, sweating, but with the potentialities of immortal fame under my arm. All the Double-Zero Group have cabled their good wishes and Schwein-Chikotsky is devoting a special number of Damnation to me on my return."

The speech temporarily exhausted Marion, and it also appeared to exhaust his hearers, for no more was said until they reached the central square. Here, getting hold of one of the Hausa soldiers who were keeping order, Campbell saw them safely piloted to the official enclosure through gorgeously clothed black masses of African humanity. The recitative of the drums was rising to a voluble finale as they took their seats.

On the beaten earth of the square the distinguished visitors were drawn up in the ceremonial horseshoe formation. There were hundreds of them—chiefs, queen-mothers, young royals, priests with their fetishes, and chiefly retinues, dressed in scarlets, greens, and purples, and over their heads, like nodding clouds, were the bright cupolas of state umbrellas. The Emperor and his suite were at one end of the horseshoe and at the other, the open end, was the chief commissioner and the official enclosure.

The chief's umbrella was particularly large, like an enormous distended parachute, blue and gold in colour with a bright scarlet fringe. It was necessary to uphold the dignity of British rule.

The chief commissioner now walked solemnly round the horseshoe—very slowly, for to the native mind authority is inseparable from a slow stately tread. Only base-born persons hurry. Behind the chief followed the giant umbrella. Behind the umbrella followed the national fetish, that is to say, the Union Jack. Behind the Union Jack came the chief's suite and—raggedly, Garrod, Campbell, the vicar, and Marion. Having completed his visit of inspection the chief commissioner returned to his enclosure.

Immediately the chiefs and the Emperor, in inverse order of precedence, returned his visit. To have waited even a minute would have been excessively discourteous.

The procession made Campbell feel slightly dizzy. It was like some nightmarish pageant. Before each chief walked, or rather danced, the sword-bearers; danced backwards, the gold-cased hilts of their swords pointed towards the chief. The chief walked slowly, not only because of his dignity, but because he could hardly support the weight of brass or gold ornaments round his neck, arms, and legs. Behind him came his retinue— attendants, hornblowers, warriors, women, musicians, stool bearers. The umbrella-carriers twirled their great umbrellas; and the bearers of the soul-horns, through which the dead enemies of the chief were supposed to speak, sounded their deep booming note. The horn was enormous, a hollowed elephant's tusk, and was hung about with a w'eird collection of bones and hair and skins.

Each chief was followed by his proud sharp-eyed queen-mother with her retinue of plump black girls. A miscellaneous crowd of followers brought up the rear of each chiefly procession.

At last, walking more slowly, more richly provided with umbrellas, more deafeningly heralded by shouts, the blowing of soul-horns, the wild beating of drums, and the clapping of black hands, came the Nga-ma-Nwama himself, Great Baloomwini, Emperor of Balooma, Bachelor of Arts.

The Nga-ma-Nwama's procession was stupendous. The sword-bearers were giants, and danced backwards like madmen while the sweat poured off their hides in torrents beneath the blazing sun. The Nga-ma-Nwama himself was almost invisible beneath his ornaments, great golden torques consisting of twisted snakes, each snake biting its own tail and the other's head. The black skin only showed in patches between the glitter of metal. The Nga-ma-Nwama's face was quite expressionless; the eyes fixed as if in an ebony mask. To have shown any emotion or recognition of the proceedings would have been most unroyal.

The Nga-ma-Nwama was muscular, but he was unable to support his metallic load unaided, nor was he expected to. He staggered slowly forwards with his arms resting on the bowed necks of two supporters, whose task it was to prevent his stumbling. Had he stumbled, a bad harvest would have been inevitable. He was followed by two men who, in a constant loud gabble, recited into his ears the history of his family since the mists of legend. Although a gabble, the slightest mistake would, in former times, have been followed by an instant execution.

Behind the story-tellers came the spokesmen. It was beneath the dignity of a West African king to speak to or hear anyone directly. All discussions take place through the medium of spokesmen. Each carried a wand of office, strangely reminiscent of Homeric heralds.

Among the spokesmen were borne the great soul-horns, hung with skulls and spattered with ancient human blood. They boomed monotonously. Beside the horn-bearers were boys with expressions of responsibility. They were all of good birth—young royals—and it was their important office, should the Emperor hiccough, as was not unlikely in view of the quantity of beer he would have to consume today, to crack their fingers loudly for several minutes, and so frighten the Emperor's soul back again into his nether regions.

Large parts of the Emperor's procession were meaningless even to Garrod, so ancient was their connection with Balooma lore. Some of the state umbrellas in the Imperial procession sheltered young royals of some relationship to the Emperor. Others sheltered fetishes of virtue, borne solemnly in copper pans on the heads of priests and priestesses, their faces daubed with white clay, their eyes often fixed in the curious negro trance.

Other followers were carrying on their heads various objects, some of which might be fetishes, others merely valued possessions. Thus the ancient horn gramophone of an antique pattern was obviously a fetish, in spite of the fact that the Nga-ma-Nwama's palace was fitted up with modern radio sets. Doubtless it was acquired in the first Balooma War. The rifles were probably just booty. Then, following the blackened stools of former Emperors, or of great queen-mothers, came the Queen-Mother and her retinue, then twelve drummers, then forty horn-blowers who, when the procession stopped in front of the chief commissioner, let out a blast that made Claude Marion jump and overturn his easel.

There was one fetish in the procession however which excited a murmer of excitement and wonder from all the assembled chiefs. Before and behind it walked a number of gaunt warriors. But the object itself was hidden by a large state umbrella whose edge was hung round with strips of cloth. Only the feet of the bearer could be seen.

Garrod nudged Campbell. "That's the Ivory Soul unless I'm a Dutchman! Look at the expressions on those lads' faces. Of course the chief commissioner will pretend to know nothing about it."

Campbell however was not so interested by the expressions on the faces of the warriors in general, as of one in particular. He was an oldish negro, evidently a man of importance. His greying hair was scant, giving him a somewhat seedy look. A scar ran down one cheek.

Campbell's mind slipped back at once to the Marion Arms and the negro peddler. Yes, it was the same scar— the same man.

"Who's that Johnny?" he asked Garrod, "the one with the scar?"

"Oh, he's the Nga-ma-Nwama's father. Quite an intelligent black. Speaks English. He doesn't count for much of course. He's only the Queen-Mother's husband. He isn't reckoned as of Royal blood."

The procession over, there was a pause, during which the solemn beat of the drums became joyous. The great ceremonial dance of the festival was about to begin. Laughter and giggles came from the huge umbrellas, hung round with strips of linen so as to form tents, in which disrobing was going on. Occasionally a black feminine arm or leg was accidentally thrust through the strips, and hurriedly withdraw, amid cheers.

But it was necessary for the dance to be preceded by sacrifice. Eggs, chickens, kids, or sheep were acceptable to the gods in the brass pans. Each priest had duly provided himself with the delicacy most fancied by his particular god, and all over the ground eggs were being cracked, chickens' necks being wrung, and lambs' or kids' throats being cut. The stools of office were positively streaming with egg yolks.

Campbell was watching the sacrifice of a chicken near him. It made no attempt to escape once it had been put on the brass pan. It stood there quietly, its wings slightly outstretched, occasionally swaying gently from side to side.

"Why do they behave like that?" asked Campbell. "Do the priests drug them?"

"It is odd, isn't it? Almost as if they were hypnotized. The blacks say they 'feel the power of the god.' If the chicken flutters at all, they say it is because the sacrifice isn't acceptable, and they don't offer it up, then. It must be something in the African breed of chicken."

"No, I don't somehow think it's that. I fancy our English fowl would behave in the same way," answered Campbell. He remembered a dark night, and an open poultry-house door, and a fowl swaying quietly in the moonlight, its wings slightly stretched . . .

The sacrifice over, the great dance began. Amid polite titters and hand claps, the Queen-Mother of the Emperor and her attendant women, including the more able-bodied of the Emperor's wives, emerged from their dressing rooms. They began to dance.

The dust rose in clouds, the heat rained down like solid brass bullets, but they danced. They shook their haunches, they stamped their feet, they pranced. The drums beat out their brazen rhythm. The drums talked. The drums sang a song of praise to the divine powers that had fructified the harvest and made the sheep increase.

Their black faces strangely blank above the white robes of joy in which they had clothed themselves, the women endlessly circled the horseshoe, their bodies apparently twitching with an uncontrollable ecstasy as they shuffled and shook, yet, all the time, as by some uncanny instinct, obeying the intricate rhythm of the thudding drums.

Round they swept, dancing as if their lives depended on it. And as the women danced, the Emperor and the chiefs watched them without moving a muscle of their faces, and their attendants and the thousands of eager black faces of the commoners behind urged them on with shrieks and shuffling.

And now the Nga-ma-Nwama, the great Baloomawini, also began to dance. Shedding his golden ornaments he advanced into the centre of the horseshoe. Without stopping their furious dance, the women gave way to him. In the centre of them his sword-bearers made a ring for him, all facing inwards, all with the gold hilts of their swords kept pointing as steadily as rocks towards him while the rest of their bodies pranced and shook and quivered with the intense movements of the dance, dancing to the royal thunder of the drums.

Slowly and gracefully, as befits an Emperor and Bachelor of Arts, the Nga-ma-Nwama danced. Stripped to the waist, crouching forwards, continually revolving in slow panther like movements, he danced the dance of the Kwama Festival, the Dance of Loosened Hearts.

And at this signal, the chiefs also started dancing, dancing under their great umbrellas. And their sword-bearers, and the blowers of the soul-horn, and the spokes-men, and the tale-tellers, and the warriors, and the young boys, they all began dancing.

Now even the common people could join in, old men and young men, grave matrons and girls, boys, and little black pickaninnies. The horseshoe formation broke up, all over the field they raced and whirled, giving yells of sudden delirious excitement, screaming war-cries, turning somer-saults, hurling their clothing in all directions, throwing spears and shields up and catching them again, throwing little black pickaninnies up in the air and catching them again, chasing each other with wild cries.

It was like a vast stampede of black humanity. The dust rose in clouds; the drums thudded like the trembling of an earthquake. For hour after hour they screamed and rioted, milled and somersaulted and yet never, not for an instant, did the twirling warriors, the cart-wheeling pickaninnies, the giggling girls, the leaping young men fail to keep time to the thud thud thud of the music that seemed to speak the voice of Africa itself.

"Phew!" said Garrod. "I've never seen a Kwama Festival Dance like this! The bug's in them properly. Well, each to his taste. This confounded dust's got in my throat, and I'm going back to have a drink. The chief commissioner's gone already. Coming, Campbell?"

"No, thanks, old chap. I want to potter round a bit."

"Dear me!" said the vicar, in another part of the ground. "I must admit this spectacle is unusual. I, wish I could get our folk dancing society here to see it.

"And yet, on second thoughts!" he added, as an almost completely naked black maiden danced her way past him. "Perhaps they wouldn't appreciate it."

"Don't talk to me of folk dancing, Vicar!" exclaimed Marion, "this is the real thing. It's stupendous. Colossal!" He extended his arms in a vague circling gesture. "I feel physically giddy and spiritually vertiginous. I don't consider I am a hysterical person, but really—" he broke off panting.

The vicar, alarmed at his young companion's tone, looked at him more closely. Marion's eyes were dazed and there was a hectic flush in his cheeks.

"What on earth is the matter, Marion?"

"I want to dance! I want to dance wildly!" exclaimed the young man, "I want to throw all my clothes off and start turning somersaults. I want to yell. I want to chase that black girl and slap her hide in time to the music!"

"But, good heavens, Marion, I have never seen you like this. I should have described you as a most self-contained man, positively repressed."

"I can't help it, this dancing has got into my blood. Boom-boom-boom." He swayed from side to side.

"Stop twitching," said the vicar sharply.

"I can't help it. The group soul has me in its grip. Boom-boom-boom—pinkety-boom!" He began to shuffle.

"Marion!" said the vicar earnestly, "I beg and implore of you not to start dancing!"

"Why not? Boom-boom-pink-pink-boomety!"

"Because if you do, I shan't be able to stop doing it myself."

The two men looked into each other's eyes. Then Marion put his arm through the vicar's with a sigh. "Come on then, we must hurry home as quickly as we can."

"And we mustn't look back," agreed the vicar. "Remember Lot's wife! . . .

With lingering steps, the two men made their way back to the Residency.

CHAPTER SEVENTEEN
A Question of Principle

MEANWHILE Campbell, less susceptible to the atmosphere of the Kwama Festival than the visitors from Little Whippering, was making his way round the edge of the ground to a kind of mud and reed pavilion. It was into this pavilion that the Ivory Soul (if it was the Ivory Soul) had disappeared, hidden beneath its umbrella and followed by a bevy of warriors carrying spears and beplastered priests waving bundles of assorted unpleasantnesses.

These guardians had subsequently been posted near the hut. But the warriors had long since joined in the celebrations. And the priests had been so frequently sustained with copious draughts of beer during the afternoon by friends, that most of them had passed clean out. The others seemed in no condition to notice Campbell as he walked into the hut.

He wondered whether he was committing an un-expiable sacrilege. But the matey behaviour of the other African gods during the day had made him believe that they had a certain generous tolerance of familiarity on the part of human beings.

The pavilion smelt rather unpleasant inside. At first it seemed quite empty. Then he heard a scuffle at his feet. He leaped back hastily. Something like a large dog was down there, but it reared up and proved to be an old woman, with a shriveled face like a monkey's. Her grey, almost silvery hair, stuck out on all sides in tousled masses and gave her in spite of her blackness an odd resemblance to an elderly "char" drunk and disorderly in the Old Kent Road.

The woman began to curse him or argue with him in a high shrill monotone. Meanwhile she made shooing gestures. As she pushed him in the chest with her unsavory hands, Campbell fell back. His eyes were now accustomed to the gloom, and he saw behind her in another room opening off this a tall object gleaming palely in the dusk—the Ivory Soul. The stool he had fished out of the well! The sight of the object made him halt, and the old woman's curses rose to storm pitch.

Suddenly a quiet stream of Balooma from the other room made the old woman turn round. She answered it: an argument began. Finally the old woman moved to a corner of the room, and with a kind of grunt sat down, resting her head on her knees so that her grey locks fell over her shins.

Campbell walked towards the other room to see who the second speaker was. It was Virginia Ridge. She was sitting on a stool in the corner, a sketching pad on her knee. Evidently she was drawing the Ivory Soul.

"Good afternoon, Inspector," she said composedly. "I thought we should meet again."

"Where have you been all this time?" he asked her. "I've

made several inquiries about you since I came to Molengi, but no one seemed to know where you'd got to."

"I've been living in the Royal Kraal. As the guest of Mr. Jones' three hundred odd wives. I've filled fifty notebooks already. Gee, how those girls can talk!"

"Is it all right for me to have a look at this stool business? Or shall I get my throat cut?"

"It will be all right if you don't touch it. Otherwise I can't say." She went on with her drawing. Her manner had been that of a guest at a tea-party when another guest comes into the room. Living at the kraal had no effect on her cool efficiency. She did not even affect the shorts of the female globetrotter in Africa, but was wearing something Campbell vaguely described to himself as "sensible."

Campbell went up to the Ivory Soul and examined it. It was a stool similar to those he had seen carried in the procession but, unlike them, it was carved out of ivory instead of wood. It was ornamented with a barbaric profusion of mother of pearl, gold, ebony, and brass. Looped golden chains were hung round the outside, and to these was fixed a variety of weird objects—stones, pieces of skull, complete bones, locks of hair, pieces of skin, little bags of leather, beans, dried plants—Campbell took out his pocket torch and switched it on the better to examine it in the gloom of the hut. Then he gave a little whistle. The top of the stool was thickly caked with blood. Round the top was wound a thin rope or string of hair, human hair, ginger hair.

Switching the torch off, he went back to Virginia.

"Have you finished your sketch? Because if so I should like to have a serious talk with you. Not in here, but in the fresh air."

"Yes, I've finished," answered Virginia. She snapped the band round her sketch book and they walked outside.

It was now the fag-end of the Festival. Most of the dancers had wandered off to their homes for the enormous meal, washed down by calabashes of beer, with which they would end the day. A few still screamed and leaped in front of the exhausted drummers and hornblowers, who maintained the steady thudding of the dance. Here and there a prostrate figure, sleeping or unconscious, told of a performer's collapse, the effect of too much beer on an exhausted frame. All the priests who could walk away had disappeared from outside the hut. The others slept. Only the old woman seemed left to guard the sacred Ivory Soul.

"But of course no native would dare to touch it," explained Virginia. "And there are only a few Europeans in Molengi. She'd knife one without compunction if he tried to lift it."

They walked on a little. "Now," began Campbell in his most impressive manner. "I think I know the whole story."

She nodded.

"I expect you do. I knew you would discover it sooner or later. It was only a matter of time. I always told the Nga-ma-Nwama you were bound to find out."

"Well, that's what I want to ask you. Why did you refuse to tell me anything? Don't you admit the seriousness of murder?"

"Not when the victim is a man like Samson. He'd already killed a native and two white men. And been the indirect cause of a good many other deaths in Balooma."

"But the horrible way in which he was murdered!"

"What if they did cut off his hair and sprinkle their fetish with his blood? He was already dead. They'd already cut his throat. It's no worse than hanging."

"That may be so. But there can be no private vengeance for murder. If everyone started killing people they thought deserved it, we should be back at barbarism again. Surely that is obvious enough."

"Of course it is. But you can't call this a private murder. Nga-ma-Nwama was acting as head of his State. He was authorized by the Baloomagara, the secret society of Balooma, to get back the Ivory Stool and avenge the murder of its guardian."

"There's no real difference. If he wanted the Ivory Soul back, he could have got it, once he'd traced it, by suing through the Colonial Office, in the ordinary process of civil law. The chief commissioner would have been only too glad to help. And if he really wanted Samson to be killed, well Samson had committed two murders; one in England and the other in Nigeria. For either he would have been hanged by the neck until dead."

"But you don't understand," exclaimed Virginia. "To have had Samson hanged would have been merely vindictive. Balooma isn't vindictive."

"Not vindictive! When they cut this fellow's throat and let him bleed to death over their fetish! If that isn't pure vengeance, what is?"

"You don't understand," repeated Virginia patiently. "When Samson captured the fetish he took away the soul of the Balooma people, just as you or I might carry away a piece of coal. He proved himself stronger than the Balooma people. He also killed one of the Guardians, but Africans don't take that quite so seriously as we do. What really mattered was the much more appalling fact that he had stolen the Soul of the Balooma people. From that moment the nation went to pieces. If you were to deny this, they would point to the years that followed as proof. Illogical but very natural."

"Well, they fished the Soul up from the well. Why weren't they content with that?"

"Because the Ivory Stool itself isn't the soul of the Balooma people. It's just its resting place. The soul has to be chained to the stool by 'medicine' and golden fetters. After Samson had stolen the stool the soul of the Balooma people passed from it into his keeping. There was only one way it could be got back. A man's soul is in his blood and hair. So the blood and hair of O'Leary had to be added to the stool before it would once again be the Ivory Soul."

"And you really think this barbarism is a justification for murder? Upon my soul, you really have shocked me now!"

"That's only because your mind is hopelessly barbaric too," replied Virginia coldly. "You think in your crude way that lives are like coins, and if one is lost to the tribe, another has to be sacrificed in exchange for it. That's the barbaric European creed, no better than the barbaric African creed!"

"I am not prepared to argue the ethics of capital punishment," said Campbell in his most official manner. "Fortunately I am only concerned in doing my duty. And I must point out that you appear to have been an accessory after the fact, if not before. Both are serious crimes under British law, and if, after I have laid information with the police here they arrest you, you have only yourself to blame."

Virginia lost her temper.

"Do you think I care a cent for your beastly British law? Anyway you're only trying to frighten me because you got the worst of the argument. You couldn't prove I knew anything about the murder, except by my own confession, and I haven't said I did know. I didn't, not actually, I only guessed. I guessed who Jones was. And I knew he had some big plans because of the sacrifice he made that night by the hen-roost. But I told him I'd not say anything, if he'd help me with my investigations in Molengi. But I told him he'd be bound to get found out sooner or later. He said he didn't mind as long as he got a clear run to Molengi."

"Then you are most certainly an accessory after the fact, and liable to a considerable term of imprisonment. And so is anyone else who helped Nga-ma-Nwama to commit the crime."

"But he didn't commit it. Even you can't prove that. He was on the cricket field at the time of the murder."

"That shows that you know rather less than you imagine. Jones did the murder himself, and his alibi isn't worth a tuppenny damn. I shall go straight from here to lay information against him with the chief commissioner, and I shall send in my report in duplicate to the Colonial Office and the C.I.D. And that will be the end of that. If the Nga-ma-Nwama isn't deposed and put on trial within the next month, I'll eat my hat."

Virginia looked at him, her eyes blazing. It was the first time he had seen her cool competence ruffled. Campbell on his side was equally annoyed, and his mood was mingled with a good deal of virtuous indignation, which may or may not have been wholly genuine.

"If you dare do that!" she said furiously, "I shall never forgive you! I thought you were an intelligent man. You're just a pig-headed, mean-minded, Scottish brute. If the Nga-ma-Nwama is deposed I shall never speak to you again!"

Campbell was used to hard words in the course of his profession, and was as a rule unaffected by them. For some reason, however, Virginia's remark got beneath his skin.

"Very well," he said, his face rigid, "if I have to choose between doing my job and never speaking to you again, what do you suppose I can say?"

"I don't know exactly, but it's sure to be something self-righteous!"

Virginia walked away. Campbell, feeling strangely depressed for a detective who had just cleared up a knotty problem by patient investigation, went slowly back to the Residency.

"My God, you look blue!" remarked Garrod. "A touch of the sun. Have a drink, old boy!"

"Thanks, I will," answered Campbell.

~§~

Carried on by his wave of indignation, the detective insisted on seeing the chief commissioner in private that afternoon.

The chief was in a convivial mood. He had with characteristic affability partaken freely of the loving cups of beer pressed on him during the Kwama Festival. As Campbell was far from being convivial the opening stages of their conversation were awkward.

"Well, what's on your mind?" grunted the chief commissioner at last, "some kind of trouble, I can see! Don't beat about the bush. Come out with it."

Campbell came out with it.

"The Nga-ma-Nwama murdered Tuffy Samson, sir," he said. "According to the terms of my instructions from the Home Office, I now formally lay information against him to that effect."

"The man's drunk," said the chief. "Good Lord! You should leave that beer alone as a newcomer."

Campbell smiled mirthlessly.

"The Nga-ma-Nwama was staying with the vicar of Little Whippering, sir, under the name of Jones. There will be no difficulty in getting evidence to that effect. I do not expect any greater difficulty in proving that he fished up the Ivory Soul from its hiding place in the well, cut Samson's throat, shaved his head, and fled back to Balooma. In this he was assisted by his father, who was also at Little Whippering under the disguise of a negro peddler."

"You are talking through your hat," commented the chief commissioner. "At the time of the murder the Nga-ma-Nwama was playing cricket."

"With all respect, sir, may I ask how you are aware of that? So far as I know, I have not mentioned it!"

"You know perfectly well how I know it, Inspector. I think the time has come for a show-down. I had an observer at Little Whippering."

"Yes, Dakin."

"Quite right. There is no point in keeping it secret now."

"Well then, sir," said Campbell heatedly, "since we are having a show-down, and still with all respect, what is your position in this matter? I tell you frankly it baffles me. As far as I can see, this pleasant heathen went to Little Whippering with the express purpose of murdering Samson and it now seems he had the support—the assistance—of a representative of His Majesty's Government at Balooma."

The chief commissioner was silent for a moment. His ruddy face was sunk forwards on his chest. When he spoke it was with a much graver tone than he had used during the rest of the conversation.

"Dakin had not the slightest idea of Tuffy Samson's presence in Little Whippering. He happened to be on leave in England, and I suggested to him that he go to Little Whippering and keep an eye on the Nga-ma-Nwama. I had heard native rumours to the effect that the Nga had some game on. I told Dakin that whatever happened, he was not to embroil himself with the local police, and that he was to do his best to keep the Nga-ma-Nwama out of mischief. Well, he went to Little Whippering. He did his best to find what our black friend was up to. He discovered it was something to do with the tenant of the Wilderness. He cross-examined two of the Nga's family he found lurking in disguise in the neighbourhood. But he couldn't find out what the game was until too late. Until the drums announced to the Nga's accomplices that the job was done and everyone was to fly for their lives. Then I admit he knew well enough. But in view of his instructions he said nothing and came back at once to Balooma."

"Excuse me, sir, but I don't think you are being altogether frank with me. Dakin's done a good deal more than keep quiet. I'm perfectly certain he has been responsible for shadowing me ever since I came to Balooma."

"Nonsense, Inspector! We shouldn't do such a thing. It would be ridiculous, besides being useless!"

"Again with all respect, sir, I must point out that ever since I came here I have been shadowed by negroes, and that I saw Dakin speaking for a long time to two of them."

"Doubtless, and for a very good reason. Please do not think I am being offensive, Inspector, but I am afraid you are a child in African matters, in spite of your uncomfortably acute perception in other spheres. Don't you know anything about the Baloomagara, the Secret Society of Balooma?"

"I do not, sir. Nothing beyond the fact of its existence."

"Well, that is the Society which is really responsible for the recovery of the Ivory Soul. The moment you set foot in Africa the drums were beating with the news of your arrival. Two men were sent at once to pick you up from the docks. You appreciate why?"

"I certainly do. They have been shadowing me ever since!"

"No, I don't think you do understand, Inspector. They were deputed to kill you at the first convenient opportunity. And you would have been killed. Every member of the Baloomagara—and there are thousands in every town— would have been pledged by his vows to help your murderers and assist them to escape. Fortunately Dakin found this out, and he solemnly warned your shadowers that you were not to be harmed. You will be inclined to underestimate the difficulty of saving your life. It would have been quite useless for instance to guard you. Death could have come by a thousand channels. It would have been useless to threaten the murderers. They would be proud to be executed for having killed under the instructions of the Baloomagara. Dakin took the only possible course. He warned them that if you were killed, the Ivory Soul would be taken back from them. It was only a bluff. If we tried to do such a thing, all Balooma would be ablaze, and every unarmed European in it would be massacred over-night. But still, as a bluff it was effective, for here you are standing in front of me unharmed. In spite of the fact that you went into the tent of the Ivory Soul! Good Lord, Inspector, do you realize the danger you ran? If when you came out from that hut, the old woman had made the slightest sign, you would have been struck down by half-a-dozen spears."

"But there was no one near—no one in sight!" said Campbell, a little astonished by the knowledge of the chief.

"Do you think the Guardians of the Ivory Soul are always visible? They were hidden in the hut, or perhaps lying round pretending to be asleep."

"But how do you know all this?"

"Listen," said the chief commissioner. In the silence that followed, Campbell heard nothing but the drums that had been monotonously and endlessly throbbing until they had become no more noticeable than the sound of his own breathing.

Boom-boom-boom, pinkety-pinkety-boom!

"White spy now speaking to old Max," translated the chief commissioner with a smile. "You get used to living in the open in Balooma! Ever since I've been in Molengi I've been listening in to the drums. At quite an early date I familiarized myself with the drum language, both for sending and receiving. Most of the messages today have been for the chiefs attending the festival, relayed from their own kingdoms. But a few have been about you, and myself, and the vicar, and so on. And so I know what you have been doing up to the time you left Dr. Ridge."

"Well, naturally, sir, I am very grateful," replied Campbell, a little awkwardly, "whatever risks you have saved me from. But still we haven't disposed of the real difficulty. I am afraid that there is no doubt that the Nga-ma-Nwama murdered Samson. I happen to know that his alibi is worthless. During the tea interval, he slipped away from the cricket field. His place was instantly taken by one of his relations—enough like him to deceive everyone, for the European is not expert at detecting facial differences in full-blooded negroes unless he lives among them. Unfortunately his relative was not so good a cricketer as he was, and muffed two catches later. When this relative came off the field, with the rest of the team, I tried to speak to him, but he fled, and ran into the pavilion. By this time Nga-ma-Nwama had returned. I have ascertained that it is possible to get into the pavilion through a window in the back, without being seen by anyone on the field, as it backs on to a wood. Jones then resumed his identity and strolled on to the field, while his relation vanished through the back door. Unfortunately for his alibi, there was blood on his hands and also on his clothes.

"There is only one thing I am puzzled about."

"I'm glad to hear there is something. What is it?"

"How did Crumbles and O'Leary get possession of the Ivory Soul and the treasure? For according to the records of the trial, the hiding place was revealed to the Administration, who restored the treasure to the Royal Family. Did they get hold of it again?"

"I have cleared that point up with the Nga-ma-Nwama. When the three Englishmen hid the treasure in the swamp, they divided it into two parts, and hid these in two separate places. They only revealed to us the hiding place of one lot of stuff. As we had no inventory, we thought we were handing back the lot. The Royal Family were much too distrustful of us to tell us the truth. In fact for a long time they thought we'd pinched the treasure and the Ivory Soul for ourselves, which helped to account for the trouble we had with the country in the years that followed. As soon as O'Leary and

Crumbles got out of prison, they recovered the still-buried treasure and divided it. Crumbles sold his share and used the proceeds in business. O'Leary took his to England but only sold bits of it as and when he required money. The rest he hoarded.

"Meanwhile he had begun to appreciate the sinister importance of the Ivory Soul, for the Baloomagara had started to get on his track already. It was no good his giving back the Ivory Soul. There had to be blood spilt ritually, the blood of the man who held it at the time. O'Leary fled from town to town, getting more and more nervous and frightened, until he settled down in Little Whippering in circumstances which he thought would make it impossible for the Baloomagara to trace him. So they would, except that Samson traced him through Crumbles, and they kept on the track of Samson after he left prison at Lagos. Incidentally this division of the treasure was another reason for Samson's rancor. He found they had taken everything instead of keeping a share for him."

"Yes, that makes the story complete. I don't think the Nga will stand much chance in a court of law."

"Well, no doubt you're right," agreed the chief commissioner wearily. "Assume the Nga-ma-Nwama is actually guilty. What do you propose to do about it?"

"That is for you to say, sir, of course. My duties are confined to making a formal report to you of my discovery, and sending copies of the report to the Colonial Office and the Home Office. Then I shall return to England. Should the Nga-ma-Niwama be tried here, I shall, I suppose, be charged with the responsibility of collecting and marshalling the evidence for your courts. The usual procedure would be for Jones to be tried in England, where the crime was committed, but in view of his special status, whatever it may be, this may not be possible. I do not even know that he can be put on trial."

"Yes, he's liable for trial all right," said the chief, "and he'll be deposed. We'll try to govern direct again. I shall resign. There will be risings. Hundreds of Englishmen and thousands of natives will be killed. Eventually the country will be pacified. Pacified, but with the spirit knocked out of it. The end of an interesting experiment!" He sighed. "But I suppose all that doesn't matter to you, Inspector?"

"No, sir, not as a policeman. It is not my business. I have a certain duty to fulfill, to discover the murderer of Tuffy Samson. I have done it. It is nothing to do with me whether the man is hanged, pardoned, or rewarded. It's out of my hands."

"Quite the approved Pilate style," replied the chief commissioner bitterly. "Do you want a bowl of water? Unfortunately life's not so simple as that. You've got to take some responsibility for your actions. The fate of this little Confederacy depends entirely on you."

"I don't see it, sir. I only have to make a report. It's up to the Government how they act on it."

"Fiddlesticks! You know perfectly well that once the Home Office and the Colonial Office have a report in their files that so-and-so murdered someone in an English village, they can't do anything but act on it, whatever they think. It's as automatic as the phases of the moon."

"Well, I don't see I can be blamed for that, sir."

"Of course not. I am merely asking you to look at the consequences of your action," said the chief in his most wooing tones. "And then not to do it. If I asked you to do something definitely wrong, it would be different. But I don't. I only ask you to refrain from an action. After all, you've cleared up a difficult mystery—the identities of O'Leary and Crumbles. You'll get lots of credit. Then as to the murder of Samson, you can tell your people that it was certainly done by a member of the Baloomagara but that it is not possible to ascertain which one. We'll back you up there.

No one is a penny the worse. We of course turn in an enthusiastic report about you—"

"I am sorry, sir, but I can't fake reports."

"Quite right, of course. There mustn't be any faking. It's just a matter of wording. I'll help you draw it up."

"I am sorry—"

"By Jove, you are certainly an incorruptible officer. I wish I could get more men like you in my service." The chief gazed thoughtfully at his blotting paper. "Take my chief of police now. The post's empty. A good job. A salary a good deal more than you are getting. And a pension. A really interesting job. Very little routine, and a C.M.G. at the end. You'd make an ideal man for the job, Inspector."

"I can only say, sir," answered Campbell stiffly, "that I've got to complete the job I came out here for before I think of my future."

"Quite. I didn't really think bribery would be any good," answered the chief as simply as a child, "but I thought I'd try it. I'm going to speak to you now, Inspector, as one man to another. As a man who has given his life to the welfare of a few million savages. God knows why. A kink, no doubt. A bit dotty. But there it is. And my Government has backed me up. Balooma has cost them a good deal, one way or another, yet Englishmen aren't allowed in it without special permission, and imports are almost nil. During the last ten years I've lost some of my best men, and had to kill thousands of natives, simply because a rascally, murderous fellow pinched the national fetish and robbed Balooma of its soul. You'll say it's barbaric superstition. Well, it's easy enough to call some deep-rooted sentiment a superstition. Come to that the British Empire is a superstition. There's only a group of independent nations acknowledging the imaginary domination of a hereditary Crown. Another superstition. There's no such thing as the British race, there's just a queer mingling of Normans, Gaels, Anglo-

Saxons, Celts, Danes, and ancient Britons, with a good many French, Dutch, Italians and Jews. Still another superstition. Yet these superstitions were real enough for men to die for them in millions during the war!"

"I grant all that, but I don't frankly see how it affects my position."

"Let's try another tack. You're a policeman. Do you believe in witchcraft?"

"Of course not."

"Neither do I. Well, supposing yourself a police officer in this country. One of your native subordinates comes to you and says another negro whom he names is bewitching him. The negro admits it. What do you do?"

"Tell them they're both talking nonsense!"

"Naturally. But then your negro subordinate takes to his bed and dies, just wastes away in spite of all medical aid. Don't look incredulous. It happens again and again. Every anthropologist will bear me out. And supposing this happens often? Isn't that witchdoctor murdering those men as much as the poisoner who poisons their soup?"

"I suppose he is, I admit something would have to be done about it."

"But what? Can you put a man to death for witchcraft, a thing you don't believe in? How could we, intelligent white men, countenance such a thing? How could witchcraft be proved at a trial, if you don't believe in it? The most we can do is to give the witch a term of imprisonment, a short one. The result is, the natives think we encourage witchcraft and every witchdoctor who has been in prison has virtually a government certificate of his powers. He can hold a whole village up to ransom."

"Yes, I can see the difficulty. Of course education—"

"In the future," interrupted the chief, "but we're dealing with the present. What actually happens now? A is dying because B, his enemy, has bewitched him. C, a friend of A, goes and spears B to save his friend's life. A, on the point of death, now recovers. Can you wonder that the D.O. feels lenient towards the murderer of this kind? Nothing we could do ourselves would save A. If we put B in prison for practicing witchcraft, the spell still holds good, and for all our intervention A dies? Can't you see that when you are dealing with so-called savages the law may well have to be different from what it is when you are dealing with Europeans? Can't you see that this is a case in point? On the one hand a rascal, richly deserving hanging, who steals the soul of a nation. Just imagine the British Empire if the Crown, instead of being a symbol incapable of death or loss was, owing to our more primitive minds, something tangible, done up in brown paper, that could be stolen. And suppose it were stolen. The Empire would disintegrate.

"That is what happened to the Balooma Confederacy. The link that bound it together was stolen. The only way it could be restored was not merely by restoring the object, that was not enough. The ritual murder of the man who had the Soul in his possession was necessary. Pure superstition, of course. A European can't countenance it, any more than lie can countenance the execution of a witch who murders by suggestion. But once the deed's done, and we know that any attempt to punish it will cause war, rebellion, deaths, can't you see that things must be overlooked, that we must turn a blind eye on the affair?"

Campbell put his hand to his forehead. He felt mentally dizzy. Only one thing seemed clear.

"I see everything you say, but I still feel it's not my business. It's your business, the business of the Government. I've found the murderer of Tuffy Samson and I must make my report."

The chief commissioner turned dark-red and his eyes became points of light. He seemed about to burst into one of his famous rages. But he controlled himself. Gradually his features relaxed, and presently he grinned.

"Well, there is nothing more to be said. Perhaps I am getting old and fanciful. Perhaps I exaggerate the importance of the matter." He got up and opened the door. "Good evening, Inspector. Pleasant dreams."

After Campbell had gone out, the chief commissioner rang the bell for Dakin. His face was now expressionless.

"I've just had an interview with Campbell. He has laid information against the Nga-ma-Nwama charging him with the murder of Tuffy Samson.

"His report," added the chief, with a bitter smile, "will be in triplicate, one copy to us, one to the Colonial Office, and one to the Home Office. Possibly it will be in quadruplicate, the fourth copy going to the chief constable in Berkshire!"

"Good God, sir," exclaimed Dakin. "What the devil are you going to do about it?"

"Nothing, Dakin. You understand my meaning? Nothing at all. This matter is between us only. From this moment Inspector Campbell does not exist for us. It will no longer be necessary for you to shadow him!"

"Quite, sir," said Dakin with a smile. "I understand!"

CHAPTER EIGHTEEN
The Sacred Lake

CAMPBELL returned to his room and sat down to write his report. Most of it already existed in draft, and it was merely a matter of assembling it with fresh data and making a formal account of the whole thing. As the substance of it has already been related there is no need to recount it here.

Campbell had already found that the train from the plantation railhead was provided with a mail van, and that letters could be posted straight into the train. He decided to post his report here himself rather than put it in the Residency mailbox. There was of course no reason to suppose that his mail would be tampered with. It would be rather ridiculous to do so, for obviously he would keep a copy for himself of whatever report he sent.

None the less he decided to satisfy his impulse, to hire a car and drive to the railhead, and so catch the evening train. He could, he found, get back in time for dinner, and he therefore slipped quietly out without telling anyone at the Residency of his intention. The garage, run by an "educated" negro, was not far up the road.

Soon he was seated in the asthmatic Ford, bumping his way towards the station.

After about ten minutes' driving, the engine spluttered and stopped. The negro driver popped out of his driving seat excitedly, and began to poke about the engine, to Campbell's mind with considerable vagueness.

Time passed, and Campbell began to get impatient. They were well out of the town, amid featureless scrub, and if the car really had broken down, he might have to walk all the way back to Molengi, and would thus miss the post.

"What the devil's the matter?" he asked at last.

"I not know, sir," confessed the man.

"Don't you understand engines?" asked the detective, as the negro started to tap the cylinder casting hopefully with a spanner.

"Not when they not go, sir."

Campbell jumped out and bent over the engine. He tried to flood the carburetor, but without success. Evidently the flow was blocked, and he looked for the filter. As he bent still lower and groped for it, he suddenly felt sick and saw a curtain of multi-coloured spangles dance before his eyes . . .

Then blackness . . .

~§~

"And where is the excellent inspector tonight?" asked the vicar. He was one of the guests at the informal dinner at the Resident's house, at which the chief commissioner presided. "I trust he has not been carried away by the spirit of Kwama? Dear me, yes. I must confess that music was profoundly unsettling."

"Do you know where Inspector Campbell is?" asked the Resident of his private secretary.

"He went out for a walk early this afternoon, sir, and hasn't returned yet."

"He shouldn't have done that," said the Resident thoughtfully. "The natives are apt to be in rather a bad temper. A hang-over. Let me know when he returns."

But he did not return. Enquiries were made by the Resident's staff throughout Molengi, but Campbell was not there. He had been observed walking down the street from the Residency, but after that not a single eyewitness had seen a trace of the white man.

At the Resident's instructions, the talking drums told Balooma of the white man's disappearance. As the following day passed without news, the Resident began to get anxious.

"I'm dreadfully sorry this should have happened, sir," he said to the chief commissioner. "One of my guests too!"

"Couldn't be helped," replied the chief philosophically. "We must do what we can. And bear up as well as we may under the cables from the Colonial Office. I've had several already. They think Balooma is like Hyde Park, and can't understand how we can be so careless as to mislay anyone."

"What the devil do you think can have happened to him, sir?" asked the Resident. "You generally spot what these blighters are up to."

"I'm absolutely baffled," announced the chief commissioner slowly. "Absolutely baffled."

He had come for a week's visit to Molengi. Three days after Campbell's disappearance, he was therefore still there, and was surprised to get an appeal from Dr. Virginia Ridge to see her.

"Dr. Virginia Ridge. Let me see, who is she?" he asked his secretary.

"She's that American anthropologist girl, sir," explained Hilton. "You remember we gave her a permit as she was to be a guest of the Nga-ma-Nwama."

"I suppose I'd better see her some time," said the chief commissioner gloomily.

"She's rather pretty," added Hilton meekly.

"All right then, I'll see her now."

Virginia came in with her usual positive walk. She acknowledged the chief's greeting curtly.

"I've come about Inspector Campbell."

"Oh. You knew him?"

"I did. He was a friend of mine. What's happened to him?"

The chief put the tips of his fingers together and bowed his head gently.

"Ah, my dear young lady," he said paternally, "I wish I could answer your question. He has completely disappeared."

"But surely you have some trace of him. You've had men investigating?"

"Everywhere, Dr. Ridge. Everywhere. You can imagine how distressed I am."

"I can imagine it," said Virginia sharply.

Something in her tone made the chief commissioner look up. Could there have been a trace of sarcasm in the words? But no, it was impossible. Merely the manner of young America.

"We must not give up hope, of course," he went on.

"But surely, Colonel, with your knowledge of the native mind, you can guess where he has gone?"

"I am completely baffled. I confess it with shame. Poor young fellow!"

"When was he last seen ?"

"No one saw him after he left the Residency."

Virginia was silent for a time. When she spoke, her remark was so surprising that the chief sat up abruptly.

"Is it necessary to feed me all these lies, Colonel?"

"My dear young lady—"

"Let's get this straight, Colonel. I'm a hard-boiled scientist with a liking for cold truth. I also happen to know the Balooma language. There isn't a native in Molengi today who doesn't know that the Baloomagara has got hold of Inspector Campbell. And they know why. Moreover I've found out, just by questioning, that he was seen to go into the garage, and was seen to leave it in a car. I admit I can't find out anything beyond that. I suppose he was taken for a ride by these Baloomagara gangsters. You must have known it too. Why not tell me?"

"But, good Heavens, this is invaluable information, Dr. Ridge. We shall act on it at once, I need hardly say. Measures will be taken at once. But why should you suppose we should have concealed this from you, had we known it?"

Virginia smiled. "It suits your book to get Campbell out of the way."

"You surely don't suggest—"

"I suggest nothing. Of course you wouldn't bump him off yourself. But it's easy enough to loosen up a bit on guarding him."

"But why should we do anything so fantastic?"

"Because he found out who murdered Tuffy Samson. Of course I knew long ago. The Nga-ma-Nwama."

"You are a very remarkable young lady," said the chief

commissioner, a little shaken. "What do you propose to do?"

"Oh, I won't give yon away," Virginia reassured him.

"I don't blame the Nga-ma-Nwama a bit. In fact I tried to persuade Campbell to keep quiet about it and go home. But now he's in the hands of the Baloomagara he's in danger. Surely you know its reputation. You must save him quickly."

Old Max met her eyes unblinkingly.

"I am sure you exaggerate the danger of what, after all, is little more than a negro friendly society."

"Colonel, is that what you called it in your paper in the Journal of the Royal Anthropological Society, Feb. 1923?"

The Chief looked embarrassed.

"Well, what are you going to do about it?"

"I assure you we are doing everything."

"Yes, I know. You have to say that. But will you get him out of their clutches? Or not? Let's know how we stand."

"You must realize that I cannot answer such a pre-posterous question," answered the chief commissioner quietly. He got up to his feet and strolled slowly to the window. "Assuming however there was anything in your fantastic supposition, well—" He turned round suddenly. "Dr. Ridge, I argued with that man for an hour. He was absolutely implacable. I did everything I could. You're an anthropologist. You understand that if he carried out his proposal, there would be an end to the peace of Balooma."

"Well?"

The chief commissioner sat down again, and put together the tips of his fingers.

"I consider the peace of Balooma is no longer in danger."

Virginia stared at him in horror. "You mean—"

"In my opinion all our efforts will be in vain. I fear indeed that he is dead now. I am, as a matter of fact, engaged at this moment in drafting a telegram to send to his relatives. I trust it will not be necessary to send it, but we mention in it how highly we regard him."

"You cold-blooded brute," exclaimed Virginia, turning pale. "Do you mean you've sacrificed this man's life"

"For a few thousand others? Yes, that would be the case, if your fantastic hypothesis were true. But I am sure you would never suppose a British official could do anything so—I was going to say 'sensible,' but perhaps that is hardly the word. 'Realistic' shall we say. In any case there is no question of sacrifice. The most your worst critic could allege is a slight relaxation of vigilance. But, as I say, that notion is preposterous. I esteemed our young friend highly, and no one could be more upset—"

"For God's sake stop play-acting," said Virginia furiously. "And let me think!"

There was a silence. The chief commissioner stared blandly into space. Then Virginia got to her feet.

"I'm going to find him, dead or alive. And you'd better not try to stop me either. I'm going to take precautions to see that if anything happens to me the whole story comes out. You won't double-cross me."

The chief commissioner regarded her thoughtfully.

"I must admit I had hardly counted on your appearance. I suppose you will think it bad taste if I wish you Good Luck. Well, I can sincerely wish you Safe-return in view of the consequences you mention. You know I should have thought that as a scientist, a hard-boiled scientist, wasn't it? you'd have seen my point of view. Unless—"

"Unless?"

"Forgive me if I am tactless. . . . Unless there was some unscientific interest on your part in the man Campbell."

Virginia flushed, but failed for a moment to find an answer. "I think you're the most unpleasant old man I've ever met," she said at last.

The door closed behind her. The chief commissioner's expression changed abruptly. He mopped his forehead, on which fine beads of perspiration had suddenly become visible. Then he rose and started to pad up and down the room in his carpet slippers, up and down, his head bent. For some reason he suddenly looked very old . . .

~§~

Campbell's next memory after the multi-coloured curtain of spangles was a sensation of being at sea. For what seemed like years he was tossed about on the surface of this sea, always floating on his back. Up and down the waves tossed him, up and down. It was a regular endless rhythm.

What made it seem more extraordinary, even to his dream-drugged mind, was that it was a warm sea, a sea of boiling water. He lay in it, burning with heat, while he rose and fell, rose and fell, in endless pitch-and-toss. The remorseless rhythm filled all his being with nausea; at times it seemed to him that he had actually vomited. And then again he was no longer conscious of his body, but only of being something vague tossed up and down on this boiling sea.

Gradually his field of vision seemed to lighten, and presently he saw up above him something solid, something material. It seemed that he stared at it for years, before it took a stable shape. It melted and dissolved into sky, rock, cloud, before he finally fixed it as some linen or cloth stuff, a hood stretched on sticks and covering his whole body.

He was quite content to gaze at it, without wonder, for (it seemed) another ten years. By the end of this time he was more conscious of his body, could realize that it was lying on a kind of bed, on its back, with this hood of linen shutting out vision.

But even now he continued to be tossed up and down on the boiling sea. The whole bed tossed up and down. It creaked and groaned with the motion. He considered this for another twenty years without surprise. His head kept on swelling to the size of a house and then contracting to a pinpoint. It was boiling hot beneath his covering, like lying in a coffin of molten lead.

Presently he heard voices, and they seemed to come from everywhere outside the covering, to be sounding in his ears, speaking strange languages.

At last, after long flashes of unconsciousness, he came to the muddled conclusion that somehow or other his bed, or stretcher, or whatever it was, was being carried. Carried by people. He heard their voices. He felt the bed sway up and down in time to their motion.

He was content to consider this without surprise for a time. His arms and legs felt like sacks of earth tied to his body. His skin seemed to have become hard and horny. He put his hand to his face, and felt something like the hide of a rhinoceros. The problem was too much for his weakened mind. He drifted into a coma again. Up and down he tossed . . . up and down . . .

Suddenly all his senses became roused with the sense of imminent death. The sea in which he was floating had become still hotter, and he felt himself asphyxiating. His breath, which had been slow and rhythmic, now came in sudden jerky pants. Collecting all his energies, he flailed out wildly with his hands, and battered at the cloth hood over his litter. It was stifling him. At last, by a giant effort of all his powers, he succeeded in yelling. Then he lost consciousness.

Once again he found himself on the heaving sea, but this time his return to consciousness was quicker. He was no longer in the bed, but sitting upright in a chair slung between two poles. His bearers were following a road that wound among jungle-clad hills. Occasionally the huts of villages could be seen among the wooded slopes. Several negroes accompanied Campbell, walking beside or behind the bearers, and above his head floated a state umbrella.

His mind was still dispersed and vague. He had the

notion that all this was a dream. It was not an unpleasant sensation. His body seemed as light as a feather, and was lulled by a comfortable drowsiness, as of one who whizzes half-asleep in a car through the country at high speed. He did not ask himself whether he was in Africa. His being was without time or place.

His head was resting against the back of the chair, and when he tried to lean forward, it fell abruptly on his chest. He seemed to have no control over it. This made him want to giggle. With an effort he regained control over it, hoisted it painfully upright, and turned it to one side.

A bearded negro was walking beside him, swathed in black robes, and bearing on his head a copper pan.

"A fetish," murmured Campbell, but somehow the word seemed meaningless to him.

Presently they came to a group of natives on the road. They knelt, bowing down their heads to the ground. A negro, walking slightly ahead of Campbell's litter, suddenly turned and looked into his eyes. The negro's eyes were extraordinarily piercing. For a moment Campbell felt all consciousness of his own personality go.

"Stretch out your hand," said the negro, in a thick throaty English, and immediately, as if without his volition, Campbell's hand rose in some stiff yet oddly familiar gesture. Then it sank again.

The road wound on and on. Occasionally they disappeared from sight of the sun along paths that led through the heart of steamy forests full of thick green plants with enormous sappy leaves and blazing flowers.

Campbell had now recovered sufficient control of his faculties to look down at himself. For many minutes he stared incredulously. He was dressed in white robes, leaving his arms and most of his legs bare. But his skin had suddenly become black, and this black skin was smeared with a kind of white clay, in barbaric crisscross pattern.

Once again he put his fingers to his face, and once more he felt a thick hide, but this time he realized that it was the coated clay covering his face.

He touched his hair. It was stiffened with clay, standing out from his head, except at the back where it was shaved. Campbell remembered dimly that he had seen priests as he was, with their fetishes, carried under umbrellas, their faces smeared with white clay. But was he a priest? And if so, how could he be also Campbell?

A strange mood took possession of his mind. For a time he believed he was dreaming—Campbell dreaming he was a priest. But that was impossible. Everything around him was too real. It was Campbell, the policeman, who seemed faint, indistinct, ludicrous. Then was he a priest who had lately dreamed he was Campbell? For a long time this seemed a satisfactory solution of the problem.

As the sun became lower and the dreadful heat, which had beaten up from the ground like a physical blow, abated a little, Campbell's mind became less dispersed. It gradually came to him that he had been drugged, and was now being carried—God knew where!

He waited, his head hanging forward on his breast as if asleep, until the next village was reached. Then, summoning all his energies, he sprang from his chair, and started to shout at the top of the voice: "I am a white man being carried off. Help!"

Hardly were the words out of his mouth before the negro with the piercing eyes sprang upon him. In his weakened condition he was unable to resist, and the man pressed a huge hand against his lips. Something was being thrust between his lips. It filled his mouth with a pungent taste. He tried to spit it out, but the negro's hand was closed firmly over his mouth.

After a few minutes' vain struggling, during which the crowd of natives who had run towards the umbrella at the first shout, hastily dispersed again, he felt his head spinning. He swallowed the substance. And then the dream cycle started all over again. He was nothing but a dream himself. A dream jogging along dusty paths through Africa . . .

After that moment he never struggled again. He seemed to have no will. A word, or a sign, from the negro with the piercing eyes, and he rose painfully to his feet, and tottered wherever he was told. It seemed as if he were a mind existing separately from his body. His body did the bidding of a brutal negro with skulls and bones hanging at his girdle, a negro with tousled blood-thickened hair. Meanwhile his mind dozed and dreamed, like a thing apart.

So far from being offered violence, he was now treated with the utmost respect. Women brought him bowls of food, and fed him on bended knees. Twice a day he was rubbed with oil. The clay was loosened from his skin. His skin was massaged with the thick black oil. And he was daubed with clay again.

Negroes, rolling up the whites of their eyes, knelt before him and pressed offerings against the soles of his feet and the palms of his hands, then scuttled away.

At the end of each day he slept in a hut apart from the village they had halted at, a hut which was almost a shrine. Four squatting black forms, outlined against the velvet night sky in the doorway, watched him while he slept, motionless sentries. They were still there, outlined against the pale dawn sky, when he awoke, and seemed not to have moved an inch. Then they fed him . . . "like an invalid," he thought, "but that is ridiculous, I feel quite well, I have never felt better, except that my body won't do what I want." And then, as they jogged again on the trail, he puzzled over the eternal problem: Who was Campbell? Was he still Campbell? Or a man who had been Campbell? Or a man who had dreamed he was Campbell?

Meanwhile the roads and paths had been getting wilder;

the clearings and sown fields less frequent; and the damp thickness of the jungle more continuous. When they came to villages now, there seemed a new air about them. Most of the inhabitants were completely naked and there was a strange wary look in their eyes. They stared at the umbrella without saluting it as it passed through.

For some time the party had been climbing steadily, up, up and up. The air grew slightly less oppressive. The path twisted from side to side; but always their goal was the wood-covered mass of a peak, whose bare sides cleaved through the covering greenery in outbursts of excoriated volcanic rock. Sometimes indeed the path they followed twisted so much that their backs were temporarily towards this peak. Sometimes it was hidden from sight as they plunged into the depths of the jungle. But always, when it emerged to sight again, it was nearer, its details clearer. Presently it was no longer a peak ahead of them; it was part of their surroundings.

They were on it.

And now the path sloped down again, down and down, and down, twisting and turning. The end of their descent was equally plain. Like a silver shield, the waters of a lake glittered below them.

The sight of this sheet of water, trapped in the crater of what was evidently an extinct volcano, aroused strange associations in Campbell's mind. The Sacred Lake of Balooma. Worshipped as the source of all things. The lake without any outlet, which rose steadily, inch by inch, year after year, until one day, so Balooma said, it would overtop its sides and wipe out Africa. Meanwhile its rise could be stemmed and propitiated. It was the lake whose fish fed all Ashanti, but which must never be fished in with spear, rod or line, or net. So sacred that neither oar, paddle nor sail might affront its majesty. The home of the Vahina. The Sacred Lake. Lake Mareptwa.

How do I know all this? thought Campbell. And to his drug-deranged mind it seemed to him that this was a proof that he could not really be Campbell. For how could Campbell, a London detective, know anything about the Sacred Lake of Balooma? He was a priest who had dreamed he was Campbell . . .

The Lake was now near. Its surface, as smooth as glass in the dead calm, looked the colour of ink, in spite of the sun on the water. It was completely stagnant. The water seemed opaque, solid. It came into Campbell's mind, and again it seemed to him that he had always known it, that the lake was believed to have a hole in the middle that led to the spirit world. The Administration Surveyor had, in fact, crossed the lake and had tried to sound the centre, a hundred yards off the shallows, but had run short of line. So its depth was not marked on any map.

Now the footsteps of the bearers were squelching as they walked over marshy ground. Several fishermen were at work on the lake. Their craft were rafts on which, lying at full length, they paddled with their arms, like a crawl swimmer, thus obeying the injunction that no paddle should disturb the Sacred Lake, or sail offend its dignity. Years of practice enabled them to achieve a fair speed, and keep on hour after hour, under a blazing sun, untired.

They were now engaged in driving fish, by skillful maneuver, along the shallows at the edge into the fish traps, consisting of plaited partitions of stick fencing, with a close mesh that served as a net.

When they saw the party approaching, several of them "paddled" rapidly to the shore. Campbell gazed at them with lack-luster eyes. He felt completely exhausted now. He was not even curious about his personality. The last dose of drug given him had been extra-strong. His head lolled on his chest and rolled from side to side with the motion of the chair.

He was laid on one of the larger rafts, and four stalwart fishermen, prone on their stomachs, two in front and two behind, paddled him across the lake. The lake was less than a mile across, a jewel set in dark-green slopes from which projected in places the bare red volcanic rock. The edge of the lake was black mud.

The fishermen chanted at their task, and the raft, as it crossed the lake, left behind it, like the stroke of a pen, a long furrow of ripples.

Lying on his back, Campbell stared up at the sky. Presently the raft altered course slightly and the rays of the setting sun shone into his eyes. He closed them. He sank into a half doze.

The raft grounded softly on the other side and he was carried ashore, still dozing. A whole night must have passed before he opened his eyes again, for he found himself lying in a hut, or rather under a roof shelter, with the sun high in the heavens. His food had to be put into his mouth. The negro with the piercing eyes came to look at him from time to time and once, when Campbell slept, rolled back his eyelids and inspected his eyes.

Campbell was thoroughly rubbed with oil and daubed with clay, and extraordinary care was now taken with his adornment. Two men, on bended knees, tied strange objects on to his robes and girdle until he was tufted all over like some grotesque Christmas tree.

By this time, however, Campbell was long past any conception of the grotesque. He was completely passive and limp, like a doll. His eyes did not focus, but remained staring into space as if fixed on some invisible object. Even apart from the blackness of his skin, the daubing of his face, and the outlandish treatment of his hair, his features would have been difficult to recognize as those of a European. They had become coarsened, almost brutal in their lack of intelligence.

It was afternoon. Outside the roof shelter several hundred negroes had gathered in a ring. In the open space stood a fetish, an almost shapeless figure hung with bits of iron. At one corner drummers had seated themselves and now, as it were spontaneously, they began to caress their drums.

Soon the whisper rose to a full-throated baying. The people began to dance. But it was not the dance of the Kwama Festival, the Dance of Loosened Hearts. It was not the dance of harvest, the dance of fruitfulness. It was some terrifying drama of compulsion. The drums, which had laughed and rejoiced at the Kwama Festival, now groaned and roared with a kind of sullen fury.

Campbell lay absolutely expressionless, as if he were deaf. Occasionally a muscle in his leg or arm twitched violently.

For hour after hour the drumming and the dancing went on, until the sweat stood out on the glistening hides of the dancers and the sun was low in the heavens. The thud of the drummers rose to a continual rolling roar. The voices of the watchers accompanied it in a shriek, while they slapped their chests and haunches furiously. The rite was a furious cry for satisfaction.

The negro with the piercing eyes, now clothed in all the regalia of a witchdoctor, stooped over Campbell. He spoke to him: a volley of gibberish. At the same time, he waved the down-turned palm of one hand in front of Campbell's eyes, up and down quickly, with a brushing movement. Then he raised his hand steadily and slowly to his own eye-level. As if tied to the negro's hand by an invisible thread, Campbell also rose, his eyes still gazing ahead, his head keeping a few inches from the rising hand.

The negro dropped his hand, and the detective stood upright, swaying slightly on his heels, his arms limply by his side. The negro walked slowly into the center of the space.

The drums and shrieking had stopped. There was complete and utter silence, except for a moment when drums, apparently beating many miles away, continued for a time after the other drums, but quickly stopped.

As the negro moved away, Campbell followed. He walked like a blind man, stepping full into a pole which stood in his way, and then blundering his way round it, with the purposeless movements of a decerebrate animal.

Arrived in the middle of the ring of faces, of which he seemed unconscious, Campbell halted. His stiffened figure relaxed and his head sank forward again. He swayed, very slowly, in time to the drums, which had started to whisper again. There was no expression on the thousands of black faces fixed on him.

Then suddenly all these faces turned one way. A slow sigh went up from the crowd.

The Ivory Soul was being borne down the wooded slope towards them, on the shoulders of the Nga-ma-Nwama. Four warriors carrying spears marched before and two behind it. Two young black virgins, tokens of its purity, were borne before it on the shoulders of the warriors. A huge scarlet umbrella shielded it. The crowd made way for it, quietly but rapidly.

The negro with the piercing eyes took the stool on his shoulders. Then he walked towards Campbell who leaned his head forward and put up his hands. The Ivory Soul was placed in his care.

Slowly, with the movements of a paralytic, Campbell started to walk. He walked straight towards the lake. The crowd made way for him again, quietly, instantaneously. The whisper of the drums flamed up again into a roar.

Campbell had arrived by the lakeside. With the uncanny skill of the somnambulist, able to perform complicated feats without a seeing eye, Campbell carefully placed the Ivory Soul on a narrow raft. Giving it a push, he lay down on it. Then he started to paddle it, dipping in each arm with the swiftness and precision of an expert crawl swimmer. With each dip the raft rocked from side to side. In spite of the weakness he had evidenced in the hut, he now paddled with mechanical regularity, stroke after stroke, without a pause.

Meanwhile the witchdoctor was following Campbell's movements intently. He seemed to be in a kind of fit. The muscles of his arms bunched and sank again beneath his black hide pulsating like the paddling of the man prostrate on the raft.

The raft was about quarter of a mile out now. Thousands of eyes were watching it. The drums were thudding in a regular rhythm to which the arms of the raft-borne man kept time.

Campbell was a third of a mile out now, and the sun shone on his arms which, cleansed by the water, showed white. Then his arms became motionless.

He could be seen kneeling on the raft. He elevated the Ivory Soul above his head and then, with a twist of his body, flung it away from him. There was a sigh from the watching multitude, and the drums gave a faint whisper of exultation.

The Ivory Soul, laden with its gold, sank like a stone. It is still sinking, says Balooma, for it fell into the bottomless pit in the centre of the Sacred Lake, the entrance to the underworld. It has long passed the abode of the spirits. Still it falls. Nothing can harm the soul of the Balooma people. No Tuffy Samson, with brutal mind and grasping fingers, can fish it up from there, as he fished it up from the shallows.

But to oversee its difficult journey through the spirit world and on and down, a guardian was necessary. What guardian more skillful, more powerful in fetish, more knowing, than the spirit of a white man? The spirit of a white man was to guard it, sent on its mission by the deity of the Sacred Lake.

For this sending they now waited.

Campbell, having flung away the Ivory Soul, lay down on his raft again, this time on his back. A little more voluntary energy had returned to him, but only a little. "All this is a dream," his drugged consciousness said; "a ridiculous nightmare. It has endured a long time, but I must wait patiently until morning."

Thus, in a dream, he floated on the bosom of the Sacred Lake, scarcely moving. The sun was sinking.

And then suddenly, as if in answer to the supplicating murmur of the drums, the strange phenomenon occurred that only once in a few years perturbs the Sacred Lake of Balooma. The waters started to swirl and boil. A thick black scum rose, and bubbles of gas rushed to the surface and burst. A strange animal-like stench hung over the lake, and as the thick scum, accompanied by dislodged water weeds, eddied and swirled about the surface, hundreds of thousands of poisoned fish floated, bellies up, on the Sacred Lake.

Normally this would be the signal for the fishermen to gather in basketfuls the strange harvest of the deep. But now they still waited, watching.

Suddenly there was a long-drawn out sigh. A streak could be seen, beginning at the far side of the lake and gradually increasing in length, directed towards the floating man. Presently the snout and long upper jaw of a crocodile could be made out.

Campbell saw it when it was a few feet away from him. It all seemed part of the dream, and though a momentary fear gripped him when he saw the jaw open and the crocodile, its fore paws on the raft, topple it neatly over, that fear vanished when the jaws closed on his flesh . . .

Soon the crocodile could be seen making its way back to shore, its prey in its mouth. Then it vanished from sight.

A great cry went up from the people. The spirit of the white man had started on its dive after the Ivory Soul, to protect it on its perilous journey for evermore. For evermore white man's spirit and Ivory Soul would fall through the bottomless underworld . . .

The sun had vanished. Night fell abruptly. The last rays of the sun revealed the tenantless raft floating idly in the centre of the lake. The lake itself still heaved and bubbled with its strange volcanic trouble.

Lighting torches, and shouting with joy, the fishermen embarked in their thousands on the rafts, to fill their baskets to the brim with the floating bounty of the Sacred Lake . . .

CHAPTER NINETEEN
Wisdom of a Witchdoctor

VIRGINIA was almost in despair. Whenever she closed her eyes she could imagine Campbell lying dead with his throat cut, or speared. All her inquiries came up against a dead end. The Baloomagara. For the native that was enough to explain everything; to prevent any further inquiry.

Certainly her several weeks' residence with the women of the Royal Kraal, speaking their language and investigating their customs, had given her special avenues of information. But the Baloomagara was a men's society. Even the queen-mothers might not know its secrets.

All that she could find out, by innuendo and direct answer, was that the head lodge of the Baloomagara was by the Sacred Lake; that the great festival of the Troubling of the Waters was about to be celebrated there; and that there was unusual activity at all the local lodges. In some way too, this was mixed up with the Ivory Soul, of which the Society was a guardian, with the right to provide the Soul's warriors, bearers, and priests.

The fact that she was among people who did not value a life and therefore could hardly be expected to give much help in the case of Campbell, was worrying enough. Fortunately Virginia was used to living among people whose codes of ethics were ludicrously different from hers.

She still believed that Campbell was alive; and though she reproached herself with making the wish father to the thought, the belief survived all reverses. Finally it became so strong that she allowed herself the unscientific luxury of supposing that, in some way, she was sensitive to his continued existence; that if he died, somehow she would know.

Nor did the chief commissioner's attitude make her give up hope. She knew that it would be alien to the queer position he had taken up, actively to hinder her in any way. She also realized that, at the most, only one or two people in the Administration would share or even suspect this attitude. From the Resident and district officers she could count on the fullest support.

In any case she now realized that once Campbell took up an attitude inimical to the Nga-ma-Nwama and his recovery of the Ivory Soul he was in grave danger. He would probably have been killed before he could leave the country in spite of police protection. At the most the chief commissioner, in some strange way, had allowed that protection to be relaxed.

Besides it was with the millions of natives, not with the handfuls of white men, that she had to deal. In this connection she suddenly remembered Garrod, the etymologist, who in his four years' residence in the wilds had acquired a thorough knowledge of the language and habits of the Balooma native and would not be handicapped as she was in dealing with a men's society.

She called on him. He was packing his clothes when she saw him. Where was he going? Back to Gorango?

"No. Up-country again," he answered. He ran a hand through his shock of hair. "God knows why! I've just had an idea about the influence of temperature change on the directive ability of *Formica hebetudiensis* which I'd like to test. I've got my bearers fixed up and I'm leaving tomorrow."

"Where are you going?"

"The usual place. A village about ten miles from the Sacred Lake. There's a huge formicary in the volcanic clay there."

He opened one of his packed suitcases and took out a bottle of whisky.

"Have a drink?"

"No, not at the moment."

Virginia sat down.

"It's about Campbell."

"Yes, poor devil! He's a write-off, I'm afraid." Then, seeing her face, "I say, were you—I mean, did you—er—" His voice trailed off.

"I liked him," agreed Virginia slowly. "I hadn't known him long. When we were together we always seemed to be quarrelling and now he's gone—" She stopped. There was a distinct danger of crying.

"It's generally like that, I believe," agreed Garrod awkwardly, "I say, I'm awfully sorry. Can I do anything? Dash it all, do have a drink!"

Garrod poured himself out a stiff whisky and gulped it down. "This confounded climate. If you do fall for anyone, you fall badly. Don't tell me, I know! Of course there's no need to give up hope, I was talking through my hat."

"Do you really mean that, or are you just saying it to cheer me up?"

Garrod looked away. "Well, if the Baloomagara have got hold of him . . . But there's always hope, you know . . . his voice collapsed into silence.

"I still believe he's alive," said Virginia obstinately.

Garrod made no reply.

"It's hopeless I suppose, and yet I keep on hoping!"

"I felt like that once," agreed Garrod. "I had a young assistant, bloke named Peterson. I'd promised his parents to keep an eye on him. One day when I was out of the camp he wandered away following some spoor or other and got hopelessly bushed. We searched for him for days. By all rights he was dead after the first night. Yet all the time I had a feeling he was alive; used to see him alive in the forest quite clearly in my dreams. Pure wish fulfilment by the unconscious of course. But still—"

"What happened?"

"I consulted a witchdoctor," answered Garrod calmly.

"A witchdoctor?" exclaimed Virginia amazed.

"Why not?"

"But, good Lord, as a scientist, you don't believe in magic, surely?"

"I don't. Though as an anthropologist you will appreciate magic is only primitive science. But I have seen enough to believe that in Africa at any rate telepathy and cryptoscopy exist."

"But how can you admit such a thing! Surely it upsets all the laws of nature?"

"There are none, nowadays. Only strong probabilities. If we discover telepathy, it is merely a new opera tor defining the unknown. Put it down to mysterious rays, if you don't like the mathematician's attitude. Or to Levy-Bruhl's prelogical participation mystique, if you want a psychological explanation. All I can say is that my witchdoctor saw, or said he saw, young Peterson, alive, in a certain place, and we found him there. Of course he may have already been spotted by natives who reported it to the witchdoctor. It's not a scientific proof. I merely recount it."

"Yes, I saw some queer things in South America," answered Virginia thoughtfully. "Odd things happen in a primitive country. Where is this man now?"

"I saw him in Molengi for the Festival. I'll get hold of him if you like. It's worth trying after all. It can't do Campbell any harm." Privately he thought Virginia had reached that stage of blank despair where a little charlatanry is welcome and comforting. And certainly the case of Peterson had been remarkable.

"But will he say anything, if Campbell is in the hands of the Baloomagara?"

"Naturally he'll be very cautious. But he's an individual old bird. He's never had any truck with the Baloomagara. In fact he resents its interfering with his perquisites. So if he can tell you something without breaking any Baloomagara regulation and getting into trouble, he probably will.

"For God's sake don't expect too much of it," he added.

"I'm not likely to do that!" she replied grimly. "I look on this as a pretty desperate joke."

As a consequence, Garrod and Virginia that afternoon were sitting in a somewhat malodorous hut while a huge negro, with a mud-stiffened beard, and covered with paint, crouched on the ground in front of them. From time to time he made circling movements with his hands, and groaned. His eyes had a certain fixed intensity, but he did not appear to be in a trance.

His assistant, a young negro boy who squatted beside him, was, however, obviously in a trance-like state, into which he had sunk, almost imperceptibly, watching the rapid movements of the witchdoctor's hands among the miscellaneous collection of "medicine" in front of him. The collection included a few belongings of Campbell's, taken by Garrod from his room.

"A simple somnambulistic trance," whispered Garrod. Presently the boy started to speak in a strange hoarse voice, full of gutturals.

"The usual dissociation of personality," answered Virginia. "Is that supposed to be a control?"

"Yes, it's supposed to be the voices of the dead, speaking the spirit language. Watch!"

The witchdoctor, turning to the boy, asked him a few questions in Balooma, which were answered in this strange guttural language, more like a Bantu dialect than Balooma. Then he picked up a wooden bowl, full of dark liquid like a mixture of blood and black ink, and put it into the boy's hand. The boy accepted it passively, and leant over it.

"He sees a lake," said the witchdoctor, translating the boy's mutterings. "They tell him it is the Sacred Lake. The white man is beside the lake. Now the white man is floating on the lake. There is a god with the white man. They tell him it is the Ivory Soul. Look! the white man has thrown away the Ivory Soul. They tell him it has sunk down, down into the spirit world. The spirits are looking after it now."

"And the white man?" asked Virginia incredulously.

"He says the white man is still there," said the witchdoctor, "there he is. He floats and floats and floats. They tell him the white man's spirit has gone to the spirit world. It is talking to the spirits now."

"Is he dead?" asked Virginia, turning slightly pale in spite of herself.

"No, O white woman, they say he is not dead, but his soul is among them. The white man's body is floating, floating. They tell him. Look, look in the corner of the lake! It is one of the gods of the lake, a crocodile god. Now the god sees the body of the white man, and takes it. He will eat the body of the white man. The white man has gone, but the raft is floating, floating. And the white man's soul is in the spirit world. Still."

Virginia had gone quite white.

"Why, you old rascal," burst out Garrod angrily. "You're making this up to scare us. It obviously can't be true. Do you think I'm paying you for a lot of rubbish like this? Crocodiles and Ivory Souls!"

The witchdoctor stared at him calmly, without resentment or fear.

"It is as the boy has seen, O white man. How should he lie, since he speaks only what the spirits of our fathers and mothers tell him? It may be indeed that they deceive him with a purpose, but what is a man, to outwit the spirits? We say only what we are told."

"You are sure he is dead? Or rather are these confounded spirits sure that he is dead? Ask them and tell them we don't want any nonsense."

"He's up to some trick," murmured Garrod to Virginia. "But I can't see what it is for the moment."

The witchdoctor spoke sharply to the boy, and then, after listening to his muttering, turned to the two.

"They say the white man is not dead. His spirit has returned from the spirit world."

"Where is he then?"

"They say find him. They have shown him to the boy. He is lying like this, underground, so."

The witchdoctor lay down and mimicked the rigidity of a corpse. "Go to the Sacred Lake and find him."

"How?"

"No matter. You will find him. For his spirit has come back from the spirit world, and so he cannot die."

"Come along, Dr. Ridge, that's enough," said Garrod getting to his feet. He tossed some money to the witchdoctor. "I was a fool to bring you to this. It's all humbug and hysteria, if not worse."

"Do you think there can be something in it? I had an odd feeling that the boy could really see something in the bowl."

"A pure phantasy of the subconscious."

"All the same," Garrod added thoughtfully.. "There may be some notion in the old fraud's mind. There's something going on up by the Sacred Lake. I could tell that from the difficulty I had in getting my bearers. I had to postpone my starting date. It's possible this witchdoctor has heard something and has passed on the information dressed in mumbo-jumbo to save himself from any awkward interrogation. There was something oddly specific about that vision."

"Then I'm coming with you," said Virginia definitely. "If you'll let me."

"All right. We're starting tomorrow." Garrod knew the ache of helplessness and felt that the American girl might be happier doing something, however forlorn the hope.

Thus Virginia and Garrod set off to the Sacred Lake together, with a party of about twenty porters. At the last moment Virginia had been able to persuade the Resident to lend her two of the police bloodhounds.

"Not that the creatures are ever much use," commented Garrod, "but it makes one feel one is doing all one can."

The animals, with the rambling gait of their breed, shuffled behind in melancholy dignity. The hot sun of Africa made speech infrequent, but Virginia found Garrod, in spite of a certain nervous jumpiness, a good companion. Towards nightfall, however, he was inclined to get a little maudlin as a result of drinking too much whisky. It seemed, however, to make no difference to the staying power of his lean and stringy frame. Virginia, who prided herself on her stamina, found it hard to stand the long treks. However, they were making much faster time, had they but known it, than Campbell and his party over the same route.

At last they were travelling down the slope which led towards the Sacred Lake. It was just subsiding after the Troubling of the Waters; and the surface was still dotted by rafts, sped by vigorous hands, picking up the helpless fish.

Garrod at once started to make inquiries. As he had expected, there was universal denial of a white man's having been there. Any mention of the Ivory Soul evoked more than a denial; a resentful glare. Garrod, knowing the native mind, had not expected anymore; but enquiries, and his own observation, showed him that there had been a feast or carnival of some kind going on the preceding day. The shores of the lake in one part were trodden down into a hard-beaten ring, showing that there had been dancing. Dancing in Balooma is never without a religious significance, and always has its own set times and rituals.

Taking this point as a centre, they started to search the shores and slopes of the lake in wider and wider circles, hoping to come on some trace of Campbell—if only his corpse. The bearers, and even some of the local fishermen, helped them with an alacrity which, more than anything else, made Garrod dejected. He did not pass on his fears to Virginia, but if there was any likelihood of Campbell's being a prisoner in the neighbourhood, the natives would hardly be likely to help him in his search. It might be, however, that they were merely acting to mislead him.

He took the bloodhounds with him. If Campbell had been a prisoner here he would probably be carried, and so would leave no trail. In any case the scent must be stale. None the less the bloodhounds seemed to "find" round the dancing place. But it led to nothing. They were soon baffled.

Presently the party was searching farther afield. Here, even if the bloodhounds could not pick up the trail, there was the chance that should Campbell be concealed by the natives in any hut or cave, they would detect the presence of a white man.

At first the hounds proved more of a nuisance than otherwise, becoming attracted by thickets or ant-hills and baying them hopefully for a few minutes. In the end they both became fascinated by a patch of earth on the bank, not far from the lake. Here they gave tongue, and even scratched the ground tentatively like terriers.

Garrod made several attempts to distract their attention,

and was about to have them taken back to the camp when suddenly Virginia exclaimed:

"Do you remember what that old man said about Campbell being underground?"

"I'd forgotten! But it's impossible. Just a moment though!"

Garrod went to the bank of the lake and inspected it carefully. Then he returned.

"There seems an underground stream of some kind here." He banged on the ground with his stick.

"Sounds a bit hollow! Cut back to the camp, boys, and bring some spades."

They began to dig. After about half an hour's digging they found they had come through to the roof of the underground stream. The dogs were baying excitedly at the hole, and presently Garrod was able to lower himself through it into the deep tunnel formed by the stream. The water was only a few inches deep, though doubtless it swelled and filled the entire tunnel in the rainy season.

"There's a terrific stench down here," he exclaimed, his voice reverberating in the hollow tunnel. "Smells like crocs. Pass me down that torch."

A moment later he gave a cry. Revealed by his torch was a figure stretched in the rigidity of death, half-buried in the mud on one side of the tunnel. The resemblance to the outstretched form of the witchdoctor in the hut was uncanny. The man seemed at first sight to be a native; his skin was dark, smeared with mud and clay. Dried blood clotted on one leg, which was doubled up under him. His eyes were closed.

A closer inspection showed that the arms were white, and then Garrod shone the torch on his face. Although distorted, and disguised with hair and paint, it was Campbell's face.

Could he conceivably be alive? Garrod placed a hand on

his chest, over the heart. He was certain he could feel a faint throb.

The stench was overpowering here, and he saw that near the dead man was a gruesome collection of carrion. The leg of a bush pig, amorphous hunks of meat . . .

As Campbell was lifted out of the tunnel, the natives gave a cry of astonishment, which became respectful wonder when they realized that he was not dead. Campbell was carried slowly back to the camp. As a biologist, Garrod knew something of medicine, and by means of massage, and injections of adrenalin when the fluttering heart seemed about to collapse, Campbell was brought back to consciousness. Long periods of delirium succeeded, with intervals of unaccountable depression. But after the seventh day, nursed by Virginia, though far too weak to move, Campbell was himself again, and able to give some account, necessarily disconnected, of his experiences. While he was still weak, however, it distressed him to discuss them, and Garrod did not cross-examine him as to minute details.

"It seems evident," Garrod said to Virginia later, "that they gave him some kind of drug that induces a paralysis of the higher centers without affecting, or only partially affecting, the sensory-motor system. In that condition he would be in a similar state to that of a hysteric subject in a hypnotic trance; that is he would have a high degree of suggestibility. He would be as easily open to hypnotic suggestion as a hysteric. It is obvious that a rapport of this kind was established. Campbell must have suffered from a partial dissociation of personality for some days. Of course all the standard hysteric phenomena have been known to the witchdoctor for ages, and there is nothing surprising in what has happened. While hypnotized, Campbell could not do anything that would be morally impermissible to his waking ego, such as murder or suicide, but he could perform certain actions without clearly appreciating their ends. This is what he seems to have done here."

"If he suffered from dissociation of personality, how can he remember anything?" asked Virginia.

"He is still living below the threshold of the unconscious. Probably as a result of his fever. You notice he is very uncertain as to who he is or how he comes to be in Africa. As his strength returns he will forget this chapter in his life, which is probably just as well for the experience must have been ghastly."

"I can't understand how he comes to be alive at all. The wound on his leg shows that a crocodile had got him all right."

"Yes, he was saved by the peculiar habits of crocodiles. They like their game to be high, and generally have a 'larder' hidden away in the bank above the water-line where they store their prey. It is not common for a man to escape in this way, but most people who have lived long in Africa have met cases of the kind. What saved Campbell was the fact that to all intents and purposes he was anaesthetic, incapable of feeling pain. Thus he did not struggle, but lay absolutely passive in the crocodile's jaws, and so was not mauled. In most of these cases, the victim loses a leg or a limb, and suffers a terrific mental shock. But Campbell remembers nothing after the moment he saw the crocodile swim towards him, and he will remember even less now. He simply lay underground for two or three days in a coma."

They had walked down to the shores of the Sacred Lake. All internal motion had subsided, and the lake was as still as the water in a well.

"Garrod, how do you explain that witchdoctor's prediction?" asked Virginia. "As a rational man?"

"There are plenty of possible explanations," answered Garrod. "Everything up to the taking of Campbell by a crocodile could have been known to the witchdoctor by rumour, by the talking drums for instance. As for the latter part, well, it could be explained as a lucky chance. After all, what did he say? First of all that Campbell was alive, that his spirit had returned to earth. A pretty general statement which your distress almost forced out of him. Secondly he said that Campbell was underground, that's another vague statement. A man is either underground or overground. Well, that's a fairly safe bet, evens. And so that is how, as a scientist, I explain it."

"And what do you really think yourself? When you're not being a scientist?"

"A rather personal question. All I can say is that in Africa these things happen, and we take them as they come. There's no explanation except—well, just that it's Africa! They would never happen in England. Let's go back to the camp and have a drink!"

CHAPTER TWENTY
End of a Detective?

AFTER he was well enough to travel, Campbell returned to Molengi with Virginia. From here they caught a train to Gorango. Garrod remained at the Sacred Lake, having pitched his camp beside *Formica hebetudiensis*, on whose abode he had already trained a complicated arrangement of burning glasses and mirrors. Most of his bearers travelled back with Campbell and Virginia.

As Garrod had predicted, Campbell had now almost lost his memory of everything that had occurred between the time he had been stunned beside the car and the time he had awakened to partial consciousness in the camp. When

Virginia repeated his own account of what had happened, he could hardly recognize it, except in the kind of dim formless way one remembers dreams. But it gave him a strange sensation of living twice through the same events to be carried back again by natives, in a chair, along the route he had travelled over when under the influence of the drug.

His experience had had at least one odd effect. It had given him a totally different attitude towards Balooma and the affair of the Ivory Soul. As is often the case with a serious illness or mental shock, it had knocked all his ethical and philosophical conceptions sideways. Or as Garrod had put it:

"Africa's got into your blood, old boy! Have a drink?"

It seemed to him quite explicable, even if extremely unpleasant, that his life should be sacrificed to guard the Ivory Soul. Not of course that he approved of it in any way, but he understood it. Equally he understood the before incomprehensible attitude of the Baloomagara towards Tuffy Samson. Most surprising of all, he understood the viewpoint of the chief commissioner. Here Virginia could not agree with him. The chief seemed to her a monstrous figure of Imperialistic wickedness. But possibly she was biased by the personal factor.

Lying back in his litter and feeling strangely unlike the enthusiastic young inspector who had set foot in Nigeria only a short time ago, he explained his new feelings to Virginia. She looked at him with a quizzical smile. With the kind of smile we bestow on friends who have suddenly seen something we have been telling them for years, and now they naively insist on drawing our own attention to it.

In the early days Garrod had been afraid that a renewed attack might be made on Campbell, as a victim dedicated to the gods. Indeed he had thought of sending a message for protection to the subaltern in charge of a near-by Hausa outpost. But it had not proved necessary. Certainly the local fishermen had assembled in hundreds outside the hut where Campbell was lying, to stare at him, but no hostile attempt was made. They merely looked at him silently out of quiet, unfathomable eyes.

It was the same on their journey back. Sometimes a group of natives would gather round the rest-house to stare, and then quietly vanish away. Nothing hostile was said or done.

Outside Molengi, they were met by an official from the British Resident, who gave Campbell a message.

"The chief commissioner has asked me to say that he is delighted to hear of your safety. He hopes to have the pleasure of congratulating you personally in Gorango."

"The old fox!" exclaimed Virginia indignantly. "How dare he?"

Campbell smiled. "Will you ask the Resident to thank the chief commissioner for his good wishes, and say that I shall call at Government House as soon as I arrive in Gorango?"

Campbell duly paid his visit to Government House. After the usual politenesses, the chief commissioner looked at him curiously.

"H'm, you seem to have changed a bit since the last time I saw you. But I suppose you're still the same sea-green incorruptible? The truth and nothing but the truth and to hell with Balooma? Well, you win! I might have known a detective from Scotland Yard would be insuppressible, even by our local talent."

"You're right, I have changed," replied Campbell thoughtfully stroking his emaciated cheek. "I'm beginning to look at things differently. It's partly the experience I've been through. Also I've been so long in Balooma now I'm beginning to look at things from the local standpoint." He paused. "When I turn in my report I shall merely state that the murder was committed by the Baloomagara. Nor shall I refer to the Nga-ma-Nwama.

"At the same time I shall send in my resignation," he added.

"Well, Inspector," said the chief commissioner quietly. "It would be impertinent on my part to thank you, for I realize you are not doing it out of any personal regard. Some day you will realize what you have done for Balooma, and what a terrible administrative tangle you have saved us from. But—forgive me if I press it—is it necessary to wreck your career in this way?"

"Inevitable, I am afraid. It is quite impossible for a Scotland Yard detective to justify his letting a murderer go undenounced, even for the peace of a nation. I see that I misjudged my own mentality. Or perhaps it has been altered by this confoundedly seductive climate. I can assure you I wouldn't resign lightly. I had hoped to settle down—marry even—but obviously this will be impossible for a little. However, there are plenty of other fields of endeavour."

Campbell reached for his hat, and was about to go when the chief commissioner detained him. Colonel Max Whittington-Hopefull-Smythe started to pad up and down in his carpet slippers, always a sign of mental strain. Then he stopped in front of Campbell.

"When I last saw you I made a suggestion. Then it was a bribe. There is no question of a bribe now. But you might think it a reward and take offence. I can only assure you—" The chief broke off embarrassed.

"Well, damn it all, Campbell! As man to man, will you be my chief of police?"

"But really, sir!" exclaimed Campbell. "My grade is not high enough! I'm too young. And I have only had experience of criminal investigation!"

"Damn all that nonsense!" commanded the chief peremptorily. "We don't want administrative fossils of the first grade out here. We want intelligent young men of any grade. Without prejudices. No red tape nonsense! I shall apply for you and I'll damn well get you. Go back to England and get well quietly."

"I think, sir, you've forgotten what's happened. Could I, as your chief of police, ever live down this last episode? I fancy prestige counts for a lot in this country!"

"Live down! What do you mean?" exclaimed the chief. "Don't talk like a fool. Look at me, fat belly, red nose, carpet slippers, varicose veins." He hit himself on the chest. "A nasty sight, eh? Yet every native in Balooma regards me as a sort of God. D'you know that?"

"Well, yes," said Campbell mystified. "Everyone knows your unique position in this country."

"Unique, fiddlesticks! Why, you whipper-snapper, you've got ahead of me. It's damned unfair. Some hard-working district officer who has spent five years in an anthropological institute, knows every native custom, and speaks the language perfectly, gets appointed to a district and the natives won't take an ounce of notice of him. Why? Because his arrival coincided with a drought! Meanwhile a young fool who calls all people with darkish skins niggers, and doesn't know or care a tuppenny damn about administration will hold his district in the hollow of his hands. Again, why? Because at his arrival they had good rains. From thenceforth he's a great rainmaker, and all the natives bring their sick and barren cows to him to touch and obey his slightest word. I used to be thought the luckiest person in this kingdom. But now I can't hold a candle to you, blast you! You're the man who came back from the spirit world! You're Great Fetish. Why when you're chief of police you need only sit in your office and the murderers will come to you. So none of this damn nonsense about living anything down. I've got to live you down."

~§~

Campbell walked back to his hotel hardly able to believe his good fortune.

On the verandah he met Marion, who expressed appropriate surprise at his survival. Marion had an easel in front of him and was painting. Campbell leaned over to look at the painting, and Marion seemed to make an instinctive gesture to conceal it. Campbell, however, had already seen the work. It depicted a thorough-bred horse bearing a pink-coated M.F.H. on whose rubicund face hauteur mingled with bonhomie. Between the horse's legs stretched rolling miles of grey-green down-country over which a pink-coated "field" dwarfed by the distance, was galloping at full speed. Above, in the large area of sky mingled the cold blues and misty clouds of an English winter.

"I thought you said something about Gauguin . . ." began Campbell.

"I know, I know," moaned Marion clutching his hair, "I can't help it. All these tropical colours and fights have had the most amazing effect on me. They've been more dazzling than the most dazzling effects of modern art. They've beaten us at our own game. And the result is I've reacted. I've come back the full circle—to Jennings. I simply can't paint anything else but horses. It's like a disease."

He gestured indignantly at the canvas. "What will the Double-Zero Group say when I send that in for our annual exhibition? What do you think Schwein-Chikotsky will say in Damnation about it? Why this tiling may end up at the Academy!"

"Perhaps when you get back home it will pass off."

"I hope so," said Marion, sinking wearily back into a deck chair, "but will my complexion ever come back? However, don't let us talk about these tragic matters."

"Where is the vicar?" asked Campbell.

"I think he's at the movies," answered Marion. "He is rather a nuisance as a travelling companion. He keeps on bleating that nothing ever happens. However, he will be quite happy for the afternoon at the movies. The film is called 'Congo Drums.'"

Three hours later Campbell was sitting with Virginia on Lion's Head, the promontory south of the bay of Gorango, and the only moderately cool place in Balooma. A breeze from the Atlantic stirred the palms, and the great Atlantic rollers climbed painfully, involved in spray, up the reddish wall of cliff. Campbell had told Virginia of his interview with the chief commissioner, and had asked her what her plans were.

"I shall stay on here a little longer, I think," she answered, "I am preparing a monograph for Themistocles on the Balooma marriage customs, with special reference to exogamy."

"Oh, yes," said Campbell. "That reminds me. What do you think of marriage?"

"What kind?" she answered briskly. "Endogamous, or exogamous? Monogamous or polygamous? And if polygamous, polygynous, polyandrous, or both?"

"Oh, just the ordinary European variety. For better or worse, you know. Richer and poorer."

"I should be glad," answered Dr. Ridge after a pause, "to collaborate with you on a personal study of this institution."

The rest of the discussion, being wholly unscientific, is not recorded here.

BRUIN CRIMEWORKS

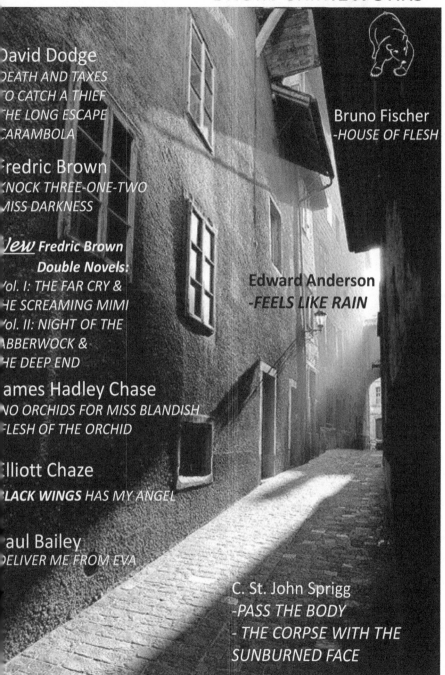

David Dodge
DEATH AND TAXES
TO CATCH A THIEF
THE LONG ESCAPE
CARAMBOLA

Bruno Fischer
-HOUSE OF FLESH

Fredric Brown
KNOCK THREE-ONE-TWO
MISS DARKNESS

New **Fredric Brown**
Double Novels:
Vol. I: THE FAR CRY &
THE SCREAMING MIMI
Vol. II: NIGHT OF THE
JABBERWOCK &
THE DEEP END

Edward Anderson
-FEELS LIKE RAIN

James Hadley Chase
NO ORCHIDS FOR MISS BLANDISH
FLESH OF THE ORCHID

Elliott Chaze
BLACK WINGS HAS MY ANGEL

Paul Bailey
DELIVER ME FROM EVA

C. St. John Sprigg
-PASS THE BODY
- THE CORPSE WITH THE
SUNBURNED FACE

Visit the scene of the crime

Bruin Asylum

Make Your Reservations Today!

The Witching Night
C. S. Cody – Booking Now

A Garden Lost in Time
Jonathan Aycliffe – Booking Now

I Am Your Brother
G. S. Marlowe – Booking Now

Dr. Mabuse
Norbert Jacques – Booking Now

Walpole's Fantastic Tales, Volume I
Hugh Walpole – Booking Now

The Magician & Other Strange Stories
W. Somerset Maugham – Booking Now

The Bat Woman
Cromwell Gibbons – Booking now

Made in the USA
Las Vegas, NV
12 June 2022

50127611R00163